Lucky Supreme

Also by Jeff Johnson:

Tattoo Machine: Tall Tales, True Stories, and My Life in Ink (2009)
Everything Under the Moon: a novel (2016)
Knottspeed: a novel (2017)

A NOVEL OF MANY CRIMES

JEFF JOHNSON

Arcade Publishing • New York

First Edition

This is a work of fiction. Names, places, characters, and incidents are either the products of the author's imagination or are used fictitiously.

Arcade Publishing books may be purchased in bulk at special discounts for sales promotion, corporate gifts, fund-raising, or educational purposes. Special editions can also be created to specifications. For details, contact the Special Sales Department, Arcade Publishing, 307 West 36th Street, 11th Floor, New York, NY 10018 or arcade@skyhorsepublishing.com.

Arcade Publishing® is a registered trademark of Skyhorse Publishing, Inc.®, a Delaware corporation.

Visit our website at www.arcadepub.com.

10 9 8 7 6 5 4 3 2 1

Library of Congress Cataloging-in-Publication Data is available on file.

Cover design by Gigi Little
Cover photo: *Morguefile*

Print ISBN: 978-1-62872-757-9
Ebook ISBN: 978-1-62872-759-3

Printed in the United States of America

Lucky Supreme

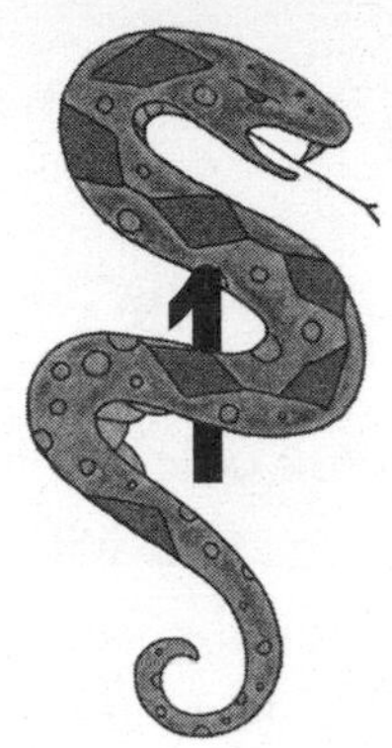

Old Town.

The heart of a city is a thick place, where the towers have their footprints, where the sugar deals get made, and where the big brains nest and the roads and freeways become arteries for something hatched in an incubator made out of random parts. But you have to keep the tumors somewhere, and in every case it has the same name. It wasn't a place where the strong survived, because they either became overnight kings and winged to higher ground, or they became part of the blur of fire and gears and something else altogether. The weak never figured into the permanent population, because the nature of the game was too constant, and there wasn't enough junk protein to make chewing the rest of the package worthwhile. What was left in between was the dream factory, where people hid in plain sight, where colossal miracles died at birth unnoticed, and where everything floated on a stagnant ocean of vice, lies, and decrepitude. The right mixture of animal stamina and imagination by the pound could take you to the far side of that sooty wilderness. Or so I kept telling myself.

"Darby. There you are." Delia looked up at the sound of the door chime as I walked into the tattoo shop. The lobby was half full of college kids banded together for numeric boldness, a few larking housewives trolling for a few drips of bad news, and one serious fucking biker. Delia was a short, scrawny punk chick in her late twenties and a mouthy but superb tattoo artist with consistently unfortunate taste in clothes. Today she was wearing black peg-legs, engineer boots covered in layers of graffiti, and a shredded old Fang T-shirt that did nothing for her flat chest. She smacked her fluorescent-green gum at me and wrinkled her tiny pug nose. What little hair she had was last night's wine maroon, a change from yesterday's hellbino blanco. "About time, you lazy fuckin' shitass."

Romanticizing the islands of neon in those places was more than easy; it was natural. It happened somewhere deep in the limbic psyche, hardwired in the marrow of the ape. Behind the wet red glaze the dream factory dreamed its hardest. The front of Lucky Supreme, alive with buzz and pulse and bent lines of glow, was about as inviting as a ruby stuck in a hornets' nest.

The romantic neon was mine. As in, I owned it.

"Up yours, dummy," I said affectionately. I pushed my way through the lobby with proprietary graciousness. "It's my Saturday. All day. But I thought I'd stop in to monkey with the stereo."

I tested the air as I made my way through the place. Tattoo shops were a balmy mix of soap and chemicals, with an undercurrent of the nervous, sweaty popcorn stink that effervesced from a waking carnival midway at noon, blending perfectly with the sweet, breathy bourbon-splatter of a backseat on a Monday night thrown in for good measure. At the Lucky Supreme, we also had all four tablespoons of

Delia's running custom perfume. She was currently trying to duplicate the heady essence of birthday cake.

In many ways our neon barrier formed the perimeter of a miniature bubble in the greater psychosphere of Old Town. If I closed my eyes, which I didn't, I might have been able to feel it and let my imagination paint the cast of characters within. Delia, a bright white spot with a great deal of internal motion, like a clock and dynamo hybrid made out of fluorescent tubes and firecrackers. Everyone else was dim in comparison except the biker, who would have registered in the eyes-closed interpretation as a big black toad. I liked to think of myself as a tidy gray rift of nothing at all, but it wasn't true. And outside of our hard little bubble were nodes of blank, songs, wings, and trashcans.

"You're just in time to settle a score for me," Delia chirped, "so snap the fuck out of it." Her chubby skate kid customer winced. He winced because she was still talking. "I think I need to market a special form of vodka that can also act as a shampoo and a lube. Righteous idea whose time has come. Purse-sized bottles. I'm calling it Early Morning Luvopoo. These douchebags all say it sounds too much like bubble bath."

"It fuckin' does," her customer whined. It was obvious that she'd been tormenting him with her train of thought for the entire time he'd been sitting there. Delia would always abuse a captive audience in lurid and creative ways. She couldn't help herself.

Alex and Dwight looked up from their stations and smiled by way of greeting. They were working on the leading edge of the college gang. The two of them were relatively new at the Lucky and still on their best behavior. Alex was a chunky half-Chinese, half-maybe-Irish guy in his mid-twenties. Dwight was a few years older, a rawboned greaser with tree-root hands and a farmer's beard jutting from a Lincoln jaw. They were on the better end of the stale sort of character that had come to dominate tattooing once it became popular enough to need them. Bold showmen or fountains of originality they weren't, and they didn't suffer from the excess of personality of the people who had been sitting in their chairs a decade ago. Delia had been with me for a rambling three years, the minimum amount of time necessary to insult me on a regular basis. She'd wormed her way into my affections in a thousand little ways, some of them possibly unintentional. It gave her an edge when it came to insubordination.

"Zombie music," I said as I passed through the iron gate in the tip wall. Delia rolled her eyes with snap drama. I'd banned Nordic metal on purely aesthetic grounds. "No undead can play guitar that fast, sweetie. Dudeboy's a fake. And Early Morning Luvopoo is way lame. Roll with Hoe Go. Great big picture of your itchy spot on the label."

"Whatevah," she replied, projecting sullen. I stopped and stared her down. She scrunched her face at me like she was trying to squeeze something out.

I continued through the bodies into the back room, where I made a passing inspection of the elaborate stainless steel crappery of cleanliness. The newer Ritter steam autoclave always gave me a tiny pulse of relief when I saw it. The old chemclaves exploded occasionally, and the popping and groaning they made through every cycle had been nerve racking. It was good that they were gone. Even cold and unplugged and sitting in a box, the sight of one still gave me pause. Clean stainless steel buckets full of deadly chemicals sitting on shiny stainless steel. The little ultrasonic tank always looked out of place in all the metal, a forlorn plastic robot scout from the future. Nothing was on and none of it needed tending, so I kept going.

The room beyond it was the secret stronghold of the Lucky operation, where sinister plans were hatched, wicked and misguided vengeance plotted, love dismissed for all the wrong reasons, where visions of nightmares and fables were put to paper. Pretty much all of it. The lounge was as big as the other two rooms combined, packed with a mad assemblage of mismatched bookcases full of art books. The cases were stacked on top of each other and rose into dusty obscurity up to the sixteen-foot ceiling. There was a graphite-smeared drafting table with a makeshift light box mounted underneath it, an old cherry-red crushed velvet sofa with matching recliners scored from the outer ring of a dumpster in a pimpy kind of neighborhood, useful for wipeouts when the night shift guys had their occasional post-shift blackout binges, and a small workbench with a grinder, a drill press, and a nasty array of soldering equipment. In the far corner was my desk, a huge antique I referred to as my office. The desk was sandwiched between two filing cabinets, decorated to total surface encrustation with the stickers of forgotten bands with lunatic names and visiting tattooers who sounded twice as bad. Gleeclubfoot, the raging punk band from no-one-remembers, was my fave music-wise, so we had five or six of their bumper stickers. One rainy night some tattoo kid named Timmy Runny had dropped off some of his magnet cards with an antlered roach head, so there were several of those on top of the mix. Runny had a crazy story, all of them did, so the stickers and magnets were a little like the spines of books that way. Ads for weirdoes, the garden flowers of the dream factory. I sat down at the desk and didn't look at any of it. Instead I waited for inspiration, which never, ever turned out to be a good idea.

With as much shit as I had to do at any given moment, I spent an inordinate amount of time sitting at the desk, listening to the shop stagger forward through another day, generally doing nothing. It occurred to me that I might be depressed, but I doubted it. Probably too shallow. Bored was a definite fit, but it was impossible to get debilitatingly bored in a tattoo shop. So I don't know why I was just sitting there. About then I realized that I was waiting for something to happen. Something wonderful. Something possibly even magnificent. Which is probably a tremendous way to jinx yourself. Magical thinking aside, there was something to be said for charting a path to that wonderful magnificent stuff. Sitting around just made me a target.

I looked at the clock above the back door, frozen since I could remember at 2:04. My social life was in the toilet. That was my first thought. I had a mild but persistent hangover. The state of the shop was a direct reflection of my inner self. Everything was broken, but not so badly that it didn't actually work in some semi-desperate way, like a redlined engine with no oil that was still screaming fast. It was out of control in a way that was hard to define, but everyone was there and pretending like it was a real business.

The back sink had about a week left before it stopped draining completely, in the same way that I had about a week before some basin inside of me became backed up with the tiny stresses of a million forgettable problems, all gathered together like a clump of hairy plastic in a drain. The light in the emergency exit sign had burned out, and finding the tiny obsolete replacement bulb could take days, if not weeks. I couldn't draw any direct parallel there, but it was a queer and telling omen. I sighed, powerless to enjoy the act of sitting, unable to settle into a state of spiritually restorative nothingness.

"Did you get my tampons?" Delia called, loud and sweet, from the front. I got up and wandered out. She was still working on the fat dude.

"They were out of super jumbo," I replied, patting her bony shoulder. "You'll have to hunker down on three or four of the regular ones."

"Heyyy," she whined. Alex and Dwight snorted in perfect unison.

"Dmitri came by," Alex said. "Right when we opened."

Dmitri was the landlord. He ran the truly morbid pizza dive down the street, a place so powerfully awful that the street crazies believed he put mosquitoes in the sauce, and those guys could generally digest anything. It was never a good sign when he came around. It wasn't just that I hated him, and I did. Dmitri was the wrecked sort of blur crazy who sent uneasy currents out around him as feelers, like an eel electrocuting his way around through muddy water. A ticking time bomb, essentially. When he finally went off for good we were all going down and we knew it.

"What'd he want?"

Alex shrugged.

"He was drunk," Delia said brightly. "Smelled like white wine. With some beer. Sweet champagne. Snails. Raging BO. Very Parisian."

"He was definitely wet," Dwight added. He gave the tattoo he was working on a boxer swipe. "Looked like the poor dude had been wandering around in the rain all morning without an umbrella."

"Portlanders don't use umbrellas," I told him. Dwight had moved to the City of Roses six months before from Denver, a place he somewhat disturbingly described as a high-altitude 'foggy' zone saturated with military radar and itinerant frequency waves. That description, that small measure of character, was why I'd hired him in the first place, but it turned out to be the only odd thing about him. It was his freshman fall in the Northwest. "That's how we bust the Californians."

I ducked out into the rain for a quick smoke, leaving Delia in charge of the rain lecture, which she immediately launched into, beginning with how constant moisture lends fortitude to mucous membranes. Old Town was in that strange twilight transition between subreality and the true Night Madness. The scuttling office commandos who'd parked in the cheap pay-by-the-week lots scattered around the area were beginning to give way to the sidewalk night shift. A couple of surly homies in watch caps and puffy plastic team coats were huddled under the awning of the old brick apartment building across the street. They hadn't been there twenty minutes before. Monique, the

Lucky's pet hooker, was savagely berating someone on her cell phone under the saggy awning of the Korean mini-mart next door. Apparently one of her boots had been stolen. She was wearing flip-flops from the Walgreen's down the street. I briefly entertained the notion of offering assistance, but Monique's foul temper was in full swing, and all she'd do was spit at me or anyone else until she went from hard boil down to her resting state of scalding steam. Maybe a day or two.

I took a deep breath of rainy street. More of the rock-and-weed tag teams were coming out a little early and vying for the best corners. The lights of Old Town were powering up, spraying the wet pavement with bright smears. I recognized the archetypes of the night watch, even if the faces changed. The haggard identity of the place had its own white pages, and sometimes, when I was just bored enough, I could see it with surprising clarity. In many ways, the goings-on would never be fully understood by anyone, but at times I was close, in the same way I'd often been close to the wrong kind of woman. I could almost hold all of it in my mind's eye for an instant and see the entire picture, but to do so would do absolutely nothing for my sense of well-being, so it wasn't the kind of thing I focused on. Especially recently.

Over the last year, I'd seen signs of "progress," and it was just like Saturday night's red dress on a Sunday morning coke habit. Little mom-and-pop places that served spinach pies and a hungry man's meatloaf dinner were relocating to the outskirts of the city, to be replaced by boutique coffee shops and upscale fusion restaurants that sold seared tuna belly and a raw quail egg with a fractal of truffled pomegranate soy sauce. Way out of the local price range, though "local," "price," and "range" all had newly flexible definitions. There were more cops around than last year, a younger, beefier variety who hassled anyone who so much as touched their zipper in front of an alley where people had been pissing for years. Parking was growing scarce with the flood of new SUVs, most of which sported at least one paradoxical tree-hugger sticker.

The net effect of pressuring the nightlife was that it made the entire culture more mean and desperate, which was why my schedule had gradually come to straddle the day and the night shift, even on my hypothetical day off. It was true that Delia could handle almost any situation, and my two night shift guys were dangerous animals, but at forty I'd been tattooing longer than all of them combined, and much of that in the dark, richly complex environment that had been Old Town in its glory days. I knew, or thought I knew, every trick in the book. I'd even invented some of them. I shot my spent cigarette butt into the swollen gutter as a TriMet bus roared past in a torus of dirty mist. Boredom breeds overconfidence.

"—cut me up some 'Bama poon," Monique snarled. She was coming my way. "An' I'm gettin' me some tape an', yo hang!" She glared at me. "What!"

"I like your outfit," I said, offering a smile. She spit and her lower lip quivered. I went back into the Lucky before she tried to scratch me.

Dwight was bandaging his customer when I went back inside. I took a moment to straighten the wooden chairs in the lobby and tidy the magazines in the bookcase, even though it would all be trashed again in less than an hour. The plants had all been watered recently. Delia's handiwork, though she'd bitch about it. I looked up at the Buddha statue with the cholo headband we kept on top of the bookcase in the lobby. As smiling and enigmatic as ever.

The walls of the tattoo shop were covered with sheets of tattoo designs known as flash, but since I'd purchased the Lucky Supreme from an old-timer with a gnarly pedigree, ours was far superior to most. Wally Langdon, the previous owner, had retired a few years before and left me with a laundry list of things to fix or destroy that were the collective result of his stunning and secretive ineptitude when it came to business, his astonishing ability to steal things and hoard them, and his amazing reinterpretation of anything that might ever make him feel guilty. Smiling Good Time Wally, forever fixated on ripping off the devil. I'd wound up with a ton of furniture he'd borrowed but never returned, most of it from me, a ton of bad plumbing and dangerous electrical work he'd traded for but weaseled out of—that kind of thing. In the end the price tag was mostly for the name and the lease and all the infrastructure I'd kept going through his reign. The only valuable stuff was the collection of tattoo art and strange artifacts he'd inherited from his former boss, who had himself started tattooing almost one hundred years before. The history of the Lucky Supreme was part of its charm. I'd never had a chance to meet Wally's former boss, who'd died a few years before I ever hit the scene, but I felt some kinship with him. More than I did with Wally, anyway.

Most of the flash from floor to eye level was mine and Big Mike's, with a good swath of Delia's incredible black and gray horror-themed pieces, but as the wall stretched up out of reach tattoo history began to appear. I had dozens of Russel Shoals sheets from the fifties, some early Lou Louis, a handful of old Rex Nightly, Blue Spears, and many more. All of them were bolted behind quarter inch Plexiglas, and in the last year I'd had expensive copies made of most of the more valuable pieces and switched them out. The originals were in a gun safe that was too heavy to move, in a storage space that was too worthless to get rid of.

Delia was chattering away about records, spraying the room in general public-speaker mode. Alex and Dwight were finishing up. The zombie music hadn't been cranked up again. Everything was stable, so I decided to do a little half-assed recon on the emerging landlord situation. I zipped up my bomber jacket and walked out into the misting rain again. Flaco's Tacos, the temple of the neighborhood oracle, was conveniently located right next door.

The Lucky Supreme was dead center in an aging one-story brick building. There was a Korean mini-mart to one side and a bar called the Rooster Rocket on the other. Both of them were the kind of unlikely operations that could only exist in Old Town, that would have never prospered anywhere else and so could never leave. The Korean mini-mart was run by an intensely private family of five, none of whom spoke a single word of English. They sold everything from crack pipes to expired Spam and had occasional special runs of mysterious items like one-dollar steaks or Big Wheels. Their clients were all low-end local foot traffic. They ran a needle exchange for the junkie population and sold Sergeant's Worm Away for dogs, Freeze Off for warts, the central components of Mexican sorcery, and CDs of action movies from Nigeria. And they sold it all without ever saying a word.

The Rooster Rocket was a hipster/punk nightclub run by Gomez, a hard Latino in his fifties who knew nothing at all about music. That part of his operation had happened entirely by accident and he ran it with entrepreneurial resignation. In the late eighties, the Rocket had been just a bar. The kid that they'd hired to wash dishes had a band and Gomez had let him play. Then the kid threw a few more shows and the booze really started flowing. After he finally ran off, Gomez had rolled up his sleeves and embraced his fate as a nightclub owner.

The entrance to the Rooster Rocket had an old ticket taker's vestibule to one side, left over from its seventies incarnation as a porno theater. Gomez had converted it into Sixth Street's smallest Mexican restaurant and rented it to Flaco. You ate standing up outside and there was room under the awning for three people. The entire food-making operation was crammed into a space with the same dimensions as a walk-in closet, proof of the miracle of Latino ingenuity and spatial acuity. I went from my awning to his with less than a foot of open sky. When I blew into my hands in front of the open window, I saw the whiteness of my breath for the first time that year.

"Two juniors," I called, shuffling a little as the cold of the sidewalk came through the soles of my boots.

"Tattoo boy," Flaco said, peeking out. He grinned at me, all gold and bridgework. His ancient face was part prune and part glove leather, and his eyes were always smiling. I'd never seen him sick or sad, not even once. Flaco's mission in life was to save enough money to pay off his tiny ranch in central Mexico and then go home. He'd been at it for twenty years and said he had two more to go. He had a wife and two grown daughters already living on the spread, raising goats and chickens and tending a huge garden they'd coaxed out of the rocky ground. "Water or soda?"

I waved at him, indicating neither.

Flaco put my order together on a sheet of wax paper and slid them out. The tacos were small corn tortillas doubled up and filled with roasted pork, diced red onion, and a type of barbeque sauce. Flaco served other kinds of tacos, but these were the only ones anyone ever ordered, and for some reason everyone called them juniors. I tossed a few dollars through the slot and scooped up a junior, leaning forward as I bit into it to keep red grease from shooting all over my pants. Over in two bites.

"The leaves are turning, man," Flaco said, peering out at the street. "Time to get my big coat out. This year, I'm thinking maybe a hat. Colorful, like the Guatemalan Rasta."

I grunted and went at the second junior, then wiped my hands on a napkin from the dispenser on the tiny counter and tossed it with the wax paper into the dented bucket beneath the window.

"Dmitri in there?" I asked, nodding at the bar.

Flaco shook his head. "No, no. He was earlier. I think our fucking landlord is losing it, *esse.* He was wearing clown pants, like the old golfer."

"Shit."

"Yes. Shit," Flaco agreed, still studying the street. "Hospital shit."

"Later days," I said, wiping my hands on my pants. It was a routine of ours.

"Better lays." His customary reply.

When I walked into the Rooster Rocket, I had to pause for an instant to let my eyes adjust to the year-round gloom after the blinding fluorescence of Flaco's window. There were a few drinkers with stamina in the dark interior, mostly local restaurant workers. Gomez was behind the bar with a clipboard in one hand and the chewed stub of a pencil in the other, checking off an order form. Gomez was a striking older man with heavy, slicked-back hair and a tidy baseball player's moustache that was as black as a charcoal briquette. His root beer eyes had a distance picked up in a history I'd never asked about.

"Hola," Gomez said. "Workin' or drinkin'?"

"Christian thimble," I replied, making the gesture for weensy with my thumb and forefinger. "Just doing the door tonight."

"You need a social life, hombre." He put his clipboard down and poured me a small shot of vodka, then one for himself.

"Seen Dmitri?" I asked, cupping the thimble.

Gomez tossed his shot back and scowled. "We need to talk about him. That man needs antidepressants. Therapy. You should have seen what he was wearing."

"I heard." I tossed my shot back and Gomez glanced at the bottle. I shook my head.

"It worried me," he continued, picking up the clipboard. The jukebox came on somewhere in the back of the bar.

Old Gypsy Kings. "This neighborhood is going somewhere else and it's taking our landlord with it."

"I'm not worried," I lied. "Got a five-year lease."

"Me too," Gomez said, his face unreadable. "But what good is that going to do if Old Town turns into café loft space, eh?"

I looked at the bar clock. The shift change at the Lucky was minutes away, so I tossed a few bucks on the counter. Gomez ignored them and went back to work, and just like that the neighborhood business association meeting was complete.

When I walked back into the shop, I knew instantly that something had happened. The dayshift guys were packed up and had their jackets on, ready to split, but they were sitting on the stools along the tip wall listening to Delia. My two night guys, Nigel and Big Mike, were just standing there, still dripping rain and holding their art bags, also captivated. Everyone looked at the door and froze at the sight of me.

"What?" I asked. The inside of my mouth tasted like snow. My vision went hyper-crisp, and everything looked like it was made out of painted glass.

Delia's little pixie face lit up with inner Manson light. Nigel and Big Mike gave me Sleepy Hollow grins. Both of them had worked for me for years, Nigel all the way back to when I was still a shit-upon employee myself.

"Aw man," Nigel purred. "It's like an early *Nightmare Before Christmas*. But without the whole movie part."

"This is gonna be raw," Big Mike chortled. "Raw like in a whole fucking buffalo raw."

"Obi called from Monterey," Delia said, sugar on sweet. She resisted a pirouette, but an ecstatic, serpentine ripple went up her entire body. Her eyes glittered with an almost confusing level of delight. Even her hair was smiling. "He was surfing in Santa Cruz today and guess who he found?"

Obi was my old apprentice. He'd moved to San Francisco a year ago, hated it, and moved farther south to the peninsula. I felt my jaw clench. The two juniors and the vodka in my stomach went from hot to foamy. Strong déjà vu. Delia enunciated her next three words in the lilting singsong parody of a thirsty baby demon.

"Jason fucking Bling."

"Who in the world is Jason Bling?"

Alex broke the long silence with a whisper. A pre-earthquake stillness had spread through the shop. Alex looked worried, buried under the totality of the mood shift. Dwight was wearing his poker face, which in his case looked a little like brain damage. Big Mike, Nigel, and Delia were all watching my face like it was their first color TV.

"A dude fixin' to shit his wisdom teeth," Big Mike said.

"A dude who would drop dead of a multiple heart attack/stroke/embolism with spontaneous cancer if he knew we were standing here talking about where he was," Nigel added. "Where he lives. Where we can find him." He rubbed his long skinny hands together. His eyes never strayed from my face.

"Jason used to work here," Delia said, gracefully taking the stage again. She began to slowly pace, gesturing with her arms with perfect posture, a small and psychotic presenter. "Couple of years ago. Flashy playboy dickhead, liked sports cars, had a big diamond earring and chunks of gold in his teeth. Dressed like a tacky pimp version of Nigel here."

"Kid would have licked out my bathtub, I asked him to," Nigel said. Nigel had rarefied taste in everything, from clothes to Italian handguns. He was tall and thin, with sharp, angular features. That night he was wearing his standard ghetto uniform: shiny black boots, black Dickies, black T, black hoodie, black jacket, and a black skullie, all of it perfectly new. He had a serious policy about wearing anything with words or color. "I was never able to teach his dumb ass a damn thing. The idiot banged half the junky strippers in this city, and I'm not exaggerating. Liked to brag he never wore a condom, too. He called rubbers 'fag bags.' Swear to God. Kid was that retarded."

"Yeah, ew. Anyway," Delia continued, "one day he just splits town, no warning, no notice, nothing. We all had to cover his shifts for a few weeks until Darby finally found a replacement we thought might not be as bad. That. Sucked. The whole thing. So a month or so after he's gone people start showing up looking for him. Bad people. I mean even worse than Big Mike. We dug around a little and it turned out that our little Jason was into some insanely stupid shit, light years beyond his VD collection. The dumbass had been moving pills out of Canada and selling them around town. He got bigger and bigger and then burned a shitload of total strangers as the grand finale."

"And that ain't all," Nigel said.

"Nooo," Delia crooned. "Our boy decided to burn the Lucky while he was burning everyone else. Look up there." She pointed to a space high on the wall, all the way up at the Roland Norton flash. Alex and Dwight looked. So did Big Mike.

"I was cleaning this filthy shithole one night a few weeks after Bling split and I noticed one of the Norton pieces was crooked. Got the big ladder out and climbed up there, since no one else ever does anything around here, and guess what I found?" She tossed her story in my direction with a flick of her head.

Alex and Dwight looked at me. Nigel and Big Mike loved this part of the story.

"They were copies," I said. "Bling had taken all fifteen of the original sheets down and copied them. We'd never have known he'd stolen the originals if he hadn't screwed up when he hung the fakes."

"Jesus," Alex said. "How . . . how'd a cretin like that ever even get a job here?"

All eyes were on me again. I shrugged.

"What are you gonna do, boss?" Big Mike asked. He flexed one meaty hand and the knuckles popped. Big Mike's huge mitts were completely tattooed and the skin over his hands reminded me of tractor tires. Every tattoo artist we knew had been looking for Bling for almost two years. The nationwide hunt was over.

I looked back up at the copies of the Roland Norton flash. I already knew what I was going to do. I didn't have any choice. I'd half hoped this day would never come.

"I'm gonna go get my shit," I said. "Mike, you're in charge of supplies while I'm gone. Alex, tomorrow morning you call all my appointments for the next few days and reschedule them. If any cops call, give them to Nigel. Delia, you're in charge of the day shift, and needless to say, none of this leaves this room."

Alex and Dwight looked a little worried as they split. They were going to get more and more worried as the night went on too, I knew, until they finally got The Fear. Big Mike and Nigel, on the other hand, quickly put their things away and started setting up as though nothing had happened, maybe with a little less banter than usual. I went back to my office corner, Delia close on my heels.

"What," I said flatly, crashing down in my chair.

"I'm going with you." Delia settled on the edge of the desk and primly crossed her hands over her knee. Her short fingernails were painted and buffed, the color of algae. A wave of birthday cake caught up with her and rolled over me.

"I need you at the shop," I said. Alex and Dwight were too new to be left alone. "I don't know how long I'll be gone."

"C'mon," she whined, squirming. She was incapable of doing one without the other. "Someone needs to mind you. You know how you get, Darby. All fuckey-shit-up. Plus I always hated Jason, fuckin' no-talent fast-money scammer piece of shit. I wanna watch what happens when you find him."

"I'm not going to hurt him." The lie was loud in my voice.

Delia laughed hard enough to blink. "Yes you are! I just wanna be there. C'mon, man, road trip." She batted her lashes. "I give an all-tonsil road willie . . ."

"Ew," I replied. "Answer's way absolutely no now. I need you here, Delia. Seriously. Someone trustworthy and resourceful has to watch my cats."

"Shit." She got up. I could tell she was disappointed, but she was also worried. She put on her big girl face and

I inwardly cringed. "And you're going to go down to the Bay Area to deal with a known scumbag and you're going to stay out of trouble? Really? And I'm supposed to believe you?"

"This is really touching, Delia."

She snorted. "I just don't want to have to look for a new job if you royally fuck up." She turned in the doorway, held her hand to the side of her head in the universal gesture for phone and mouthed "call me." Then she flipped me off as an afterthought, made the gun-blows-brains-out gesture, gave me the clown frown, split.

"No boyfriends at my place," I called after her. "Or whatever you call those things before you eat 'em. And use toilet paper! That's what it's there for!"

On the way home, I listened closely to my car's engine. I'd bought the BMW through a customer of mine who worked as a mechanic at a dealership. They got well-maintained trade-ins all the time, and the mechanics picked them up to make a little cash on the side. The car sounded good. It was a late nineties 530 wagon, not at its most glamorous with an overflowing ashtray and random papers, shop supplies, and assorted crap all over the seats, but it would hold up through the twelve-hour drive.

I pulled up in front of my place and sat in the warm car, thinking. I thought about the drive and how I wanted to leave before sunrise. I thought about the rolling hills four hours south, and lonely Mt. Shasta just beyond it. The Kingdom of Cannibals. Zombie Country. Big Dead

County. A scenic place to make sure to check the oil before you ever passed through, because breaking down out there would be worse than breaking down in Compton at three a.m.

After the government had run the weed growers out of southern Oregon and Northern California, a thousand tiny meth labs had taken their place. The hippies turned grim, picked up guns and hammers and saws, lost all their teeth, and started listening to Motorhead, the whole nine yards. Most of the women who weren't scarecrows had become Walmart fat and their heads all looked curiously primitive, as though the speed had rearranged the bones in their skulls. All of it had gone straight to the lost episode of *The Twilight Zone* and points beyond. The small-town newspapers in that region read like fictional horror tabloids.

I thought about that and listened to the rain on the roof of the car, but mostly I thought about Bling, and how I'd be standing in front of him in less than twenty-four hours. I could see why Delia was worried. I was paranoid about what I was going to find when I went into his hiding place and I had every reason to be, because if the idiot was still alive, that meant he'd gotten better at being what he already was. Two years had given Bling time to develop into a mightier kind of shithead. That he was still alive was direct evidence.

My two cats were milling around on the porch as I walked up the steps. One of them was a Manx named Chops, a truly ugly, heavily muscled creature who trundled like a miniature rhino and fought successfully with dogs. His tail looked like a misshapen thumb. I'd paid a few hundred dollars for him at an exotic animal farm and I suspected I'd been ripped off. The other cat was named Buttons, an orange Maine Coon, also enormous, dripping wet and purring without a thought in his head. His big, unfocused eyes looked like green grapes. I sometimes thought poor Buttons had confused himself with some variety of forest mushroom. Delia had renamed them Pinky Bong and Dillson.

I let them in and they rampaged over each other to their food bowl. I'd lived there for almost a decade and it showed. The living room was crammed with inexpensive antiques I'd picked up at random with the intention of restoring. An old walnut armoire I'd found a few years before was my best effort to date, more of an experiment. There was also a huge 1940s AM radio with a crack in the top, a couple of wooden bookcases with brass hinges and glass doors, and a fat gray sofa I slept on sometimes. Next was the dining room where I never ate, dominated by a six-seat walnut table where no one ever sat, a piano I never played, and two freestanding brass lamps that may or may not have had been plugged in. Some of my more important curios were in an old china cabinet. Off to the side was the spare room, where I kept my collection of books, fossils, cool rocks, and trinkets, plus my drafting table. Past the dining room was the kitchen, the bathroom, and my bedroom. The ceiling had cracks in it and so did the walls. It was the kind of place that made all my old junk look good.

I sat my bag down in the living room and got a beer out of the fridge, carried it into the spare room. I sipped and looked the books over for a minute, then pulled down a coffee table volume entitled *Vintage Tattoo Art, Volume Three*. It had come out a year ago and somehow I wound up with a free copy. It was yet another art book showcasing the pitiful stylings of early tattoo artists, now in vogue for commercial reasons. I sat down and cracked it open.

They were definitely far from the great illustrators of their day. The majority of the work was poor beyond belief, almost as if monkeys had been given blunt crayon nubs and ether and then been pointed at a blank wall, but the author had included a vast amount of interesting historical information, painting a blurry, distorted portrait of an era in tattooing few people alive could remember. Tattoo culture should have been using it as an example of something unfortunate that had been overcome—like a crippling childhood learning disability or devastating juvenile obesity—but instead it was being spin-glorified because it was easy, and easy made stupid-level money fast for the new legion of rookies. It was how Ed Hardy got into the mall. Buttons came in and wound his wet body around my leg, then flopped out on the floor at my feet, trilling softly. I opened the book to the page I'd almost torn out when I first saw it.

On page 127 was a single image from a sheet of Roland Norton flash found in England. It was a splendorously ugly watercolor thing, featuring a few lopsided anchors, a lame spider web, a crooked star, and an androgynous skunk with a flower in its three-fingered cartoon paws. Coffee stains. A patch of mold on one corner. Yellowed overall. Underneath it was a caption, 'Roland Norton, Panama, 1955.' Even the handwriting was kindergarten. Just like mine, but not from my collection.

It had taken me three weeks to track down the contributor, an English tattoo artist by the name of Wes Ron working in the outskirts of London. Like me, he had inherited a checkered slice of tattoo history when his mentor retired. I'd only told Delia what I had learned next, after I'd sworn her to multiple levels of secrecy. It was the reason she was concerned enough to want to tag along on a twelve-hour drive.

"Piece of old-school shite, mate," Wes Ron said when I'd finally gotten a hold of him. "I don't know where we got it, just mess from the old boxes in back. But I tell you what, when that *Vintage Tattoo* book came out some wog bought the piece, twenty thousand US. Nip in San Francisco. Maybe Chinese. Only one I had, fuckin' pity too."

I told him that I had a few pieces lying around to pump information out of him. His advice:

"I tell you what, mate. Lot of calls after the nip. Some of 'em offered larger figures than what I got. Who the fuck knows why anyone would want that old stuff, but the value is going up, up, up. Hold out for the highest bidder. Wish to fuck I had."

I snapped the book closed. Buttons looked up at me and blinked.

Old-school flash had been going up in value for the last decade or so, but I'd never heard of any of it trading hands at those prices. Up until Bling's theft was discovered, I'd felt reasonably secure in displaying the originals in my collection at the Lucky. They were bolted behind Plexiglas and too high up to reach without a ladder. And of course the Lucky was almost always open and staffed by some hard boys and girls. In the few hours in the dead of the early morning, when it was closed, it was still reasonably secure. The new cops were the only cars out at that time, and the big windows gave them a good view of the interior of the tattoo shop. The doors were reinforced, and the windows themselves were skyscraper stock, bordering on bulletproof. They were the building's most modern feature, installed at Wally's behest before he left, one of the few sensible things he'd ever done, though since it had been my idea I'd been the one to arrange the entire thing. One of Nigel's ex-girlfriends had bounced a brick off one of the windows only two weeks ago and managed to knock herself out when it hit her in the head. The only person I'd ever known who could break into the Lucky was me. And I knew lots of people.

So the only way to steal original art, a rare tattoo machine, or even a ballpoint pen from the Lucky during Bling's time was to work there. He'd run the Monday day shift solo. I imagined he'd shown up early for once and in a mad scramble unbolted the covers on the Norton collection, copied them at one of the dozens of places downtown that could pull it off, and then made the switch. In my mind's eye I could easily see him, sweating, giggling to himself, dragging the ladder back and forth while he snorted coke off the back counter. It was an eight-hour window, more than enough time. Everyone estimated that even a moron like Bling could have pulled off the entire operation in less than three. Nigel could have done the entire thing in forty minutes. Bling had left on a Monday night, probably on the same day he'd made the copies.

And he'd vanished without a trace. All of my people at the Lucky had called every tattoo artist they knew across the country and put the word out that we were looking for him, and for a time we were sure that he'd turn up somewhere. We even sent out pictures. But the months began to stack up. People forgot. Other weird things happened, and after a while only a handful of artists were on the lookout for a tall, mouthy kid with some old-school flash and a ridiculous name, one he'd probably changed anyway. We had turned over every stone to find out what his real name was and came up with more than a dozen possibilities. At some point I'd given up any hope of finding him without ever even knowing it.

I shook my head. Bling had probably lost himself in the endless labyrinth of shops on the East Coast for as long as he could stand it. It had been a mistake to come back west, but after two years he probably thought it was safe to work out of a small beach town in central California. Chances were that Bling had seen the book, but Wes Ron had no memory of ever speaking to him, though he allowed that it was certainly possible. Like many industry hacks, Jason Bling had been extremely fond of old-school tattoo designs, naturally because they were so incredibly easy to do and it made him look good when he did marginally better. It also didn't bode well that he was so close to San Francisco, a place where a person with a known interest in collecting the obscure Roland Norton could be found. In that light, it was entirely possible he'd sold the pieces off more than a year ago.

I sipped beer and listened to the rain on the window, the purring of feckless Buttons. The refrigerator clicked on. It was peaceful. Dusty. Dark and calm and quiet. It made me sigh.

I had to go and find out. I drained the rest of my beer and let my gaze wander over the other books. If Bling still had the flash, fine. I'd take them back because they were mine. If not, I'd find out who he'd sold them to and take it up with them. They were stolen, after all. I didn't want to get the law involved in anything I was involved in, but I would if I absolutely had to. However unprecedented it was, it seemed like I might actually have some legal legs to stand on. It seemed at least remotely possible that I wouldn't be arrested instantly, though remotely was the key descriptor. I almost always got arrested, and every time it added to my record, making it more likely in the future. I'd seen my record, and there were things on it I had absolutely no memory of ever doing. Thinking about it made me shake my head. I'd arrest me too, and I knew it. I had a completely unpredictable track record. In the best light, it was possible that a jolly cop with Santa Claus qualities would just think I scored high on whimsy. But there were no best lights, and no cheesy sheriffs either.

And there were other reasons to be concerned, of course. Equally serious ones. Another thing that worried Delia, even though she hadn't said it out loud, was that I'd trusted Bling. I'd given him a shot, tried to nurture him, and generally done the best I could by him. And the fucker had burned me. Beyond vengeance, there was the simple fact that from a purely business point of view, I couldn't let it slide. The only reputation you could have in the tattoo world that was worse than a thief was that of an easy mark.

Jason Bling had duped me and he had to pay. My reputation was at stake.

The code of the gentleman tattooer—or lady tattooer—was a work in progress, and no one had written the definitive pamphlet as of yet, but the salient points were gradually becoming more common. Much of it stemmed from the paranoia of the inheritors of tattooing's Golden Stone Age, a loose and lawless period between the beginning of time and 1990.

Shit-talking had taken on an entirely new mysterious form, for instance. If you knew, to the point of being positive, that something potently shitty was going down at another tattoo shop, you were supposed to be deliberately vague and noncommittal, to the point where it looked as though you had suddenly spaced out. It was intended to send a simple message: I am in no way associated with that place. This was generally and often accurately reinterpreted as, "That hell pit is on a well-deserved doomsday death spiral and it will suck you in if you approach. Red flag! Red flag!"

It went on and on. The knowing look paired with "people sometimes work there for years" meant a happy, stable outfit. "That's a lively place" meant someone was drinking way too much, and the awful admonishment "The kids these days, aw man, to be twenty-five again" meant obnoxious galore, you will be babysitting the boss's new tattoo protégé, who will lecture you at length about how great he is, how he's as tough as Bruce Lee, and how there are two full moons every month, but people are too stupid to figure it out. No amount of money is worth turning into a killer.

The traveling tattoo artist is common enough and always had been. It's America. People move, sometimes freely. But subconduits existed inside the greater information superstructure, a changed thing with the Internet. So there was a chance that the Bling scenario could have this conclusion:

X: "Going to Portland. Might hit up the Lucky Supreme, see if they need anybody. You know anyone there?"

Y: "Nah. They were looking for some dude a few years ago."

X: "Really? Why?"

Y: *(darkly)* "Dunno."

Translation: Someone stole something valuable and they got away with it. And if X just happened to be the wrong sort of character, it retranslated as "Suckers."

I pulled out my cell phone and scrolled through the numbers until I found Obi's. He answered on the first ring.

"Hey boss, you get the rockin' good news?"

"Yeah." Obi still called me boss. "You're absolutely sure it's him?"

Obi laughed. He had a good laugh, a deep, joyful thing that never had anything bitter in it. Delia thought he was on the simple side, but he was happy, so she was only half right at best.

"Oh yeah, I'm positive. I'd recognize that douchebag anywhere. He's a little fatter now and he lost that white rapper thing he had going, but it's definitely Bling. He's all gussied up like a fifties Pony Boy greaser now. Even picked up a restored Chevy lowrider somewhere. Real fire-breathing monster with his dream couch for a backseat."

"Did he see you?"

"Not even, man. I was surfing outside of Santa Cruz all morning. Around noon I went to get a burrito and saw this new tattoo shop in a fucking mini mall. I was going to check it out when Bling pulled up, fucked with his hair for a minute and then unlocked the place and put out the OPEN sign. I watched for a little while just to make sure it was him and then I split. You're coming down, right?"

"First thing in the morning. Should be there around ten tomorrow night."

"Right on, man. You wanna crash at my place? You have to. When was the last time you slept on anyone else's couch?"

Obi's wife was a truly lovely woman, warm and kind, but also the worst cook I'd ever encountered. Portland could make a food snob out of anyone, except for that one woman. Worse still, she didn't seem to know it, and Obi was too nice of a man to ever tell her. Her famous olive and onion casserole was a thing that left the tongue version of an afterimage. They also had a kid now, a little girl named Lisa. They called her Gigi. They had a happy life. There was no point in getting them close to anything like Bling.

"Nah," I said. "I don't want you involved. I'll get a hotel in Monterey and visit Bling the day after tomorrow. I can't risk staying in Santa Cruz. I don't want to run into him before I'm ready."

"Suit yourself," Obi said. "Call me when you get in and we'll meet up for drinks."

We talked a little longer about his wife and their daughter. He told me once again at great length about her first smile, the state of her newly emerging teeth and what he was doing to comfort her in that regard, the varying quality of her poop, how she was progressing with various educational toys, and finally how he wanted to design a line of clothes for toddlers with tattoo motifs.

It was a little after ten by the time I finally got off the phone. I stepped out onto the porch and lit up a smoke and watched the rain. My thoughts rambled slow and directionless as I watched infrequent cars hiss down the street. Gradually, the happy vibe Obi had left me with dissipated.

Delia was right. I was five nine and 160 pounds. Jason Bling was fifteen years younger than me, several inches taller, and at least twenty pounds heavier, and he was a dumpster-style brawler who was fond of guns. His wicked temper ran right alongside his total lack of common sense. So there was little doubt it was going to be ugly. And it had to be, just because of the ambiguous gentleman's code, and characters X and Y. Because it had to play out as X, "They were looking for some guy (no name) who had some of their old flash. They have a rad collection. Check it out." Translation: They got their stolen stuff back. Those guys and gals roll solid. Serious inquiries only.

That translation was a big part of my job.

3

I seldom use an alarm clock, so when it went off at six a.m. it shocked the cats nearly to death. For an instant I thought the awful beeping siren meant that a dump truck was backing into my house. I ripped the cord out of the wall and briefly marveled at the cruelty of the machine. It had a backup battery in it, so it kept going. It seemed unreal to think that anyone had invented it, and ghastly and absurd that most people woke up to one of them every morning. The cats settled back down into their warm spots, sullen and suspicious, once I had well and truly broken the clock. It was a questionable start.

I made coffee in the dark kitchen and dressed quickly and pulled on a worn pair of steel-toed engineer boots. When the coffee was ready, I filled up a thermos mug and sipped from it as I packed my duffel bag. I tossed in enough clothing for three days, as I doubted I'd be gone longer. If I was, I could always do laundry at Obi's and risk his wife's poisonous vegan hospitality. I added my sketchbook and a few mechanical pencils in case I got bored, plus two steel ball bearings from a merry-go-round for when Bling got mouthy.

In every way, a gumball-sized ball bearing is a superior weapon. You can throw it at point blank range to great effect, hold it in the sleeve of a sturdy jacket and use it as a sap, or even wrap your fist around it and hammer away at the soft parts of a person. It wiped off easily with a little spit or some rainwater, and if you ever got caught with one, it was much less of a hassle to explain than a blatantly obvious weapon like a gun or a knife. I always claimed that I'd just found it and thought it was cool, and it worked because it was. Delia said she could hide an even dozen inside of herself somehow, and maybe, maybe she meant her stomach. A metal ball also bounces off of things, like people for instance, so you can pick it up and use it again. A bullet cannot be fired twice. A metal ball can be hand fired forever, again and again, and it won't break, catch, run out, or backfire, and it doesn't need a silencer. It could roll right through the grates in a rain gutter. It did weird and unpredictable shit to the underside of the car behind you on the freeway if you dropped it out the window. It's dependable that way. Plus the ball bearing has epic style, which appealed to my vanity. It had in fact become a symbol for me.

It was still dark and raining when I started the BMW. I stopped by an ATM and withdrew a couple hundred bucks and then headed in the direction of the Lucky Supreme to drop off my spare key for Delia.

When I drove over the Burnside Bridge I looked down at the river, just like I always do. The Willamette was a wide, slow expanse of black, dappled with the reflection of the gold and white pre-dawn halo of downtown. Sometimes at sunset, if the angle of the light was just right, you could see big gobs of oil rising from the bottom and dispersing on the surface in vast, prismatic pancakes. A massive Korean tanker was docked at the grain silos on the east side. They had always been a good source of premium hash and opium, back when I cared about that kind of thing. According to Nigel, the Russian tankers were the new smorgasbord. Every drug known to man, explosives, and they filmed their own porn on location.

Old Town began at the west end of the bridge and spread north. I drove slowly through the crumbling Chinese dragon gates and angled up to Sixth Street. It was a strange wedge of city at any time, but it was particularly unusual just before sunrise. The streets were nearly empty, so the place had an eerie, post-apocalyptic ghost town feel, mostly because all of the trash was new: a visual paradox. The nightlife had wrapped it up and vanished like roaches into the bigger cracks, and the daytime office crowd had not yet put in their manic appearance. Flaco's Tacos was sealed with battered aluminum slats. The Rooster Rocket was dark, the front door triple locked and chained. It looked like it had been abandoned for years. The fluorescent banks in the Korean mini-mart were out, and it looked like a derelict junk shop full of broken plastic patio furniture. It took light to bring that place anywhere close to convincing. Only the Lucky's neon and the streetlights burned at that hour.

I sat across the street from the shop and studied the place. It was dark inside past the neon in the windows, and I almost never saw it with the lights out. Delia opened on most days, and when she didn't one of the new guys did. Big Mike or Nigel were always there when I left. The neighborhood was changing around it, but even powered down and empty the place still resonated, like the center of a new spider web. Critical avenues of strange energy intersected at that point.

I let myself in and wrote a short note to Delia, reminding her that my bedroom, specifically my bed, was off limits, especially if she had crabs, and that she could help herself to the beer in the fridge. I taped the note and the spare key to her locker. Big Mike had mopped just a few hours before and the place was still humid and heavy with the smell of floor polish and mop juice.

There was nothing left to do. I looked at my station and as an afterthought I took a handful of blue nitrile gloves and stuffed them into the interior pocket of my bomber jacket. I gave the place a final once-over from the doorway and then locked up.

Once I hit I-5 south, my pensive mood lifted a little. Most of the early commuters were inbound for the city center, so as I headed south the road was reasonably clear. I fell in a few hundred yards behind a fast-moving semi, far enough back to be clear of its swirling mist cloud, hit the cruise control, and settled back in the big leather seat.

City gradually gave way to suburbs that in turn gave way to industrial parks. I blew through it all, sipping black coffee and ruminating. When I finally hit scan on the radio, I came across a three-block set of the Doobie Brothers, which struck me as a good sign. After the alarm clock episode I'd been waiting for one. A gray sunrise was in progress when I hit the base of the Siskiyous and started climbing.

I-5 stretched from Canada to Mexico, and I'd lived within earshot of it for most of my life, been lulled to sleep on countless nights in different periods of my existence by the sound of its ever-running river of engines. I'd hitchhiked up and down it two decades ago with some hippie woman whose name I couldn't remember. I'd almost died on it twice and fallen in love with a Lisa in one of its roadside bars. The best peach I'd ever eaten had come from a fruit stand off of I-5. Three of my friends had disappeared down it, headed for the fabled country called "That Way." My brother had vanished on it, headed north.

Unfortunately, the stretch between Portland and Medford was probably the most visually bland stretch of that great road. From Portland to the California border in October it was a straight shot of spent agricultural fields cut down to hard nubs poking through the mud, groves of fruitless trees shedding mottled leaves, and assorted hangar-like aluminum farm buildings. Hours of rain-swept monotony before the sudden transformation around Ashland and the edge of California. Medford was where Cannibal Country began, and it thickened from there.

I stopped in a tweaker shithole called Roseburg four hours south of Portland, found a burger joint, and went through the drive-thru. Normally I'd look for a taco truck, the kind of place that sprang up around the migrant workers in those parts and were reliably good if you had a stomach properly callused from years of Flaco's juniors, but I didn't have time to prowl around and sniff one out. Instead, I wolfed down a bland jalapeño cheeseburger in the parking lot, leaning up against my car. The only thing worse than fast food was the LSD-inspired Disneyland decor in the places, so a rainy parking lot filled with big new Ford pickups and a scabrous beater Pinto put the highlights on brunch. When I was finished, I tossed the garbage in their bright plastic can, washed my hands off on the rainy hood of my car, and hit the road again.

It stopped raining about ten minutes from the state line. Around noon, I took off my jacket and put on some Ray-Bans from the Lucky's lost and found that I kept in the glove box. I turned the heater off. I'd just lit a cigarette and was thinking about sneaking a road beer when my cell phone rang. Delia.

"Where you at?" she asked.

"Just hit California. The sun came out pretty much instantly. I'm actually wearing sunglasses right now."

"I can't believe you made me stay here. You know what I look like in a swimsuit?"

"I dunno. A thirteen-year-old tranny?"

"Ha ha. Fuck you. I got your key and the colorful note. I'll feed Pinky and Dillson when I get off."

"Thanks. What's going on up there?"

"Alex rescheduled all your appointments for the next few days. None of them rebelled because he told them you had something on your scalp you needed lanced. Sympathy all around. My idea, of course. I'm booked and so is he. Dwight is on walk-ins."

I knew that Delia thought Dwight was a limper, and her stand-in management style always pushed things right to the edge. She would spend the day coaching him on everything from setting up and breaking down his station expeditiously to eating faster. So the new guys were going to be really happy when I got back.

"Any sign of Dmitri?"

"Not yet." Delia sighed. "You didn't find him yesterday?"

"Didn't look, so no. Gomez was worried."

"You didn't see the pants, Darby. You didn't smell him."

"Yeah, well . . . if he comes in don't freak him out."

"I won't! God! Have fun in sunny California while I run your excuse for a life. Sunglasses my ass."

"Smoochay," I replied. I blew a kiss.

She hung up.

I hit the edge of the Monterey peninsula just after nine in the evening. I'd been there before when Obi first moved down and then a few more times afterward. I liked the place and I knew my way around well enough. I took the exit to the Marina District and on impulse drove by the shop where Obi wound up. Jane Western's Original Tattoo was closed for the night and the windows were dark. It was small, with only three artists in residence: Jane, Obi, and a cool kid named Pedro, but it was a quality operation. They drew all their own flash, though they had a few sheets that were gifts from other artists, including a sheet of mermaids I'd drawn, but they did mostly custom work, from noon to eight Monday through Saturday. Obi was happy there. He planned on opening his own place in a year or two, and that was part of the reason he'd left Portland. Like any good apprentice, he didn't want to compete with the shop he'd learned in.

Jane Western herself was somewhat typical for a woman in the predominately male field of tattooing. Intelligent, highly focused, generally impressive. Tough. She was my age—around forty—and enjoyed triathlons and tinkering with her collection of vintage jukeboxes. She also went bow hunting for bear or possibly moose in Alaska every year with some of her cop friends. Her house, Obi once told me, was decorated with old movie posters and furnished with many items she had made herself. In another life I might have asked her out on a two-week date to Mexico, but in this one I was too scared.

I rolled past the place and then down streets lined with old whitewashed Spanish buildings with terracotta roofs, wind-sculpted coastal pines, and the odd palm tree. Beautiful. The kind of place I could fall in love with every morning. The Portola Hotel was at the edge of the marina, a short walk from the plaza and the pier that jutted out into a sleepy bay full of old sundowner sailboats and sea lions. I parked in the brick turnabout in front of the hotel and checked in at the front desk. A smiling Sri Lankan woman with dusky skin and enormous hazel eyes gave me a cookie and then ran through the perks. At around three hundred a night, it was more than a little steep, but since Bling was going to be footing the bill, I decided to live a little.

I walked through the lobby with my duffel bag, skimming through tight clumps of well-dressed men and women. The entire ground floor was given over to a brick floored atrium with towering citrus trees and perfect potted plants. Soft piano music wafted out of the lounge as I punched the arrow on the nearest in the bank of elevators.

The room was spacious, with a small sitting area, a bed designed for three people and their two guard dogs, a massive flat-screen TV tastefully concealed in a towering wooden cabinet, and a minibar located just before the sliding doors that led to the smoking balcony. After I dropped my bag in the middle of the room, I opened the little bar refrigerator and spun the lid off of a mini of Johnny Walker Red, dumped it into a waiting glass, and tapped Obi on my cell phone.

"Boss!" he shouted joyfully.

"I'm here," I replied. "Over in the marina and I'm fucking starving. Meet me at the Crown and Anchor in half an hour." There was no way was I going to eat the leftovers of whatever poor Obi had for dinner.

"On my way," he said. "Welcome back to the Gold Coast."

I took a quick shower and changed into black jeans and a clean black V-neck T-shirt. It was a clear night and still warm that far south, so I took a ball bearing out of my coat and put it into the front pocket of my jeans, leaving my jacket behind. A lot of tattoos were showing, but it was a reasonably hip town. Delia had redone the old dragon spiraling up my arm, turning it from a dated late-eighties mess into a truly fantastic creature cavorting across a cloud-streaked sky webbed with lightning. The band of roses on my wrist could have used an overhaul, but it had sentimental value.

Outside, I walked a little ways away from the doors and lit a cigarette. The night felt perfect, that magical temperature where I couldn't even feel my skin. The air smelled like citrus and the ocean. I started walking, a slow, relaxed amble I noticed instantly. I wasn't on vacation, I reminded myself, and at the same time I didn't care.

The Crown and Anchor was just around the corner. It was a basement establishment with an English pub motif: dark wood, brass, plaid carpet, and shelves full of knick-knacks like pictures of old sailboats and dinner plates depicting past Queens and foxhunts. I'd always wanted to go on a foxhunt so I could steal all the horses. It would make the right kind of picture, anyway. I knew from my last visit that the prime rib was excellent and they had imperial pints, plus a good selection of scotch. The waitress guided me to a booth with high wooden backs and took my drink order. Obi arrived minutes later.

"Dude!" he shouted.

I stood up and we hugged. Obi was a hard six feet with an expressive Nordic face, close-set blue eyes, an almost comical Superman jaw, and hair so blond that it bordered on white. His beaming face was sunburned and peeling across the bridge of his nose. I'd given him endless shit about sunscreen over the years and so had everyone else, but he was evidently still set on the tan he would never get.

"How was the drive?" he asked, settling across from me.

"Not bad. I have that weird sloshing feeling, like I'm still in the car."

"You obviously need strong drink."

The waitress arrived as if on cue with an imperial tankard of Harp and a tumbler of Macallan on the rocks. Obi ordered a pint and we both went for the prime rib, medium rare. That he was hungry so late was tacit proof that a variation of the onion and olive casserole had been on the menu at his place.

"So," he said, rubbing his hands together and grinning.

"So," I replied. I downed the scotch and sipped the beer. The road slosh receded a few degrees, like the beginning of a shift to low tide. A nice little campfire lit up below my sternum and radiated out into my T-shirt.

"I did a little calling around, very discreet," Obi said. He looked both ways and leaned in a little closer. The Crown and Anchor was a loud and lively place at that time of night, but I appreciated his caution. "The shop he works at is called the Smiling Dragon Tattoo Emporium. Bling calls himself Richie Rad now, if you can believe anything so fuckin' stupid. The place opened a few months ago, a real turnstile. I had my buddy Jim go in and look around. Your Norton stuff isn't in there. Nobody knows who owns the place, but it doesn't look like Bling does or he'd be lording around like some Rockefeller in a gold sequin dinner jacket. Plus, you know, guys like Bling . . . He's on the run from so many people he can't open a PO box."

Obi's beer came. He took a mighty slurp and smacked his lips. "So what's our plan?"

"I'll drive over in the morning and check the place out. Hopefully Jason'll be working, or whatever it is he does there. When he's done I'll follow him home and make it up as I go along."

"He'll freak if he sees your car," Obi said thoughtfully.

"I'll get a rental at the airport."

"You can use my van if you want," Obi offered. "Man, I want to go with you." Obi had only worked with Bling for three weeks, but it had been more than enough. It was also possible that Delia had called him and put a few ideas in his head.

I shook my head. "It's better if you stay out of it. I'll just pick up a rental. With any luck this will all be over with tomorrow night."

Obi cocked his head with a wry smile and raised his glass. "Well then. To Lucky Supreme."

I clinked his glass with mine.

After a huge prime rib dinner I said good night to my old apprentice and strolled along the waterfront to the pier. I'd passed the halfway drunk line somewhere, but stopped within sight of it, so I felt good, but not bad-tomorrow good. White sailboats rocked gently on the calm water in their bird-shit-spattered mooring slips. A seal belched somewhere in the darkness, and a thin fog was spreading in off the calm water. I lit a cigarette and walked up to the railing and leaned up against it, spit into the water.

Sounds carried through the moist air, and scents as well. The lapping waves of the briny harbor mingled with the lemon trees and the cooling herbal sap of sage and rosemary. Distant laughter from the restaurants on the pier combined with the plastic grinding of wheels as the Mexican dishwashers towed huge garbage cans full of spent oyster shells and shrimp fins to wherever they took them at the end of the night.

The nightlife around the marina was wealthy and young and often very beautiful. The thrum of expensive sports car engines wired out of the fog behind me with increasing frequency as I smoked, and that sound would grow with the heartbeat of ten-dollar drinks and fake tits and quality coke as the evening took its ever-changing form. But right then was the median time, my favorite and most familiar twilight, the magic place between two worlds in one place. It made me a little homesick for Old Town, which would have been both sad and disgusting if my mood hadn't been just right. It made me feel rich instead, in the way that borderline broke people sometimes do.

4

The fog had burned off by nine a.m. I sat on the brick patio on the ocean side of the Portola eating breakfast from the buffet. Cantaloupe, some grapes, a single strawberry, and black coffee struck me as healthy, but I was picking at it. I was never much of a morning eater, but it was probably going to be a long day with a potential for serious physical activity and a surveillance diet, which I assumed meant no food, so I felt obligated to try.

Two slender women in spandex and knee pads rollerbladed past, heading for the bike path that led to the aquarium. Long hair and long legs. I watched their retreating backsides from behind the anonymity of my lost-and-found sunglasses and considered that it would be timely to get laid. The quality of the late October light was a rich, buttery yellow, sharper than the sunlight in Oregon, but still with that Vaseline fantasy blur that gave the west coast part of its orangey seventies movie quality. A light breeze ruffled the fruit trees and potted bamboo. A few more athletic women bladed past. The Portola buffet served mimosas with really good orange juice. I didn't want to go anywhere at all.

I trapped a few bucks on the table under my coffee cup for the Mexican busboy and caught a cab in front of the hotel. The small airport was less than ten minutes away, and it took less than five to rent an anonymous white Camry from Avis. I picked up a map, even though I didn't really need it after Obi's careful instructions, scribbled laboriously on the Crown and Anchor napkin in my pocket. It was just after ten thirty when I hit the freeway for the forty-minute drive to Santa Cruz.

I'd been to Santa Cruz. In the late eighties I'd worked briefly as a butcher in Alaska, chopping salmon for the lower forty-eight in a fresh freeze factory located on a spit of land outside of a little town called Homer on the Kenai Peninsula. It hadn't been all that bad, though I'd never considered doing it again. Everyone lived in tents on the beach. The other butchers and the freezer crew guys and gals were from all over the country, and every night after work we'd gather around big flat bonfires and drink beer and do bong hits, dreaming out loud about what we'd do once the season was over.

A lot of those young adventurers went to Thailand or India, sometimes Nepal. They did the same thing every year. If they ran low on fish cash they would bomb into Amsterdam and sell coke to other Americans for a few months. Sounded fun. My plan was less prosaic, but I was eighteen and I didn't know anything about the outside world at the time. When the factory closed at the end of the season, I hitchhiked all the way down to Santa Cruz with some hippie chick I'd met up there, the first white girl I'd ever seen with dreadlocks. She was a little older than me, in her midtwenties, and about as spaced out a woman as an eighteen-year-old boy/man could ask for. We stayed in a crappy motel on the beach with a kitchenette for a few months, eating beans and rice and shagging like lusty animals in a perpetual spring mating season for stoned mammals. I smiled when I thought about it, and when I did I realized my face had been locked in zero all morning in spite of the view.

Santa Cruz hadn't changed all that much in the intervening years. It still had an artsy, sleepy beach town feel, but the effect was somewhat diminished by the new prefab crap sprouting up between the old buildings. Even the venerable brick structures were showing symptoms of the same American retrofit virus that was running through Old Town—if it was old, slap a plastic sign on it and call it good until the bulldozers arrived.

I found the Smiling Dragon Tattoo Emporium based on Obi's directions, pulled into the parking lot of a Chinese food place across the street, and studied the place. It was even worse than Obi described.

The Leering Snake Turnstile Graveyard was the kind of tattoo shop that I most feared and despised, even without stepping through the door. It was in a mini mall as described, sandwiched between a Vietnamese hair-and-nail salon and a video game outlet called Gamestar. A tattoo shop in a mini mall, or even worse a full-sized mall, was deeply wrong on many levels. It not only spoke of poor taste and the damning commercialization of the art, but the actual owner was almost certainly an extra-shitty member of the already shitty Wall Street class, showing up for some profit and sporting humiliation now that the brutal work of cleaning up after Wally's generation was done. The sign out front was predictably huge, not neon but some kind of cheap Malaysian thing that you might find dangling from the facade of a franchise tire chain or a diet hoagie place. An art prison, churning out license plates, where custom was a word from a different language, children's coloring book was as good as you would ever get, and every shift was exactly, precisely eight hours long. Getting there early or staying late could be confused with joyful enthusiasm, and that kind of attitude would make everyone suspicious.

Inside, I knew, there would be three or four high-speed hacks like Bling, stencil jockeys who paid more attention to their hair than they ever did to learning how to draw. The walls would be covered with Sailor Jerry knockoff flash, primitive, flat, watercolor garbage interspersed with sheets purchased off the Internet, and maybe a dozen or so imitation Ed Hardy generated by the most ambitious ape in the mix. I rolled the windows down and slouched low in the seat, lit up a cigarette.

Three minutes before noon, a cherry-red '67 Chevy low-rider rumbled into the mini mall parking lot. It was an expensive ride, with chrome spinners on the wheels and dual tail pipes that rumbled close to the frequency of the devil's voice. I sat up a little, my heart rate rising pleasantly. My hands were instantly sweaty.

The Chevy door yawned open like a coffin lid and out stepped Jason Bling. A feeling of immense delight bubbled up through my thundering chest and I almost laughed out loud.

Bling was a big kid, and he carried it with a trademark, slightly bowlegged swagger. Some people had cat spines, some dog. Bling was rigid Doberman. He was dressed as Obi reported, in some kind of rockabilly getup; a new white T-shirt with a pack of cigarettes rolled into the sleeve and straight-leg jeans folded up four inches over construction boots. The look was complete all the way up to his shellacked pompadour.

Bling flicked the tail end of a cigarette in front of the hair-and-nail place next to the shop and unlocked the front door. A few minutes later, the lights came on inside and the CLOSED sign in the window turned around.

Bling's new place of scab creation was open for business. I sure liked his car.

Two more artists showed up in the next few minutes, both of them decked out like Bling. One was a fat guy driving a Honda motorcycle and the other was a small, hard-faced kid driving what had to be his girlfriend's Mazda. There was a stuffed panda dangling from the rearview and a PINK sticker on the bumper. I pegged the kid instantly as the artist in the group. He was carrying an art bag, so he'd been doing homework, which meant he had appointments. One foot out the door headed up into the real game, plus he had an actual girlfriend, so he and Bling undoubtedly hated each other. Possibly useful.

At one o'clock Bling came out and smoked another cigarette, talking on his cell phone the entire time. It was an old pattern of his I remembered all too well. When he'd worked for me, he'd spent as much time on his cell phone as any fifteen-year-old suburban cheerleader. I'd considered his two-cell-phone phase mildly humorous at the time. He leaned against the side of his car and jabbered, occasionally tossing his head back in flamboyant, hair-flipping laughter. A couple of very young women in flowery shorts, flip-flops, and halter tops went into the Smiling Cash Machine and Bling followed them in, pausing briefly to hard-scratch his crotch through his jeans.

Around four, I finally drove down to a mini-mart a few blocks away and got two bottles of water and a few beef and green chili taquitos, then I parked just a little up the street and continued the stakeout.

Just after six Bling ambled out, hopped into his car, fired up the V8, and headed north. I pulled in behind him a few cars back, put my sunglasses back on, and slouched to the side.

Eventually he pulled into the gravel parking lot of a newer-looking bar called the Madison. He was still on his phone as he locked the car and checked his hair and teeth in the reflection of the window. Satisfied, he sauntered inside.

The parking lot was relatively full for a Thursday and I had to take a fierce leak after the two bottles of water, but I decided I couldn't risk going in or even losing sight of the Chevy. I was peeing into one of the empty bottles when my cell phone rang. Delia. I tucked the phone under my chin.

"Tell me you found him. Tell me you found him and robbed him because he already sold your stuff or lost it." I don't know how I could hear her holding her breath, but I could.

"I'm looking at his car right now. I'm also peeing into an empty water bottle."

"You mean you're touching yourself even as we speak? You're lucky this isn't Microsoft or I'd sue your pervert ass."

"You wouldn't believe this. The idiot is dressed up like an extra from *The Lords of Flatbush*."

"Hmmn," Delia mused. "It's a step up from Vanilla Ice."

I grunted and meat-tapped the mouth of the bottle.

"So what's next?"

"How are the cats?" I countered. Delia sighed explosively.

"Fine! Pinky bit me already, but in his defense my fingers smelled like French fries."

"He does that because you make him happy. Just don't try to touch him while he's eating, and don't try to stop him when he's having his toilet water. He hates that."

"Duh."

There was a long silence.

"Be careful," she said finally. Her tone was different. "I just talked to Nigel and Mikey. They want you to call as soon as you're done. I'll be at your place getting sticky stuff on your crappy porn. Waiting. Pacing."

It was my turn to sigh. "Call you later. Promise." I thumbed the phone off.

Bling came out of the Madison a few minutes later, accompanied by a meaty Mexican guy with an oily, cratered face and a tiny ponytail, wearing a Nike track suit and lots of gold jewelry. They got in the Chevy and talked for a few minutes. The Mexican guy got out and went back inside the bar. Bling sat still in his car for a moment and then his head dipped out of sight once, then twice. Snorting coke, off a knife or a CD cover. He checked his nostrils in the rearview and rubbed them, fired up the Chevy, and gunned it out of the parking lot, spraying the other cars with loose gravel to mark his exit.

Bling drove faster then. I followed him down Water Street, slumped low, only a single car back. He took a left at Poplar and roared up the hill, blasting his horn at a minivan that tried to change lanes and then at a sturdy old woman at a crosswalk. I dropped back a few cars, just in case the coke had already made him paranoid. It had certainly made him more aggressive.

That was why I almost lost him as he rounded a corner and took a hard right through a red light. My molars hurt as I hit the gas and took the corner thirty seconds behind him, pushing the little four-cylinder rental. I caught sight of the Chevy a few blocks down, roaring to a stop in a parking space in front of a seedy cinderblock one-story apartment complex. I came to a stop behind a van just up the street and got out, pulling my bomber jacket out behind me.

Bling was on his cell phone again. This time I was close enough to hear him laughing at something, a throaty, contrived thespian spaz of a thing that never sounded friendly. He kicked his car door closed and flipped through his keys as he approached an apartment door. I came up quietly behind him, head down.

"Late," I heard him say. The parking lot was conveniently empty of people. He slid his key into the lock and swung the door open. As he passed through the doorway, I put on a burst of speed and raised a hand like I was waving to him, in case anyone was watching out a window. I caught him square in the center of his chest with the heel of my boot as he turned to close the door, knocking him backward into the room.

I nudged the door closed behind me and locked it without taking my eyes off of him. Bling was lying on his back, clutching his chest, clucking out a dry heave sound. He let out a pitiful moan and glared up at me. His eyes went wide with the shock of recognition.

I pulled on the gloves from the pocket of my bomber jacket and then took out a gleaming ball bearing and held it up to show him between my thumb and forefinger.

"Hello," I said softly. "Fucker."

All the lights in Bling's apartment were off. No TV. No radio. We were all alone, which was good, as it meant I wouldn't have to beat the shit out of one of Bling's girlfriends for trying to shoot me.

"Assault!" Jason Bling choked. "Your ass is going to fucking prison!"

He started to fish something out of his hip pocket and I nailed him hard in the shoulder with the toe of my boot. His cell phone skittered across the filthy linoleum floor. Bling let out a hiss.

"Real shithole you got here," I observed. Most of his stuff was in cardboard boxes with the lids ripped open. There was a stack of pots and pans on the floor of the kitchenette to my right. The only other furniture in the entire place was a king-sized poster bed from a low-end eighties porno flick in the center of the single bedroom, with a large plasma-screen TV propped up on milk crates at the foot of it. The walls were bare white with handprints and general smears. Bling's clothes were scattered on the floor around his Cadillac bed, and it was obvious that he'd been walking back and forth over them, leaving flat trails of unwashed feet and parking lot grease. The entire place smelled like sour Chinese mustard and ripe ass. In an instant, I realized

Jason wasn't planning on moving any time soon. He'd never bothered to unpack.

"Where's my Roland Norton flash?" I asked quietly, standing over him. For whatever reason he was mad as hell. I cocked my head, curious.

"Fuck you!" he screamed, his face twisted with fury. His wind was already back.

"You wanna call the police, you stupid prick? I do. I know three things right now, Jason. One, you have some coke in your pocket. I know you do because I saw you buy it. Two, I have a signed statement in *my* pocket from everyone at the Lucky Supreme saying that they will gladly testify against you for the theft of the Roland Norton flash"—a lie, but it sounded good—"and three, I know a pill-slinging fuck-up like you doesn't have a bank account. Noooo, not you. You have a great big wad of cash in here somewhere, don't you buddy? Maybe a shitload of pills in the same box? Bet that'll look sweet when the cops find it." I took my cell phone out. "Got your little rolled up pussy nuts in order?"

Jason deflated like a balloon. His expression morphed from homicidal wrath to weaselly furtiveness in a single heartbeat. His eyes flicked for an instant in the direction of the kitchenette. Busted.

"I didn't steal a fuckin' thing from you, Darby," he said with all the firmness he could squeeze out of his chest. "I have no idea what you're talking about. Just get the fuck out of my place. Get out of here and it's like you were never here at all. You're a psycho, man. Full blown. You slipped in your head somehow. I get that. But you better just go."

He made his voice gentle. "Go and get some help man, like from a shrink or a—"

"Wrong." I started mock dialing. Bling's eyes bugged out.

"Wait! Just fuckin' wait a minute!" I could see the gears in his greasy head spinning like the wheels in a slot machine, hoping a stall would land him on the triple cherry. I waited.

"Well?"

"That's kind of a puss move, isn't it?" he said, a hint of a sneer touching his lips and eyes. He edged back a little. The red in his cheeks was draining away, replaced with white as blood pooled around his organs. Bling was getting ready to fight. "Calling the cops?"

"It's either that or beat you within an inch of your life and then tear this place apart. You know I don't like cops, but I don't feel like getting all sweaty. Plus these are my favorite pants." I took a deep breath. My hands were shaking as I flipped a cigarette out of my pack. Jason noticed and cracked a telling smile.

He came up fast, swinging a haymaker with his good arm. I lifted on my toes and then dropped into it and hammered him in the soft underside of his breadbasket, my first two knuckles wrapped around the ball bearing, angled down a little so that the weight of my descending upper body mass was behind it. A great whoosh of smelly air gusted from his gaping mouth and he went down again. I kicked him hard in the side and he instantly vomited. Then everything seemed to pause. He seemed dead for a moment, and then one hand scrabbled out in a blind palsy through his slimy white puke, like he was groping after a key.

I dropped on him, ripped the chain off of his biker wallet, tied his hands behind his back, ran the clip under his belt and hooked it. There was a single disco-era lamp in the living room on the floor by his bed. I ripped the cord off and tied his hands again, using the rest of the wire to loop around his neck in a half-assed ghetto hog-tie. Bling struggled as the cord bit into the underside of his prominent Adam's apple. His sweat tripped it back and forth over the bump, so I pressed my knee into the center of his back and cinched the cord tight in place on the underside, leaving him just enough room to breathe.

Bling watched me out of the corner of one rolling eye, coughing violently, as I picked up his wallet. I riffled through it, my heartbeat loud in my temples. No bank card or credit cards, no driver's license. Lots of little slips of paper with women's phone numbers and a small stack of Smiling Dragon Tattoo Emporium business cards. The card for a car detailing place. Another one for a barber shop. Three hundred and forty-six bucks. I pocketed the money and dropped the wallet in the puddle of puke, splashing his face with a fan of droplets. Bling let out a choking protest.

"Dinner's on you," I said, even though he was too stupid to catch my little joke. Sometimes I break the tension just for myself.

His keys were in his left pocket. I dug them out and looked them over. One of them was a round, toothy nub, the kind that usually fit into a bike lock. I read the writing on the side. Sentry. A safe key.

"Bling, Bling, Bling," I tutted. "What kind of idiot are you to keep a crappy safe key on the ring you carry around in your pocket? You think your zitty coke dealer pal in the tracksuit never noticed? You're damn lucky I came along when I did."

The safe was in the kitchenette, bolted into the back of the cabinet under the sink, so poorly hidden behind a reeking, overflowing trashcan that I'd have found it in less than a minute, even if he hadn't given it away by flicking his eyes there when I brought up his stash. I swept the trashcan out, scattering rotting take-out boxes across the floor. There were maggots, which sharply, instantly fucked up my already terrible mood. Bling moaned and cursed behind me as the smell filled the place.

The snub key fit neatly into the lock of the squat plastic safe. I flipped the top open and whistled at the bundles of used bills. On top of them was a shiny new gun. I took one of the bundles out and skimmed it with a gloved thumb. An even thousand, mostly in twenties. There were sixty-one bundles in all. I scooped them out and set them on the counter. It was only a moderate amount of money when it came to yuppie houseplant drugs and about a third of the value of my Roland Norton collection. Below the bills were two plastic bags, one packed with Valium and a smaller one with a few hundred Oxycontins. I left the drugs for the moment. When we got to the question and answer period I could hold them hostage over the toilet.

"Your moonlighting gig is pretty much twenty-watt, kid," I called in a casual voice. "I need a bag of some kind for all this cash, Bling. Where you keep 'em?"

"Fuck you," he croaked.

I walked past him and stripped the grubby pillowcase off his bed, then went back into the kitchenette and shoveled the money into it. When I was done I walked back into the living room and kicked over one of the boxes. CDs, clothes, and assorted junk scattered across the floor. It took less than ten minutes to thoroughly destroy the place. No Roland Norton flash anywhere. No artwork of any kind. Not even art supplies. Bling struggled a couple of times as he got his breath back, but quieted down again whenever I paused to look at him. There were two closets in the place, both empty. The bathroom was a nightmare, with a moldy shower curtain and a toilet bowl full of orange water with a black and green freckled rim. Bling was out of toilet paper, but there were a few fast food napkins on the back of the toilet. A forever dry toothbrush sat in a little nest of hair on the edge of the sink. I was glad I was wearing gloves as I probed around and finally opened the medicine cabinet. No toothpaste. Just an empty bottle of aspirin and a tube of cherry ChapStick with no lid. When I was done bulldozing the entire place a second time, I settled across from him on top of an upturned milk crate.

"Showtime, scooter." I gestured at him with the gun, patted the rolled-up sack of cash in my lap. "You want to keep this money, you better tell me where my flash is."

"Untie me," he wheezed.

"Nah."

"Jesus man, you have my gun! I think you broke something in my chest, Darby. I need a fucking cigarette. Please!"

I thought about it for a minute. It would be stupid to untie him, exactly the kind of stupid Delia had warned me about.

"Fine. You do anything dumb and you die like half the other jackasses with a gun like this." I pointed at him with the barrel of his shiny toy. "With every single bullet in your own motherfucking piece."

It took five long minutes to get the chain and the cord off of him and I wasn't gentle about it. When I was finished, Bling lolled onto his side like a beached tuna and then flopped over on his back. His puke was getting all over him. Obi was right about the gut he'd grown. I lit a cigarette for him and stoked the cherry before I tossed it into his lap from five feet away.

"Fuck," Bling whined, plucking it up and smacking his jeans where it had come to a smoldering rest. He took a long drag and coughed, then eyed me.

"You better not have sold my stuff," I cautioned.

"Sure as fuck did." Bling took another drag. "Had to." He blew the smoke in my direction and stared at me through slit eyes. There was a white gob of whatever he'd retched up earlier stuck in the corner of his mouth. "Do what you're gonna do, Darby. Just get it over with. We had a few laughs, me and you. I know what you tried to do for me. But all this shit? You don't understand, man. Walk away. If you walk away, it'll be like I paid you back a hundred times over." His hand was trembling as he hit the cigarette again.

"I know you were running pills out of Canada," I said. "I know you burned a bunch of scumbags and split town. I don't need to understand anything about you, kid. It would make me dirty somehow if I did. But predicting you, now that's a different story. I knew, I just fucking *knew* your place would look like this. Just like I can predict that everything you say will have some kind of wrinkle in it."

Bling didn't say anything. Amazingly, his smug expression returned, this time with watery, world-weary, sad eyes. It was strange and surprising to see something so complicated on his face. Reveling in his fate, the kind of magical tragedy that only happened in movies and to him, and there was actually something real about it. He held up the cigarette and studied it like it was a pet insect.

"I knew right when I saw you that this shit was finally over," he began. "I don't even fuckin' care at this point." He tried for a sigh and coughed instead.

A messy, distorted truth was about to come out of him. I could feel it. I watched and listened, motionless, transfixed in spite of myself.

"Got all fucked up with the wrong people," he continued. "I always do. But this time there's no way out. I'm still working this shit off every day, like a . . . like a slave or a prisoner, I guess. Indentured servitude, like the Irish guys in the old days. They wanted your Norton flash, don't ask me why. They wanted it all. I always thought it was some ugly shit, especially compared to some of the other old stuff at the Lucky." He shrugged and coughed again. "Who the fuck knows."

"Who'd you sell it to, Jason? Tell me who has it and I might mail this money back when I'm done with them." I said it calmly.

Bling's laugh was a mean bark of disgust aimed at both of us. "Not a fucking chance, Darby. You, that slick fucking soulless bastard Nigel, Big Dummy Mike, little psycho fuckin' Delia . . . You may be a pack of badasses, dude, but these people would eat your livers with fava beans. No fuckin' way. Just let it go." He took a breath. "I'm really trying to help you out right now."

"Jason," I said. I could hear the tiredness in my voice. I leaned out and whipped him over the top of the head with his gun. He screamed and shrank back into a ball, as far back into the trash around him as he could get.

"I said no fucking way," he said firmly. He glared at me, all angry dog in a hot car. "They have pictures of my parents! Pictures they took of them sitting in their backyard, dude. They were eating. Laughing. Pictures of my sister and her three kids at a park. No way, Darby. That's the one bridge I can't burn. You maybe can't understand that, but try, dude. Just fuckin' try."

Bling's jaw quivered. I knew from that look that I could beat on him all night and he wouldn't talk until the very end, but Jason knew I wasn't a killer, that I wouldn't, couldn't go all the way to monster, that he would never see his death in my eyes as I beat him to the edge of oblivion with no intention of stopping. That true, unfakable x-ray stare was the only thing that would get him to spill his guts. And from the look on his face I knew that whoever had the Roland Norton flash definitely could go there and keep going, all the way back to his mommy and daddy and points beyond. It didn't mean that it was true, just that he was sure of it. I was suddenly sick of that room, sick of looking at him, sick of the smell of his vomit and the rotting trash. The aura of desperate scumminess was getting inside of me and fingering things.

"Jason Bling," I said slowly. "You might have a soul in there after all. You can't fucking imagine my surprise."

He stared at me with those dog's eyes.

"Just sit there," I continued. "Sit there for an hour. A week. Don't ever get up again. Don't pick up that broken phone and monkey around with it. Don't do anything at all, because I will know. I will, and then I'll have to come back, and if that happens we both change forever." I paused. "I'm gonna leave now, but I want you to think about something, fool. You know why I don't blow your worthless fucking brains all over that pile of shit behind you?"

"No," he replied sullenly. I leaned a little closer and stared as far as I could into his empty head. It was so empty I flash-hallucinated that I could see right out his ass to the seat of his pants. My glimpse of his soul had come and gone. His face went so blank that for a moment I could see what he must have looked like when he was a little boy, before he took all the wrong detours and lost his map and became Jason Bling.

"Me neither." I got up and backed up to the door, the money under my arm, the gun pointed at his face. Bling raised his hands and then slowly reached down and withdrew the small bag of coke from the breast pocket of his T-shirt, his glassy eyes never leaving mine. I backed out, lowering the gun to my side, leaving him in his personal darkness as I closed the door on what he considered a life.

On the drive back to Monterey I checked the rearview every thirty seconds. There was no way Bling would try to follow me, especially since I had his only gun and I'd been convincingly sincere about what would happen if he did, but there was a chance that he had the spine to look out the window at my rental and get the license plate. The hard calm had left me on the walk to the car and I was shaking a little and my stomach felt like it was full of flat beer. The rings of moisture under my arms were getting cold and sweat was trickling freely down my ribs. I lit a cigarette and rolled the window down, letting the freeway-speed ocean breeze scour away some of the stink of the last hour.

The sun had set while I was busy. I tried to call Obi on my cell phone, but I couldn't scroll with my thumb. I cursed and tossed the phone on the seat, then tried the radio, but I couldn't hear anything with the windows down. So I smoked and tried to keep the cigarette from being blown apart.

That hadn't worked out too well, I thought. I glanced at the fluttering, greasy pillowcase on the passenger seat. The gun was underneath it. I cursed again and smacked the wheel with the flat of my hand. A mixture of shame and self-loathing rippled in itchy waves through the meat of my body. I felt fevered. Infected.

Jason Bling was no better than an animal from a drainage canal. No smarter, no more noble. His life was a malarial rampage of pussy, drugs, and the constant scams that linked it all together. And he'd dragged me down into his Darwinian sewer with no effort at all, and for at least one evening I was just another sorry creature in Bling's shit-eating food chain, one clever rung higher than he was. That was why I walked out with the money and the gun and enough information to work with. Because I'd played his game, and I was better at it.

Deep down, I wanted to believe in some kind of world where no one beat the hell out of anyone else for stealing something crappy. Where no one got tied up in a puddle of puke. Where I didn't sit in front of someone and ruin a part of both of us while I openly wondered about murder. The evolving mystery of the crap in question just made it all a slightly different shade of wrong. I was under no illusion that I would ever hold incense and hug turtles and contemplate the dawn with the Dalai Lama. It was way too late for anything like that. But for years I'd been feeling like the level of deranged corruption around me was at the maximum level I could tolerate without lasting damage, and my personal threshold was exceptionally high. When it spiked beyond a certain point, I couldn't swallow it anymore. On some psychic level I was puking as I drove, a hard retching purge, but I couldn't get it out. It never came out. It always stayed in me somewhere, every single time.

I tossed my cigarette out the window and lit another one. The lights of Monterey flickered through the groves of eucalyptus trees and I got a sudden wash of Saturday Night Howl. Neon. A clean hotel room. Bars with clean people, doing their drinking in clean clothes out of clean glasses. Music. Women with nice shoes and day jobs. No scabs in their lipstick. No chance they had ever met Bling. It didn't matter that I'd be the worst person in the room.

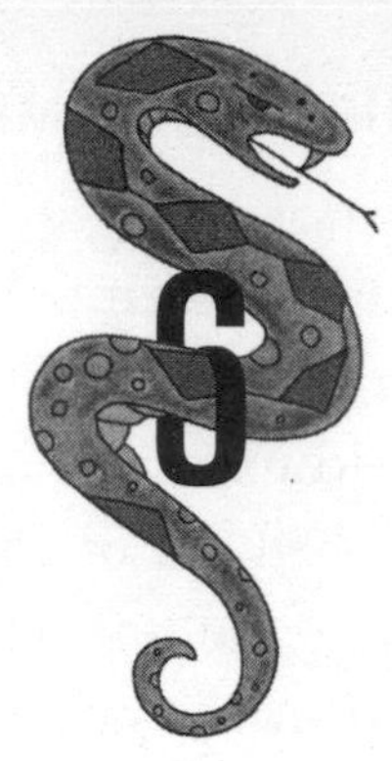

When I got back to the hotel, I parked the rental in the garage down the street next to my BMW and locked it. It would have been nice to put the money in my car, but it didn't have a trunk and there were security cameras everywhere, so the spare tire compartment was out too. I walked up the sidewalk to the Portola with Bling's gun in my bomber jacket and the pillowcase full of money tucked in a roll under my arm. Delia would call it one of the weak parts of a plan that had already devolved into improvisation. I was glad she wasn't next to me, scowling in that way she had when I risked making something already bad worse.

None of the perfectly crisp employees or sunburned vacationers looked at me as I went through the wide lobby to the elevators, every one of them amazingly unaware that I'd just beaten and hog-tied a worthless scumbag and stolen his drug money. I rode in the elevator with a German tourist and her short-shorts teenage daughter. When I looked down to avoid their eyes, I noticed flecks of Bling's puke on my pants. I didn't raise my head until the doors opened.

Back in my room, I took a thousand dollars out of Bling's stash and locked the rest of it in the hotel room's closet safe with the gun. Then I took a long, boiling shower, scrubbing my hair and my hands over and over again. The top two knuckles on my right hand hurt a little where the ball bearing had been when I pounded Bling's soggy beer gut, and my hip was stiff, probably from the drive down from Portland, but the hot, sulfurous water soaked into my joints and I gradually relaxed.

When I turned the water off I could hear music in the distance as a dance club fired up their sound system a few blocks away. I got the aspirin out of my bag and popped three, then walked naked over to the window. The night looked peaceful, restively devoid of angry prostitutes and scheming thieves. No obvious drug dealers or pimps. Not a junkie in sight. Not even any desperate old people. A couple holding hands strolled past below me, maybe going to dinner.

I dressed in the best clothes I'd brought with me. The black Armani jeans were getting faded, but it was dark. The black V-neck sweater from the Myer and Franks after-Christmas sale still looked good. I needed to get out and get into a higher class of trouble. If nothing else, I could get drunk enough to forget why I was getting drunk, and that had spiritually medicinal value all by itself.

In the elevator I checked my face for bruises, because you never know. You can bruise your face after a fight of any kind just by rubbing it too hard. There weren't any, but the bulging wad of twenties in my pocket was throwing off the cut of my pants. When the doors opened I headed across the huge tile lobby to the bar, still decompressing.

The bar turned out to be a little too upscale for my taste, which wasn't really much of a surprise, but the designer had also gone for a blend of cozy with a dash of sports bar in a misguided attempt to please everyone. A bar needs character, but not a schizophrenic one. It confuses people prematurely. There was a gas fireplace in one corner, surrounded by low driftwood drink stands and glass coffee tables and plush chairs. Across the expanse of wine-colored carpet from the fireplace, an immensely vulgar plasma-screen TV was silently broadcasting a sports channel. No one was playing the polished grand piano to the right of the entrance. They were piping in an almost subliminal level of Casioed Billy Joel.

The place was only half full, even at nine thirty on a Saturday night. I ordered a smoky martini at the mahogany and brass bar and turned on my bar stool, surveying the room. It was depressing, but in a hygienic way.

Some kind of convention was evidently going on, at least in the hotel. Most of the other drinkers were wearing nametags, a dead giveaway. The bar crowd was predominantly male, guys in their mid-to-late forties, with big mushy office bodies tortured by red meat and 24 Hour Fitness. Collared shirts, huddled in tight groups and drinking expensive white wine or Midwestern bar standards. The scattering of women were all hyper and shiny, with TV hair. I'll never know why, but women with too much glittery jewelry always struck me as birdlike, but in a chicken rather than a sparrow kind of way. An intense, peyote-level scrutiny of my formative memories on the subject might have dredged up my introduction to the concept of gizzard stones or something equally ghastly, so I never thought about it.

There were a few people at the bar itself, mostly obvious locals chatting quietly with the bartender. One of them was a woman in her early thirties wearing most of a uniform, possibly a waitress from one of the numerous local bistros. She was pretty, with shoulder length straight black hair and a long, lanky figure. I smiled at her and she looked away. She was talking, so I slipped into eavesdropping mode.

"—Mary and I was like, good God, girl." The bartender was an older woman with gray in the wings of her hair. She nodded sympathetically as the woman continued. "I mean, the terminals are updated every six months. I can't screw around with her tickets every fuckin' order."

"You should take a shift at this place," the bartender said, looking over her shoulder. A ticket chattered out of the black plastic module on the bar top by the drink condiments as if on command. She plucked it out and showed it to her. "Check that out. No abbreviations, but all the stuff at the bottom? Everyone hits the rush button. And when they tip me out, you think this constant drink crisis ever comes up? Why would I even bother to mention it?"

A couple of bar drinkers peeled off for a table. The bartender started filling the emergency order that had just come in, either from room service or the restaurant next door. The waitress looked at me again.

"I can't stand computers," I offered as an opening. She smiled and stirred her drink with a straw. It looked like a rum and coke, a drink I'd only consider if the world was ending in thirty seconds.

"Can't do a damn thing without them," she replied. "So you aren't with the software convention?"

I picked up my drink and moved to the stool next to her. She gave me a grin that said I was being an idiot. I ignored it and looked innocent, even perplexed.

"No way," I said in a low, conspiratorial voice. "Who are they?"

She laughed softly.

"Computarians." She turned and looked at the other drinkers. "We have conventions around here every week, sometimes two." She looked me over, the laugh still dancing around her eyes. "What are you doing here?"

"Art," I said expansively. I tried to look thoughtful and then I thought about Bling.

"Hmm," she said, watching my face.

"It's a rude environment sometimes. Very competitive."

"Do you like it?" she asked, sipping through her straw. Her lips were thin and painted a dark, flaking red. I shrugged.

"It's probably better than, I dunno . . . what did you say these people are up to?"

She shrugged back. "Premier Telecom Applications. That's what the geek sign in the lobby says, anyway. Probably routers or satellite code crap."

"Ah," I said, brightening. "You understand that kind of thing?"

"I'm working on my business degree. So no. But I've been serving them all night at the bistro up the street." She lowered her eyes over her drink.

"I bet you know where to eat around here," I said. I looked over the bar. "And maybe get a few drinks. This place is kinda sleepy."

"Maybe," she replied, smiling in earnest.

My cell phone rang a few times that night, but I didn't answer it. It turned out that Carina and her boyfriend of several years had broken up a few months before. Around two a.m. I left her little beachside apartment and checked my missed calls. There was one from Obi, two from Nigel, and eleven from Delia.

I called Obi first and got his voice mail, a happy, family kind of message with the kid squeaking in the background. Nigel's number went straight to voice mail. Then I called Delia. She answered on the first ring.

"Gettin' some poon?" she asked in a slurred voice.

"Just finished," I said. "What are you up to?"

She yawned. "Went out for drinks. Played old Atari games at that arcade place downtown. Lame. When you didn't call, I actually figured you were fine. You would have called right away if you got shot or something. Or the cops would have. Or the morgue. A veterinarian you were holding hostage."

"I'm walking through Monterey trying to find my hotel," I said. It was a nice night, not too cool, with a salty breeze touched with rosemary and cotton candy. I told her about it.

"Did you find Bling?" she asked when I was done.

"Oh yeah."

"You kicked his ass, didn't you?"

"Yep."

"Goody," she said sleepily.

"It really wasn't that bad," I said. "He did puke."

"Right on. So do I need to worry about the cops showing up at the Lucky in the morning?"

"I doubt it," I replied. "I didn't get the flash back, but I have an idea who might have it." I saw the Marriott sign off in the distance. The Portola was right next to it. "I guess I'll be down here for another day or so. How's the shop?"

"Fine. Today was solid. Your cats miss you, but I'm on the couch and they're both laying on me. Little piggies." She yawned again. "You need to get a TV."

"Not really."

"Nighty then. Don't be stupid."

Back in the hotel I crashed on to the bed with my clothes on, properly spent. Carina's perfume was all over me and my mouth tasted like I'd eaten a hairy boxing glove, so I stripped down, had a shot of gin from the minibar, and took a shower.

With a towel wrapped around my waist I went out on to the balcony and looked over the sleeping city, my mind drifting randomly over the blurry events of the day. Delia was right. I couldn't really afford to be stupid. I was pretty far out on a limb, walking the wire with no safety net. I could feel it, even through the booze and the fucking and the exhaustion. "Don't be stupid" was solid advice.

But I was on a roll.

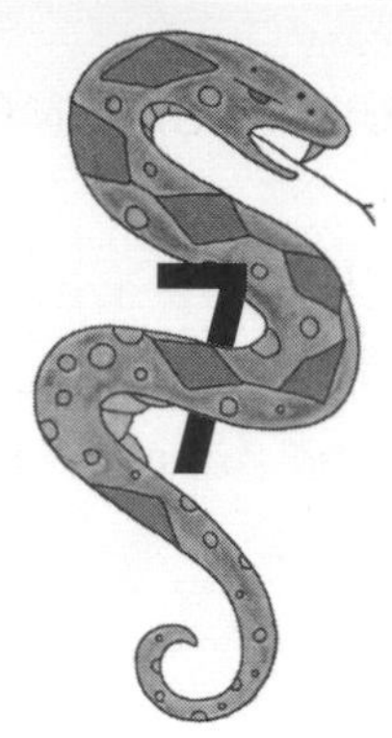

7

My cell phone rang at nine a.m. sharp. Gold light flooded the hotel room, bright on my eyelids. I groaned and scooped the phone off the nightstand and looked at the number, rubbing my face. It was Obi.

"Hey boss! Hangover?"

"Oh shit," I muttered. The sound of his impossibly happy voice was like an ice pick scraping across the inside of my dried-out skull. I fished around in the back of my mouth and pulled out a curly black pubic hair.

"Good!" he continued. "I'm glad you're having a good time, dude. I bet you even smiled once or twice. You probably even got laid. You get your stuff?"

"No," I replied. "I . . . there was, see, I . . . shit." I sat up and shook a cigarette out of my pack, then staggered out the sliding door onto the balcony and lit it. The sharp breeze woke me up a little. "Obi, I need a little favor."

"Alka-Seltzer?" he asked. "The woman asleep in your bathtub needs a ride home?" That was one good thing about an old apprentice: they always felt like they owed you. Forever.

"I need you to tap your client base. Get someone with connections to find out who owns the Smiling Dragon Tattoo Emporium. The actual building." Most working tattoo artists had a list of customers with specialized backgrounds. I had a massive one, and I'd trained Obi well, so I knew he'd been picking up Monterey names as he went.

"No prob. Actually my broker can do that. Or this law librarian I tattooed that works in real estate. She'd be good. It'll take about an hour after I get to the shop. Is one o'clock okay?"

"'S fine." I padded over to the miniature coffee maker in the alcove outside the bathroom and stared at it. The little machine was bleak. Mournful. Oppressive.

"So, what, you going to look up Bling's boss?"

I decided against attempting the coffee machine and turned away. "Yeah. Bling said something that made me think, right after I'd kicked his stomach out. He was still working off some kind of debt. Every day, he said. Like a slave, or a prisoner. I need to know who runs that place and who owns the building. Everything."

I had room service bring up a twelve-by-sixteen cardboard shipping box and a pot of coffee, and an hour later I was showered, dressed, caffeinated, and standing in line at the Marina post office with the bulk of Bling's cash. I taped and labeled it at the weight desk by the priority envelopes and passport forms. The money actually smelled bad, like old milk, fish oil, and rotting tarps. The box was addressed to me at the Lucky Supreme. On the way over I'd stopped by a scenic pond with some swans gliding over the surface and underhanded Bling's gun into the still green water.

Once the package was sent, I drove back to the airport and returned the rental, then took a cab back to the

Portola. I was still shaking the hangover and needed a walk, so I wandered out to the pier, pausing now and then at the vendor stalls to look over the displays of saltwater taffies and seashell sculptures. Finally, I got a second cup of coffee and the local newspaper and sat down on a bench in the sun.

I had Bling's money, but it was a fraction of what people were paying for Roland Norton, Panama 1955. It wouldn't hurt to press it a little further. I still felt bad about yesterday, but it was hard to feel truly moribund sitting in the sun and staring out over the ocean. Maybe I just didn't want to go home, I realized. Obi had found a fantastic little piece of America. I chipped away at the newspaper and drank coffee. After a while I took out my sketchbook and half-heartedly scribbled and sketched at the edges of a few of the sailboats.

Sketchbooks came in all shapes and sizes. I favored the black ones with the hard, durable covers, the size of a hardback book. On impulse I flipped back to the first page and traced the dark trail of the last six months. It was like a diary written in hieroglyphics.

The first pages were always tense in a sketchbook. It was bad juju to have something crappy or thematically off too early, so they almost didn't count. In this one I'd drawn skulls, the first one with heavy shadows, a few cracks, no real time invested, and then on the next page another one. It was apparently skull number one's girlfriend. Floppy hat with a flower in it, clown makeup made out of playing card hearts and spades, diamonds and clubs. Scattered around the base of it were coins set on their edges, with comic book motion lines to make them spin. Hard to remember, but probably girl problems.

Two pages of coiled snakes. Then four pages of guns, smoke curling from the barrels, smeared Gotham skylines behind them. Crows with no trees to land on. An owl head on a stick. A ten-page study of antlers, mostly deer. A mummy, no background. Necklace of eyeteeth, three pages of toads, some realistic eyes, a red wine finger painting of something, I couldn't tell, maybe gears, a second run of toads, a five-page spread of poisonous fantasy mushrooms, crows again, and a duckling with a distended fish mouth underneath it. Then . . . a sailboat. I looked up.

It was in no way the reflections of a positive mind, not until the boat. The water was sun dappled, tips of eraser white on the graphite water. Slow, easy clouds gave the sky some character. It hadn't occurred to me to draw the boat on fire in a hurricane, a tornado bearing down on it, shooting out a medusa halo of lightning as it came, tsunami waves on all sides.

Maybe it was evidence that I had skipped out of a rut I'd been in without knowing it. Strange times can do that. I looked around at the place I was sitting. It was beautiful. Perfect light, the smell of the ocean. Obi was right to live in this place. I probably couldn't. If I tried, it would only be a matter of time before I got used to it all, and every day, the feeling that I was somehow too conspicuous, that all the strangers could tell that I was the strangest stranger of them all, would wear me down and start to piss me off. I couldn't fit into Obi's paradise. I was just a visitor to places like this. Point of fact, I'd already beaten the shit out of someone, perved out with a waitress, mailed drug money to myself, and carried around someone's gun all morning until I threw it into a pond. And I'd been there for twenty-four hours. Plus, I was sitting on a bench plotting mayhem, dark imagery in hand.

I sighed. Big Mike's sketchbook was unusual in some ways. He used Sharpies instead of pencils. Nigel didn't sketch in his so much as write. Lists, phone numbers, drafts of insulting letters he was going to send, with a few pictures here and there. He tore most of the pages out as he went, so when he was done with one, it left a trail so secretive that any psychiatrist or future historian would give up instantly.

Delia liked sketchbooks that were slightly larger than mine, which made sense as she was smaller than me. Almost all of the pages were drawings of birds, but there were also pages of what looked like textile patterns. I sometimes painted, but I almost always gave them away when I was done. Big Mike did the same thing. Nigel never painted or did any kind of art outside of tattooing. He was a collector. But Delia was a serious painter, and a sculptor as well. She kept that part of her life to herself, and I wondered about that, not for the first time.

Obi called a little after one o'clock.

"Done," he said. "You got a pen?"

"Shoot."

"The Smiling Dragon Slaughterhouse is owned by Nicholas Dong-ju of Dong-ju Trust in San Francisco. He owns the entire mini mall, including the hair place and the video game store." Obi reeled off the San Francisco address and I jotted it down in my sketchbook.

"Thanks," I said. I snapped the book closed. "I'm going to drive over there now. Call you tonight when I get back."

"Right on," Obi replied. "You know Beth would love to see you. Wanna come over for dinner?"

"I'll pick up something on the way back. No telling how long this might take. But thanks, brother."

"Cool." I could hear the disappointment in his voice. Obi wanted to share his pain.

I got my car out, gassed up, and hit the freeway. Within twenty minutes I was back under heavy clouds. San Francisco cloud cover was different than the rain ceiling in Portland, or anywhere else for that matter. It had a cursed feel to it, old and heavy and tired, the kind of sky that was likely to produce wrecking fogs and scummy sleet, maybe even a frog storm. The sky didn't seem as much like a ceiling as a sad helmet with advertising on the far side. It started to rain ten minutes later and the traffic slowed. I flicked my lights on and surfed through the local radio stations, smoking and thinking.

It was entirely possible that Dong-ju was the same Asian resident of San Francisco who had purchased the Roland Norton piece from Wes Ron in England. Totally possible. Whoever he was, he had money, real estate, and at least three businesses. Only a powerfully eccentric weirdo could take an interest in Roland Norton's bug-eyed, semi-retarded garbage, but San Francisco was notoriously full of them, so it could also easily be a dead end. I mentally shrugged.

There was more to consider, of course. The business entrepreneur owner of a tattoo shop factor. It was like a vegan owning a steak house, or a Republican owning a bookstore. They just didn't know what the fuck they were doing, and they always tended to zero in on the profit margin, at the exclusion of more important things, like art and its progress as a thing without a giant dollar sign on it. Dong-ju could represent a higher octave of this problem. This time I shrugged with my face.

It was all extended speculation, but if he was in fact the guy I was looking for, then the opening card I had to play was a pretty good one. Dong-ju had more to lose than I did, plus he had Bling on a financial leash, so he'd get paid in the end one way or another, no matter what. He could either pay me the balance and take it out of Bling's ass, give me my flash back and take it out of Bling's ass, or have me and the cops in his hair for as long as it took, and then he could take his frustrations out on Bling. It was worth a shot to talk to him, no matter how I looked at it.

Traffic finally let up at the suburban outskirts of San Francisco proper. I exited I-80 and headed over a mossy old concrete bridge down into Harriet Street. The gloomy energy of the place was getting hard to fight off. From there, I entered an increasingly shitty neighborhood that grew a little worse with every block. The rain thickened and slowed, smacking the hood of the car in slow, fat drops. Streetlights flickered to life, hours early, and shed a lonesome, crappy glow on everything as I slowly drove, making a cautious approach. It surprised me that San Francisco still possessed run-down industrial areas. Gentrification had erased or upgraded most of it on the West Coast, especially in high-priced regions like the Bay Area. Run-down industrial was hard to find in Portland, and when you did find it, it was filled with artists and their strange support ecologies. Cheese makers and tiny print shops hid in the warehouses, cafés and snotty restaurants down the alleys. Nothing like that was going on here.

Dong-ju Trust proved to be the most uninviting bunker in a stretch of them when I finally found it. The building was an enormous, squat thing with rust-streaked gray paint and patches of exposed concrete. There was a parking lot with a sagging chain link fence on the east side with a new black Lincoln Town Car, a white pickup, and a newer tin shed. There was space in the lot for a dozen or so cars and a truck or two, but the rest of it was empty and it looked like it had been that way for a long time. The roll gate was locked and chained. The caged windows of the building were caked with years of soot and set too high to see through. Above the dented steel door was an address in nail-on numbers, but no company name.

I sat in my car across the street, having second thoughts. There were a few yellow lights on inside, their urine glare completing the welcome. It was too bad I'd tossed Bling's gun into that pond, I thought. I could easily picture bodies inside the place, or a horrible Dickensian factory with emaciated child workers. Towering boxes full of bullets. Crates of unstable landmines. A deluxe meth lab. Mannequins. The ball bearing in my pocket was the exact variety of dumbass Delia had warned me about. I took it out of my pocket and pushed it down in between the seat and the seat back.

A produce truck slowly rumbled past a block down, riding extra low on the springs. I got out and locked the car.

The rain wasn't especially cold and the air smelled like rust and wet fruit trash. I flicked my cigarette away as I went up to the door and then just stood there staring at it for a minute, getting wet. Bad shit was behind that door. I could feel it. There was a battered plastic pad with a speaker grate and a black button on the wall next to it. I pressed the button and heard a distant buzz inside.

"—es?" came a static-lashed woman's voice.

"I have something to discuss with Mr. Dong-ju," I shouted into the speaker grate. "Roland Norton. Panama. 1955. Like, proto art."

"—pointment?" I could barely hear her, but I picked up bored.

"No, I don't. I'm sure Mr. Dong-ju would like to talk to me. I'll only be in town for another few hours."

"—oment please."

I stood in the rain and a lonely minute passed. Then another minute. I pulled up the collar of my bomber jacket. Two minutes after that I blew rain off my face and pressed the button again.

The door opened immediately. A short blonde woman in jeans and a T-shirt scowled out at me. She was maybe a hard thirty, with a used-up coke nose and a Russian whore's makeup. Her washed-out blue eyes looked tired and glazed with Prozac. I looked down from her bad stare. Flip-flops. Pink toenail polish.

"Come on," she snapped.

I followed her into a small space cordoned off by chewed-up corkboard office dividers. It was ten degrees colder inside and the air smelled like mildew and bad coffee and menthol cigarettes. She sat down at a small desk with an office computer and an untidy pile of papers, sucked some coffee from a paper cup, and tapped the keyboard.

I was about to say something irritating when the steel door opened behind me and a big wet guy in a long black leather jacket rolled in on a cloud of cologne, wiping rain from his flat boxer's face with both of his huge, scarred hands. He didn't look Korean when he focused his small, piggy eyes on me.

"What do you want." There was a crescent-shaped scar under his left eye and the eye itself was a little drifting and scummy. His teeth were small and uniformly gray. Dentures.

"I'm looking for Nicholas Dong-ju," I replied.

"We know already," the blonde said in a nasal twang. I flicked my eyes at her. She scratched the side of her mouth with one long fingernail, stretching her lips into an 'O' the way women do when they apply lipstick. She glanced under her fingernail.

"What for," she asked. It didn't come out with a question mark. The big guy stepped closer. I nodded and held my hands up in surrender. His hard face settled lower down into deep ugly.

"I think there's been a mistake," I said calmly. My pulse was ramping up. "I have reason to believe that Mr. Dong-ju might be in possession of some property that for a variety of reasons he might not want."

The big man squinted.

"Wrong answer," the blond droned, still bored. The big guy rolled his neck and flexed his hands.

"Look," I said, hands still raised, taking a step back toward the blonde, thinking human shield, "some shithead who used to work for me might, and I mean *might,* have sold Mr. Dong-ju some stolen property. Artwork. Stolen from me. I could easily be wrong. I just wanted to ask Mr. Dong-ju a few questions, that's all. I seriously don't want any trouble of any kind."

I could throw the blonde and then maybe the computer next, then use the desk as a vaulting point to get over top of the divider behind it.

The big guy snorted and shook his head. I found my center of gravity and bent my knees ever so slightly. He picked up the change in my posture and his good eye widened. He smirked. Barely.

"Get out."

I walked carefully around him, just out of reach of his gorilla arms. Behind me the blonde tapped away at her computer, the entire episode already forgotten. I backed up to the door and opened it, stepped out into the rain, and turned.

There were two cop cars on the street, one in front of my BMW and the other one behind it. Four cops in rain gear were right outside the metal door waiting for me. They looked pissed.

"Hands up, asshole," one of them said, raising his flashlight like a baton.

Someone hit me hard from my left and flattened me against the wall. I was cuffed, fast and tight. I didn't resist as I was escorted to the lead cop car across the street. The cop who nailed and shackled me was kind enough to duck my head so I didn't bang it on the way into the chicken coop.

I sat there, heart pounding, my face iron with cold fury, while the four cops stood around and talked things over, sweating me. A couple minutes later they broke up and two of them went back to the second car. The other two got in up in front of me.

"Name," asked the cop in the driver's seat, hard eyes in the rearview. His partner twisted around and gave me the opening glare of the 'We already don't believe you' routine.

"Darby Holland."

"We need some ID," the same cop said. "That BMW yours?"

"Yep. Wallet's in my back pocket."

The cop in the passenger seat got out and came around, opened the back door.

"Lean," he instructed. I leaned over so he could get to my wallet.

"Anything sharp in here?"

"No."

"No needles, pocketknife, anything like that?"

"No."

"You sure?"

"Yes." The suspect junkie burglar speech.

He pulled my wallet out and returned to the front seat. Both of them were bored as they ran my license. I watched through the window as one of the cops from the car behind us went to the steel door of Dong-ju Trust with a note pad and pressed the buzzer. The blonde opened it and let him in, smiling and bobbing her head, a grateful and concerned citizen.

"Lot of cash," the second cop observed, holding my wallet open for his partner to look into. He turned and gave me a flat stare. "What are you doing here?"

It was time to think fast. It wasn't the first time I'd been shuffled into that particular seat, so I was ready. That's what the sweat time was for when used wisely.

"I'm on vacation," I snapped, irritated. "Someone told me there was an art gallery around here. I was trying to find it."

"An art gallery?" They exchanged a look. "This is an industrial area. Most of these places are storage."

"I'm from Portland," I replied, "as you can see from my driver's license. Tons of our galleries are in the industrial areas. Use your fancy computer and google it. It's sort of the thing these days."

The cops sighed together. They'd evidently heard all about it already. Passenger seat gave me an appraising look. "We got a few calls that someone meeting your description was prowling around looking at gate locks and testing doors. Looking through windows. That you? Trolling for art galleries?"

"This was my first stop."

A third cop car pulled up. No one got out.

"Mind if we search your car?"

"Go right ahead," I replied. I relaxed and stared out at the rain.

He put my wallet on the dash and came back and got my keys, going through the whole sharp thing again. The cop from the second car joined him in the search and they rooted around in the BMW for a few minutes. Eventually they slammed the doors and locked it again. The cop that had gone into the building came out and they all held a short conference across the street.

"No luggage," passenger cop said when he got back in. "Where you staying?"

"The Portola Plaza in Monterey," I replied. "The pass key is in my jacket."

They looked at each other again. The results from my driver's license on their computer could not have been in any way helpful to my cause, but there were no outstanding warrants, just a long list of bad shit I'd done and much more that I might have.

"Get him out," the driver said.

The passenger cop pulled me out of the back and took the cuffs off, then handed me my wallet and keys.

"You want to find an art gallery? Google it, genius. We better not find you around here again." He gave me a tight smile. "Hope you enjoyed your stay, and drive safely back to Portland."

My knuckles were white on the steering wheel as I drove. No one followed me, and for some reason that made me even angrier. I'd walked right into a sweet little burn. It had everything. Tidy, efficient, clever, and free. Bling had obviously had some coke-fueled episode after I'd left him, reviewing everything he'd said on rewind and fast forward until the paranoia bit down on something hard. Then he'd called to let them know I might be coming. I should have known when the burned-up blonde had kept me waiting so long, and then the big guy was dripping wet when he showed up. I'd been played, and now I couldn't even go back without a major hassle. The cops had my license number, description, history, and every reason to fuck with me. Sweet indeed. And smart. It also sent a very clear message. I'd found the right guy.

Telling my version of the truth to a bunch of wet beat cops had obviously been out of the question, for many reasons other than purely aesthetic ones. Something about me never inspires confidence in law enforcement types, and I felt the same way about them. It showed. My record made me an unreliable witness to anything, an unbelievable giver of statements, and a reliable source of bad news. In this case, all true once again. I'd just lost a hand without ever getting to the poker table, like I'd been mugged at the casino door, a casino where I would be gambling against big money and was sure to be robbed anyway.

I considered going back and pounding on the door of Dong-ju Trust like an idiot maniac, then just winging it. It was such a powerfully reckless, stupid idea that it would catch them by surprise. I wanted to burn the fucking place to the ground right after I stomped that crusty bitch's computer into a million pieces. Setting me up with a pile of cops was not only infuriating, it was dangerous. People got shot that way all the time, especially people like me. And cops didn't shoot anyone just once anymore, either. They kept firing until their guns were empty, probably because of something to do with paperwork, and there had been six of them. That was a lot of bullets. I swallowed and tried to let the fire settle into coals. It was time to regroup.

Some brilliant, next-level, RAND Corporation reasoning was called for, with a considerable amount of Israeli tactical know-how and probably some high-end, otherworldly spy gear. What I had instead was a package of skills designed to survive at the lower end of things and honed by being there for so fucking long. So basically none of that. I considered the situation from various angles. Brilliant reasoning did not honestly describe my thought process, I knew. Tactical know-how just sounded perfectly awful, so no again. All I had in the way of next-generation spy gear was my metal ball. Lame.

Amazingly, the biggest mistake so far had not been mine after all. Nicholas Dong-ju had shown his level of game and given me time to think, and I was going to make sure his ego's error cost him. I had days to plan and a staff of my own that made the floozy and Eye Goo Dude look like sissies. I knew who had my stuff, and that was enough for the moment. And Bling was going to get another visit from me.

I lit another cigarette, somehow cheered by the train of thought. I was getting back into my element, mostly because there was nowhere else to go, true, but I had a destination. I had a feel for the situation. It was a sketchy one, but it was enough to work with. I knew who had my flash, and they knew I knew it. The fuse was burning and that was fine by me. I'd been assessed as some kind of scumbag who could be stalled by the cops and turned aside. People were always so incredibly surprised to discover that they were in fact right about the scumbag label, and that the brand had not only been painstakingly earned but came with an entire package of hard to deal with, completely unexpected bullshit.

My life had been a snake nest of burning fuses for as long as I could remember. People in general planned and planned their entire lives, creating structures to live inside of, the bigger and more complicated the better. They were waiting to retire to start living. A much smaller percentage of people never made a single big plan at all and cruised the ineffable instant, with a loose idea of a possible future. I was a different and almost completely foreign kind of mechanic in that respect. The perfect plan was the kind that had every chance of success, but if it fell apart it had the potential to explode and create a beautiful chaos to navigate at speed, and that was generally the secret goal all along. Every politician knew the same thing, which was maybe why I couldn't trust a single one of them. Most every working artist of any kind did, too. It could be a bad thing to rub up against. The future had no substance. It didn't smell like anything, it didn't make noise, and it had no color at all. Not until it happened. And I was usually right there waiting when it did, with my collapsing plan.

I punched scan on the radio and let it ride until I hit a doo-wop station. Nolan Strong, the Five Keys, the Penguin. I liked how people could really sing instead of scream in those days, not that the screaming was entirely out of step with the times. My hands felt good on the steering wheel as I gripped it. I felt strong. In the aftermath of all the adrenaline, my face felt mobile and clean. My breath came with a long, even lightness. Even my dick was a little hard.

A song was like an idea. It came and then it was gone, leaving an echo inside of you. My plans in the nest of fuses always resembled layers of those echoes, a thing Delia glimpsed from time to time and understood on some level. And you could replay a single song and add it to the symphony, but it was never exactly the same because you changed a little in between listenings, and the world always changed around you as well. A sketch was like that also, an assemblage of rough lines, the bridge between something part dream and something final, but still viewed differently every time. I found myself smiling at the quantity of the madness I carried around inside me.

I knew what I wanted. The ghost of something was already lifting from the ground. My opponent had emerged from a place of potential hiding with an attitude. Fine. He'd manufactured a crafty little trap on the fly using the cops, some kind of Slavic monster, and a retired whore. I had far more dangerous things up my sleeve. I had the Lucky Supreme. And I had Old Town, in all its glory.

I pulled into the parking garage at the Portola Plaza just after seven. My last night in Monterey looked like it was going to be a foggy one and it was only getting worse. My cell phone beeped a few times on the drive back, but I'd ignored it, lost in thought. On the short walk to the hotel I stopped and sat down on a bench and checked my missed calls. Obi, Delia, and Big Mike. I somehow didn't want to hear any of their voices.

I thought about calling Carina, the tall waitress I'd met the night before and ridden like a fancy bicycle, but I was still in a strange, contemplative mood that was in mid-transition to something else. Instead I lit a cigarette and stared out into the dark. I thought about how occasionally I was sick of Portland, and how I'd never left for good because I suspected that wherever I went would eventually wind up feeling the same, just with different weather. I would always wind up in Old Town, no matter where I was. I also ruminated for a period of time on tattooing itself, and how I landed in it flat on my back, too tired and featherless to fly anymore.

Once upon a time it had seemed like the only option, the only way to scrape together enough money to get a safety margin. Poverty had left a canyon of a scar in me, I knew, and there would never be enough of the right kind of dirt to fill it in. I smoked and watched the night.

When I was fifteen, I'd gone almost two weeks without food at one point. I'd fallen all the way down into the deep end of the gutter and all the things in it had come alive around me. Down that low a kid can still taste pretty good to some people, even a real skinny one. A bag of bones, thick hair and big eyes, with more than a little of that special, desperate kind of tired is highly marketable meat. And the butchers and the counter girls were just as hungry as the fat man with the bib. I shot my cigarette far out over the water and lit another one. I don't know why I was remembering it, but there had to be a reason.

After my mother and sister left to go live with some distant relative with room for two, my older brother and I had wandered around before we each decided that the other one was too much of a burden. Work for him had revolved around his taking as much as he could of whatever I could scratch together from odd jobs and petty crime, the kinds of things I was capable of without an ID or a wallet to put it in. He wasn't lazy or greedy. He was damaged. When I hit the first really hard stretch he lit out for a legit paycheck, but he didn't need me tagging along. The saddest I'd ever been was the day he finally split, madness in his eyes. He might have been a lot of things, some good, some bad, but he'd loved me.

The city was Denver. It was there that I first caught the tail of the animal inside of me, the wild thing that sometimes came out of the brittle and contrived shell of a proper human, and there was never any getting the fucker back in. Society can be much more exclusive than most people will hopefully ever realize. A night came when I was standing in the snow in broken shoes and a stolen coat with no pockets, staring past a neon CLEAN sign through the window of a Laundromat at an ashtray full of juicy, lipstick-ringed menthol butts jutting from a cat litter pan. My eyes had refocused on the alien, awful reflection of my face, all eyes and cheekbones. I was a cartoon parody of a thousand things that would never be. Me. I'd failed the admissions test and would not be joining the cast of society's comedic fantasmadrama. Blink. Still there.

The night that happened to me, I boldly went after the ashtray anyway; huge revelations aside, I needed those cigarettes. It was warm in the place and the chime above the door sent a painful shock through me, but I didn't want to stay for long because I knew it would make my feet hurt if I warmed up. Some biker chick had been sweeping up and busted me halfway through my scavenger hunt. Her smile had been the smile of a horny serpent, full of lust and something I was later to recognize as dollar signs.

A foghorn called in the distance, pulling me out of my reverie. I smoked and looked at the unlit boats, remembering, knowing it was a bad idea but letting myself do it anyway. We'd chatted, the green-haired biker lady and I. She invited me back to her place. I knew she was thinking sexy street boy. It was the first and last time I fucked for food, and I got ripped off. What I got instead was a chance to live for another week when she introduced me to an amateur magician named Riley the next morning. I chuckled, then stopped.

Riley had been an affable sort of killer who was part of the local specialty food chain, one rung above the woman I'd desperately torn apart with the last of my strength the night before. She'd been the feeder. Riley was the warden pimp, the gardener, the salesman with everyone's shoe size. Later that night I met Riley's patron, a wealthy restaurateur with an enthusiastic taste for boys just like the boy they thought I was.

The whole thing was unbelievably corny. I'd known as soon as Riley whipped out his first magic trick, after my meal ticket had vanished like the cigarette in Riley's hand, exactly what was in store for me. What they could never have known was that the bait in the trap was all I had left, and the rules that had put me in that situation in the first place were the rules I'd just abandoned because of my random reflection in a Laundromat window. Reeking of skanky biker chick pussy and shivering all the way into my spleen, I was delighted to snort their cranky coke, which had been a terrible mistake for them. It had been like giving fast-acting rabies to a dingo.

The night had not played out well for Riley and the big rape guy. I'd escaped with all the coke, a big bag of weed, ten bottles of assorted pills, a pair of gold-plated fingernail clippers, sixty-two dollars, a bleeding scalp, and a crazy plan. Over the next few weeks I'd lived off the spoils of my first operation as a nonhuman. I tracked Riley and the biker woman, whose name I never knew, and I'd found it delightfully easy. When I'd found an even dozen of the kids who went before me, I rounded them up and proposed my plan, in the cinder block living room of Travis Kentucky, the dime bag champion of Macadam Park. Blackmail. And when it was done, I'd kill Riley and the woman and rape dude.

I got up from the bench to head back to the Portola. There was a bar off to my left, down a walkway. I started walking, taking my time, unable to stop remembering.

I'd risen that week to the status of king. Those poor, starving, tapped and rolled boys had trusted me, too. With the last of my money I'd gotten us all cinnamon rolls and we'd smoked seedy weed, and for a night an astonished hope had come back for all of them. A little of it even seeped into me, and I'd marveled at it, a gummy foreign thing struggling out of a fiberglass cocoon inside of me. We'd talked about escape, where we were going to run to and how fast. The memory of those faces, lit from within, mobile and hot, the flashing broken teeth and bright glassy eyes and dirty hair, all of it haunts me.

The next morning we went to work like a team of hardened juvenile street commandos. Jacob was a fourteen-year-old kid whose parents died in a car crash outside of Boston, and this was his second escape. He'd hit the streets in a permanent semi-psychotic flight to get away from his pervert uncle. It was clever Jacob who found Riley. My troops were fanned out in a giant grid, with me in the center, ready for the word, and it was Jacob who brought it. He went to round up everyone else while I went to give Riley our terms.

Riley was still in the phone booth where he'd been spotted minutes earlier, laughing with lunatic hysteria and pounding the wall, wearing a bright yellow jacket. For some reason I can remember the jacket very clearly. It was a ski jacket, with zippered pockets, a shiny canary color, with a bright red collar. He dropped the phone when he saw me and ran, but he went straight down the wrong alley right off the bat. When he realized he was cornered, Riley dropped into some kind of martial crouch and then I was on him. The fight was over in less than three seconds and ended with my knife at his neck. I gave him our terms, even though I'd wanted to see his spine worse than I'd ever wanted anything. Ten grand or I blew the whistle. A measly ten fucking grand. I stupidly listed off the names of everyone who was ready to testify to impress the gravity of the situation on him, how truly fucked he was, how my research had been so complete and so perfectly damning. Riley agreed to pass the information along and meet me with the money at one a.m, in the Dunkin' Donuts by the college. He'd said he was sure it would work, that it was great we were stopping the guy, that if it hadn't been him acting as the lasso man it would have been someone else, that he was truly sorry, that I should gut the biker whore. He'd said a lot of things, white foam at the edges of his mouth. He even wanted in on it. On the special nights, when he failed to find the right kind of urchin, he got a whipping and a really savage buttfucking. In the beginning he'd been fine with it, but he limped a little sometimes anymore, so he was game for an escape plan and some payback.

Jacob's body was found in a dumpster three hours later.

An hour after that, three more went all the way down. An insane biker and a brass knuckle Mexican were sweeping up. I tried to find any of the others, but the night had turned into a nightmare of sirens and freezing wind and garbled rumors of the body count. They knew my name and it was everywhere. Even bill, Darby Holland. Three bills, Darby Holland. One grand, Darby Holland.

They all died, but I didn't find out the final death toll for an entire year. When I couldn't find anyone left alive and every scumbag had run straight to a payphone at the sight of me, I'd stolen a car someone had left idling in front of a 7-Eleven. By the time the last of those young lights winked out, I'd been on my way to Portland, a place I'd heard about from someone else, who had heard about it from they couldn't remember where. A place with trees and hippies, café jobs, kind and gentle prisons, bridges, and all the wild berries you could eat. Cherry trees. In Old Town I'd found a familiar ecology, but I never tried for the role of king again. I never got back in the shell, either.

I sighed. A little of the fantasy feel of the foggy night, the cleanness of the plaza, the soft sounds of the water, and the rich smell of the sea settled back around me. The bright lights of the bar were closer, and I could hear people laughing inside. Letting my mind wander around the edge of a potential crisis kicked up the oddest tortures every time. It was the same for everyone, I knew, but for me the rawness of certain years made daydreaming at night a bad idea. Delia knew some of those stories, and thankfully she'd never suggested therapy, probably because she feared that in some way all those things were too much a part of me, too wrapped around my core to peel away to any good effect. Then again, she might have been worried that I'd get arrested.

The bar was half full. I ordered a scotch on the rocks and carried it outside to one of the patio tables. It was peaceful enough.

The logic behind gutting my way through some twisted version of American apelife in Old Town had its roots everywhere. There was some kind of reason why that memory came to the surface with such instructional clarity, and the wheels in my head coughed it up around midnight and drink number five.

All planning aside, all the twists and turns, feints and blinds, potential tools and bridges for gaps, all of it was semi-worthless in the end. The same thing that kept me trapped in my world was the very same thing that gave me my best advantage. My survival rate. The doors to the history inside of me closed and the bar came alive, like someone had turned up the volume.

It was the escape artist who always won. Always. Even if he was escaping back into the same box he just broke out of. I left the bar and walked, and for a solid hour I enjoyed the nowness, a spirited and occasionally whimsical impostor in a twilight paradise, unashamed, smoking cigarettes and touching the salt air with my eyelids and fingertips. We were all born at some moment to ourselves, and for me, it was in the window of a Laundromat with a neon CLEAN sign. A rich, splattery smoothie of signs and omens and tellings to be sure. Maybe it was finally time to embrace it, and maybe it was just a long wire of PTSD. In the end, it probably didn't even matter.

But I was glad I couldn't see my reflection.

Early the next morning I dumped a generous load of Bling's cash at the front desk. Then I gassed up the BMW, got a large black coffee, three packs of smokes, two donuts, and some teriyaki beef jerky, and headed back to Portland, the rising sun to my right. The coastal pines were magnificent at dawn, sculpted by a steady wind, brushed into gnarled organic fans, and the intermittent glimpses of ocean were fields of gold crested with shimmering silver blue. The gas station coffee tasted good because of it. I found a jazz station and slumped into a relaxed road posture, hit the cruise control. BMW seats were designed for men much fatter than myself.

The fog burned off as I busted into the desolation north of Sacramento an hour later. The random, jangling pieces were all settling into place in my head. Being partly distracted by the mundane task of driving kept a lid on the past. Doing nothing at all was something to avoid for a few days.

The dawn gave way to a bright morning, so I put on my shades and thought about Delia, how she'd still be sleeping, and how flagrantly evil it would be to call and wake her up and tell her in poetic detail about the phenomena of sunlight. Straight-up lying would have to cover the scenery, however. Outside it looked cold, with barren fields, groves of deadish trees, and rocky patches with huge metal barns that could have held anything or nothing at all. Maxwell to Red Bluff, all the way to Redding an hour after that. By noon, I'd left the flats of the valley and I was climbing into the forest again. As I approached Mt. Shasta, my cell phone rang, breaking me out of the meditative road trance. The shop.

"What's up?" Big Mike asked. Mikey never came off as bubbly, but at least he didn't sound depressed.

"On my way back. Should get in late tonight."

"You get your stuff?"

"Nah, but I know who has it. I'm still thinking about what comes next."

"Bummer. Or good. Delia wants to talk to you." He handed the phone over. He'd been a decoy. It was a trap.

"I tried to call you last night, asshole." She didn't sound irritated. Just tired and disappointed.

"I know. I sorta had a shitty day." I told her the entire story, pausing every now and then when she let out a sulfurous string of curses. While I was talking, I heard the door to the back of the shop open and close, followed by the familiar creak of the chair at my desk. I could almost picture her sitting there with her boots up.

"Motherfuckers," she neatly summarized when I was done.

"That was pretty much my conclusion, too."

"I told you I should have come with you." Petulant.

"You sure did. And now you can rub it in for the rest of eternity, add it to your list."

"So now we're on the lookout for cops *and* imported criminal scumbags?" Incredulous.

I thought about it for a minute. "No more than we usually are, I guess. Not yet. Actually, probably. So yes. If Bling called the police about the whole beating robbing thing, I would have been arrested in San Francisco or Monterey, and I bet this Dong-ju guy thinks he's chased me off. But . . . he knows I have his location, some shit on him, that kind of thing. He isn't playing ball my way, but I'll bet he's playing something. Look at it this way. He's entered the tattoo world somehow, with that idiot shop and Bling on a leash. We aren't old-school villains like Wally and the carnival burn squad, but he has to know that this isn't like fucking with the neighborhood Kinkos, either. He's in the game, and I guess we have stuff he wants. But until we know more, let's be kinda quiet. The last thing we want is to give Nigel any reason to start packing a gun again."

"I guess. Where you want me to leave your key?" Annoyed.

"Keep it for now. It's a spare."

She gave me a detailed report on the cats and how she'd changed their box, which had been shamefully overdue for it, and was just launching into what was sure to be a long, graphic account of why her butthole was tender when I cut her off, claiming I had an incoming call.

"Lies." She hung up.

I caught up with the rain again around sundown in Northern California. The gas tank was three quarters empty and the jerky was gone, so I took the Shasta exit and spent a few minutes roaming around the strange little town looking for a station that was open. The vibe was creepy, in a mountain witch kind of way. Most of the storefronts were dark, even though it was early evening. The only places open were flagrantly hippie, UFO-fearing teahouses, militant lesbian cafes advertising granola bagels and vegan three-bean soup, and a truly scary antiques place with teddy bears all over everything and a pale old woman in a faded dress, staring out the showroom window like a ghost. No bar neon anywhere. A hot dog stand would have been burned to the ground in that place.

I finally found an open gas station after a long hunt and pulled up to a pump. I was paying at the counter when I glanced up at the security monitors while I waited for change. There were three grainy black and white screens, one on the pumps, the second on the register, and the third monitoring the lot behind the store where they kept the propane tanks. There was a black Lincoln Town Car idling out back. I squinted. It looked familiar.

"That your car?" I asked the clerk. He looked up at the monitor and laughed.

"I work at a gas station, dude," he replied. He was a zitty kid with shaggy brown hair, maybe sixteen and in serious need of his first shave. "As in I drive a skateboard. Probably just some dude taking a nap or beatin' off."

"Huh." I looked again. "He been there long?"

The kid glanced up again and then shook his head. "Just pulled up. Happens all the time. Not really worried about a guy in a brand-new Lincoln like that stealing propane. Saw a dude in a Jeep get a blowjob out there last week. One time, I swear I saw this lady change her diaper out there, and I mean *her* diaper, dude. She was, like, way old. Left it right on the ground, too."

"Bummer," I said. The kid smiled.

"Good one."

I took an extra twenty out of my wallet and passed it to him, then jotted my cell phone number out on the back of a Keno card and slid it across the counter.

"Do me a favor," I said, nodding up at the monitors. "If that car leaves in the next few minutes, try to see who's driving it, will you? Then call me."

The kid looked skeptical, but he didn't put the twenty down. "I don't really do that kind of thing, man. I just, like, work here."

"Right," I said, smiling easily. "It's just that . . ." I leaned in a little. "I think that I'm being followed. Some crazy bitch I can't shake. Wants me to meet her family, do my laundry, whole fuckin' nine yards. We only went out once. I didn't even kiss her."

He glanced up at the monitor again. "She hot?"

"Not really. Sort of hairy, you know? Questionable skin, smells a little like scalp. Local hippie. I'm just down here for a few days to hit the slopes. Met her yesterday and she followed me around the whole time. Damned woman is going to ruin my vacation. I even feel like a dick just talking about it."

"Got it," he said. The twenty and the Keno slip disappeared. He smiled hugely and I had to smile back.

I hit the road again with one eye on the rearview. The Lincoln didn't pull out behind me, but ten minutes later I spotted headlights less than a quarter mile back. Traffic on the road was thinning out. If the Lincoln was following me, it would be harder to do it without being noticed from there on out.

My cell phone rang and I hit receive.

"Looks like you're clear, dude," the clerk from the gas station said. "I went right out there and looked in the car after you split. I mean, I could use a crazy chick, hairy or not."

"It wasn't her?"

"Nah. Some big dude. Had a weird fucked-up eye. Probably just passing through, like I said. Rude as fuck, though."

"Thanks."

"Yeah, so I'm working tomorrow night. You see this girl again, maybe scrape her off on me, know what I'm saying? Name's Ron, but the ladies call me Ronnie."

"If I see her." I hung up.

I had the cruise control set to seventy, but now I clicked it off and slowly accelerated up to ninety. The BMW handled well on the rain slick road, but even so I was nervous and getting more so. The Lincoln kept pace with me and I swore like a sailor. I hit one hundred, my knuckles turning white. The trailing car kept up with me.

I knew from the drive down that we were about to hit a long stretch of nothing. It stood to reason that the driver of the Lincoln suspected from my speed and Ronnie's stellar reconnaissance that his cover was blown, though he made no move to overtake me yet. He was either waiting for me to lose control and wreck, or he was unwilling to drive any faster.

A lone truck stop came into view and I braked hard and took the exit. The Lincoln was less than a hundred yards behind me when I pulled into the brightly lit parking lot and cut the engine, directly in front of the place. The Lincoln cut its lights and idled in the darkness at the edge of the lot next to a bank of semis.

I got out and rushed into the truck stop, then made a beeline for the restrooms, sure I was being watched through the truck stop's wraparound windows. Maybe he'd think that I was desperate to take a leak or had a sudden case of diarrhea and that his cover was still intact.

I washed my hands and looked in the mirror. Same old face, but pale, and the vein in my right temple was really pulsing. It was strange, but at that instant I realized I should start moisturizing in the near future. The restroom was empty. I thought better of being alone in there and went out quickly, hand cupping the ball bearing in my jacket pocket.

I glanced through the windows as I walked casually into the dining section. The Lincoln was still out there, unmoved, exhaust gently seeping from the tail pipe, a moist silhouette with a glittering edge. I took a seat in a booth where I could keep an eye on both the parking lot and the front door.

The truck stop wasn't busy. A family of four were eating burgers a few booths down. In the booth next to me, four big truck drivers in flannel shirts and mesh-backed hats were hunkered over their table, carving away at thin gray steaks and scooping up powder and milk mashed potatoes and fluorescent green peas, grumbling quietly about gas prices and deer hunting. A scrawny, incredibly dirty kid in his late teens wearing sunglasses and neck to foot denim was drinking coffee at the counter and chatting up the waitress, who detached from the counter and drifted in my direction. A few other people were scattered through the place, reading the local tabloid or staring out at the rain.

"Hey hon," the waitress said. She plopped a sticky plastic menu down on the table in front of me. She was a stoned, chunky dishwater blonde in her early twenties, with a spray of acne in a bong-hole circle around her mouth. She might have been pregnant in the way she leaned back to take a little drag off her belly. "Coffee?"

"Sure," I said. I turned over the cup on my paper place setting.

"Rainy, huh?" She had a faint southern accent. I've never understood how so many Okies found their way into Northern California roadsides, but they were everywhere on that lonesome stretch of I-5.

She sloshed some watery coffee into my cup and wandered off, pausing to refill the cups at the trucker's table as she passed, holding her lower back with one hand as she smiled and gave up a little banter. I picked up the menu and looked it over. It wasn't promising. When she drifted back past I went with ham, three eggs over easy, and hash browns.

The food came on a greasy white platter ten minutes later, and with it inspiration. I dumped Tabasco on the eggs and wolfed them down in three bites. The hash browns were a basic grease and potato matrix, so I shoveled them up as well. The ham had a faintly green and blue prismatic sheen on one end so I left it alone. The Lincoln never moved.

The truck drivers got their thermoses filled before they hit the road. I sampled my coffee and shuddered.

"Hey, dudes," I called out. "Those your trucks out there?"

They looked up from doctoring their thermoses with nondairy creamer and sugar packets. Their heavy faces were gray with exhaustion. I gave them a solid frown.

“Not that it’s any of my business, but you see that black Lincoln parked out there next to your rigs?” I tossed my head, eyes still forward.

As a group they peered out into the rainy parking lot. One of them adjusted his hat, pulling it lower over his oily hair.

“I’d keep an eye on that one,” I continued. “Guy was just monkeying around testing cab doors out there. Tracksuit, it looked like. Fat dude. Might be waiting for someone to head out there alone. ’Course, maybe you guys know him.” I shrugged and took another sip of coffee.

They paid and pulled their coats on, grumbling to each other and glaring suspiciously out into the rain. I could sense their group vibe going from stale to shitty.

“You sure?” one of them asked, squinting at me.

“What I saw,” I replied.

They walked out in a loose formation. I watched as they conferred in the door alcove for a full minute and then they headed straight for the Lincoln, marching slowly and with purpose. When they got to the car one of them rapped on the driver’s window.

I tossed a twenty on the table and slid out of the booth, keeping low. The dirty kid and the waitress watched me with blank expressions.

“Keep the change,” I said. I went into the little concession area that wrapped around the side of the place, where they sold everything from maps to cowboy hats, fossils to snake bite kits. I waved at the cash register girl and went out through the side door.

Immediately I could hear raised voices over the rain. I sprinted out past the gas pumps away from them and circled back in the darkness behind the semis, stopping just behind the last one. I knelt in the cold gravel and mud and peeked under it.

The four truck drivers had surrounded the driver of the Lincoln. I could only see their legs; four sets of work boots and faded jeans, and in the middle the long, stout tree trunks of a man wearing giant Reeboks and track pants. But I recognized the flat voice.

"I didn't touch anything. Fuck off," said the big guy from Dong-ju Trust. I wondered how long it would take him to figure out that I had handed his own trick back to him, a variation on the one he had used to get me into the cop car. Too cutesy by half, I thought.

"You mind staying here while we look through our cabs?" one driver asked.

"We aren't looking for any trouble, fella," another guy said, calmly but forcefully. "No need to call in the law. Let's just stay put while we check everything out."

"Don't!" someone shouted.

There was a blur of motion. One of the truck drivers went down hard, and then another. The blows that echoed through the parking lot sounded like someone smacking the side of a cow with a baseball bat. A third truck driver went down. It looked like the last one had a little more scrap in him, getting in a few good gut kicks before Dong-ju's man locked up with him. There were three sharp smacking sounds of forehead to face and the last trucker dropped.

I could hear the big guy panting. He stood there for several long seconds while I held my breath. Then he kicked the last guy once in the gut and started walking toward the truck stop.

I waited in the lee of the truck axle, watching his retreating legs. He didn't seem to be in any kind of hurry. One of the truck drivers groaned and then made a terrible, high-pitched keening sound. I peeked around the edge of the muddy wheel and watched the Russian enter the truck stop. He looked around the diner and then calmly made for the restroom when he didn't see me.

I scrambled over and checked his car door. I hadn't heard the beep of an alarm, but I cringed anyway as I grabbed the handle. It was unlocked. I dug my keys out of my pocket and picked one at random, the key to the laundry room at my duplex. My hands were shaking as I rammed it deep into the ignition and snapped it off with a violent jerk. I scrambled out and slammed the door, then sprinted back into the gloom behind the semis, moving fast, back toward the gas pumps. I paused in the lee of the last truck. My car was less than fifty feet away.

I watched as the man in the tracksuit made his way through the place, head swiveling back and forth. Everyone inside looked relaxed. The brief episode in the parking lot had gone unnoticed thus far. I watched as he finished his casual inspection and glanced out at my car. Satisfied that I wasn't in it, he walked slowly back out into the rain toward his Lincoln. He knew I was going to Oregon and probably reasoned that he could wait up the road until I passed and catch me there. The Cannibal Country no-man's-land around the Oregon–California border was a perfect place for a fiery high-speed wreck with a few bullet holes tossed in. Any law enforcement would just write it off and go back to donuts and Internet porn if he tossed a couple of bags of meth around the wreckage, which was the cop-tool brand of clever they had rolled out thus far.

When he was close to the Lincoln, I made a mad and silent dash to my car, key already in hand. I was in and peeling out in reverse in seconds. I cranked it hard right and stomped the brakes, then slammed it into drive and floored it, rooster-tailing gravel with the headlights out. I looked up just as he slammed his car door. I didn't know if he could see me as I roared past, if he looked up an instant after his key wouldn't go into the ignition and he realized he was trapped in the middle of nowhere, but I shot him the bird and almost lost control of the BMW. When I flicked my eyes over the rearview the flash of tableau was perfect. My would-be murderer was standing with the car door open, staring. Behind him, the dirty kid and the waitress were under the awning. He was pointing. She was on the phone.

I ripped out of the parking lot and down a long empty road and up the on-ramp before flicking on the headlights. There were no other cars on the road, so I pushed it up to eighty-five and hit the cruise button and tried to catch my breath. I lit a cigarette and cracked the window. Smoke swirled into the night and I suddenly, inexplicably laughed. And I couldn't stop. After a long minute I hit the changer on the CD player and cranked it up. Doobie Brothers boomed out of the speakers.

A few miles later, two highway patrol cars roared past me going the opposite direction, sirens wailing and lights flashing, followed a mile or so later by another speeding patrol car and the first ambulance. I clicked the BMW up to ninety. The level of trouble I was in had just gone up significantly, I knew. But there was no telling what was going to happen anymore, so I was back where I belonged.

My apartment had been dusted.

I dropped my bag on the floor by the door and went straight to the refrigerator. There was a note from Delia, written in her perfect Palmer script.

"Dearest Dickhead, I got you beer and there's a Reuben from Ken's in the fridge. You better have brought me something really fucking good. Like a dildo full of Mexican jumping beans or a cowboy hat with horns. Welcome home, D."

I got a beer and poured myself a shot of Corner Creek, then went and sat down at the dining room table, which shone with a gentle gloss and smelled like a lemon polish I didn't have. Both of the cats jumped up, sniffed my drinks and my forehead, then lay down, purring and yawning, like I'd been gone for an hour. Delia spoiled them so thoroughly every time I was gone that my absence was probably a plus in their worldview. When I'd gone to Seattle for a few days last summer, she'd made tiny paper hats for them and sent me dozens of pictures on my cell phone. It almost seemed like they were posing for her.

I took my boots off while I drank and then restlessly prowled around the place in my socks. The bed was made, the bathroom was spotless, the towels folded in three like in a good hotel. Everything was exceptionally clean. There was nothing for me to do. I always cleaned when I got home, as a way to reclaim my space. I felt like I was living in Delia's place, which I could only imagine as I'd never been there. I was living in Delia's place, decorated with all my stuff. Somehow it didn't bother me that much.

I wandered around a little, sipping beer and snooping around my own place, looking for signs that Delia had been probing around. I had plenty to hide, but most of it was so confusing that I could hide it in plain sight, which I did. I drifted over to the armoire, opened it, and peeked in. Still messy. No sign that she'd been there. Too bad. Then I went over to my curio cabinet and opened one of the glass doors. Everything was where I'd left it, so I opened the other door. There were dozens of objects, but one of them had been moved. It was one of my favorites and I'd sketched it many times, but not anytime recently. She evidently had. I took it out and studied it.

It was a small brass cannon, Civil War. A toy. The spokes on the two wheels may not have been period correct. In fact none of the features were probably accurate, but it *looked* like a Civil War–era cannon, and that was all that mattered to me. It would have looked okay on a pirate ship, too. The little brass man who loaded it probably had a little brass musket. The lines along the barrel had a kind of perfect flow. The nub at the base was like the nipple on a pacifier. I put it back and closed the doors.

In the living room, I took my sketchbook out of my bag and flopped out on the couch, my drinks on the polished coffee table on coasters I'd never seen. The street was quiet outside. The cats lay down around me and I drew sketches of them wearing an assortment of comical hats. As I did, the yellow lines faded from the inside of my eyelids and the drinks smoothed away the rumble of the road in my bones. I let my mind wander a little over the collection of the ideas I'd entertained since the truck stop trick.

Trouble was going to follow me all the way into Old Town, I was sure of it. Absolutely certain. The only question was when and in exactly what form, how large and how tight. I was betting on either fast and brutal or some kind of esoteric rich guy tactic designed to flummox a dumbass of my description long enough to go for a sterile solution.

In the morning, I decided, I would play the king one more time. But this time not with an army of rag tag orphans. I smiled grimly as my gritty eyelids stuck. This time I'd mobilize all of it. Every gutterwad junkie, every scuzzy shitbag I'd terrified into smiling at me, every customer with grit, and of course the prostitutes. The worst, mouthiest, most violently insane prostitutes Old Town had to offer were a match for anything under the moon. And I let them use the bathroom at the Lucky. I had a real army at my disposal this time, a spooky one comprising the most desperate savages and purely venomous, murderous psychos available, every one of them looking to put a scar on the face of gentrification, The Man's face.

Dong-ju's face.

Old Town looked just as I'd left it when I got there in the morning. The same group of black guys were hustling the corner of Sixth and Couch, way late or switching to the day shift. Lenny Bobo, almost dead but smart as hell, his laughing fat protégé Tony, some fresh ex-con named Onion Max with roaches in his soul, and Bob, who had the malt liquor shakes and a bad cough. An old guy with wild hair and destroyed skin named Carlos was railing about something, shaking one skinny fist at the sky. Business people skirted through the hookers who had struck out the night before and been turned out again for the early bird specials. A big and tall tranny named Brenda was among them, reputedly a hardcore blowjob mystic who could fit a beer can in his/her ass for twenty bucks. Flaco's was closed.

It had only been a few days, so I hadn't been fearing some kind of remarkable civic transformation. When I cut the engine in front of the Lucky, the only change I felt was that my shoes had already let in a little rain and I'd forgotten to shave. The Lucky's sandwich board was out and all the interior lights were blazing. Delia's red Falcon was parked out front and so was Alex's old Jeep. I could see Delia through the big picture windows, vacuuming the lobby.

"Mr. California," she said as I entered. She clicked the vacuum off and started winding up the cord. She was wearing a fetching ensemble of shiny black plastic pants, pumps, and a child-sized tuxedo shirt that showed off her belly button and the wing tattoos ramping up from her camel toe. "How are Pinky and Dillson?"

"Fine." I set my bag down. "Thanks for taking care of everything."

"They're like our babies," she said, beaming up at me. "Assuming you had motoring sperm and I could give birth to anything but a chupacabra."

"Natch. What you been up to?"

She shrugged. "Stickin' it to the man, dodging the crabs, running your life for you. The uze."

I winked at her and carried my bag into the back. Alex was sitting at the light table working on a design and listening to his iPod, probably so Delia wouldn't talk to him. I patted him on the shoulder as I passed and sat down at my desk. My schedule said I had two appointments, the first at one, the second at four. Both of them had been lined out already, so I'd be shading and coloring all day, which I preferred. Outlining a big tattoo, for me, is a boring drag. The really fun parts were drawing it in the first place and then making it *pop*, bringing in the light and dimension. I'd gone through phases where I felt the exact opposite, so I'd reverse it again.

For once Delia wasn't blasting some kind of music warfare that I'd have to shut down and endure the wrathful aftermath, which could sometimes last all day. Her new crush was Empire of Shit, a local punk band who made amazingly crappy live recordings, possibly on a cell phone. Instead we listened to Slayer, which I could only just tolerate. I gloved up, dropped some tubes I'd scrubbed out a few days earlier into the ultrasonic to blast out anything I might have missed, tossed the gloves and washed my hands, then gloved up again and set up my station. All of my gear was in two easy-to-clean metal boxes. One held dozens of small plastic bottles of pigments from various companies, the other all of my sterilized, packaged tubes, needles, and a bank of five tattoo machines.

Some tattoo artists collected tattoo machines, which always struck me as a waste of money. Five good ones were probably more than anyone really needed, especially if you could tune them properly in a short amount of time. Beginners and small-time operators often hoarded a large collection of the expensive things, most of which they only used once or twice before going back to the ones they were the most comfortable with. Like many professionals with more than a decade's experience, I preferred to spend that money on bad women.

Delia was set up at station one and Alex was in station two, leaving me room in my favorite corner, the one farthest from potential battle at the door. They both had early appointments, so once they were working I answered the phones and talked to the walk-ins. The iPod hooked up to the stereo had gone from Motorhead to jazz. People were laughing and having a good time. The vibe, that hard to generate mood, was growing storybook, when Delia switched the music back to her new fave.

"Empire of Shit is getting—" I began.

Delia screamed, a high, piercing shriek of harpy warfare.

"—to be one of my favorite bands ever," I finished. She glared at me. The room slowly unfroze.

The ultrasonic dinged. I rinsed the entire thing out and ran the tubes once more through straight water and then bagged them and popped them in the sterilizer. As

I did, I looked at the maintenance record on the bulletin board above it. It was Nigel's job to change the water and run the mineral descalant through the autoclave at scheduled intervals, but I sometimes did it if he'd been really busy. The fumes were murderous, rumored to take months off your kidneys with every whiff. He'd changed the water yesterday, the record marked in his tight, even script.

I reflexively checked a few other things, even though I didn't have to. An artist reusing needles often scraped them through the Alconox, a white powder that went in the ultrasonic. I checked it for lines. None, and I felt bad. The encounter with Bling had left me suspicious.

There were a ton of ways to bust an artist on the grift. The ones who were always low on ink but never borrowed any, who ran everything really close to the wire, were almost always cheating. When they were counting pennies, usually most of the pennies were mine. The artists who took heavy deposits and were hard-ass, merciless sticklers about them, penalizing any customer who made one of a thousand errors, like showing up ten minutes late or canceling by leaving a message after hours, were playing the same scam as the banks, so they obviously couldn't be trusted. I didn't dig further than the Alconox. The people at the Lucky didn't deserve my paranoia, especially considering what I had to tell them later.

Everything was cruising along nicely, so I popped out for a smoke. Flaco was open, so I strolled over to catch up on the local news.

"Nice day, eh boy?" He leaned out his window. We watched cars hiss through the rain together for a companionable minute. Most people walked past with their heads down and their hands in their pockets. The new people, the vanguard of the yuppie expansion wave. The Old Towners were furtive and hugged the walls, or marched with their heads high, or zombied straight forward, or danced or capered or prowled. An endless variety of locomotions. A cold wind ripped along the street. I eventually turned to Flaco and nodded. Flaco showed me his gold teeth.

"Just made some *lengua*," he reported. "You want?"

I made a gimme motion. Flaco's *lengua*, like the goat or the brains, were only recommended by him when they were especially good. He saved anything teetering on the edge of food poisoning for the gentry. I watched him work, rubbing my hands together and blowing on them.

Flaco piled glistening brown slices of the rich, stewed tongue on a couple of doubled-up junior corn tortillas and sprinkled them with cilantro and onions, topped with a squirt from one of his squeeze bottles of sweet chili BBQ sauce and a final squeeze of lime. He slid them out on wax paper with a flourish. Two bucks.

"How's Dmitri?" I asked. I picked up one of the juniors and bit into it. The tongue was so tender it fell apart, except the tiny ribbons of chewy buds, left on for texture. The BBQ chili sauce had a long, seedy burn. I leaned forward to spare my shoes. The drops of grease and sauce whipped away in the wind.

"Loco." Flaco watched me eat with a tiny smile on his wizened face. "He came sniffing around yesterday.

Fucked with Gomez. I think your sweet little Delia charmed him into guilty penis confusion. The Lucky was spared."

"Really?" That was news. I snagged the second taco.

"Oh yes. He came out of Gomez's very angry and went into the Lucky, but Delia had him right back out, doing her happy dance. He was fawning over her like a bad grandfather when he left. You know she goes to the same gym as my neighbor's daughter?"

"Didn't know that," I replied. I finished the second taco and Flaco passed me a tiny, worthless napkin. I scooped up the wax paper with it and shot the wad into Flaco's empty trash bucket. It blew right out and disappeared.

"Loco, eh?" I tossed a fiver deep into the counter.

Flaco nodded, snatching it. "Yes, my friend. He gives me the sleepless nights."

"Seen Monique?"

Flaco shook his head in disgust.

"Smiles? That scuzwad Barnie?"

Flaco tossed his head. "Holed up in the Burger King. Too fuckin' cold out there."

"Cool. Do me a favor and keep an eye out for expensive cars full of great big guys with guns. Tell Smiles the same thing, Barnie too. Tell everyone. The Lucky has rich meat swinging its dick at us. Finders keepers. They carry fat rolls and who the fuck cares if they go missing 'cause they're way out of towners. Plus, whoever helps the Lucky, well, let's just say what goes around comes around."

Flaco raised his eyebrows. "Free food money. And a lucky charm."

"Bingo," I said. "Later days." Flaco saluted with the fiver. "Better lays."

My one o'clock was a woman named Mary Little. She was in her late twenties and very trim, wearing Columbia sportswear on her day off. She worked as some kind of MRI specialist, or maybe she was a physical therapist. To my great shame I'd always been powerfully attracted to her type: the no-makeup hiker chicks who drove Jettas and wore sensible clothes, had good educations and a nice family in Boston. I smiled at her, because a hug would have obviously been out of line. It was one of those moments when I wished I smoked weed and smiled more.

"Hi." She shook her hair and took off her raincoat. "I heard you were in California?"

"Totally was," I replied. "Thanks for being easy." She was one of the people who had to be rescheduled. I was glad Delia had been kidding about the scalp lancing cover story.

"Whateva," she sassed. "My aunt Judith was in town anyway. We did the whole Portland thing."

"Saturday Market, Voodoo Donuts, shit like that?"

"Bunch of little foodie places I've never even heard of. She watches the food shows."

We chatted about nothing at all while I set up, taking my time. Delia powered down her chatter and watched me, occasionally smirking. She knew about my uptown girl fetish and thought it was wildly entertaining.

Mary was heading for divorce and she was a hopelessly polite shit talker, the worst combination in ex-wife material. I set up my shader and all of my ink caps, nodding and occasionally sighing at the list of her husband's atrocious sins. He wanted to have kids. She had her career to consider. There were glass ceiling issues in the bedroom. He watched sports. He liked his car too much. His sister was a bitch. He wanted to get a dog if they didn't have kids soon. He was needy.

Not surprisingly, Mary was getting a tattoo that made the most of her supple figure, probably to drive him mad. Tasteful. Big. Muted tones. The Cadillac of wallpaper. The image was taken from a wrought iron fence she'd seen somewhere in the south while on vacation with the poor fucker. I'd made it look like aging brass, but lighter, almost like brass smoke. We were working on the highlights. It ran up her side, so I caught a few brief glimpses of her possibly fake tits, which were absolutely perfect. Each time it happened, Delia glanced over and tried to catch my eye so she could make humping motions with her hips and roll her eyes in mock trance ecstasy. I ignored her.

"Mary, I'm absolutely so fuckin' sorry to hear about this," I said finally. "See, you have a classic problem here, Chica. Your douchebag, what's his name, he sounds all right, really, if you can find matrimonial bliss with a dude who likes his mom too much, wears your shit out with the pep-pep-peppy sort of crap he's probably up to so he doesn't have to think about how soul crushing his life is. You're just horrified he wants to spread the boredom around like low-fat butter on white bread with no crust."

"Exactly," Mary said, almost hurt that I understood so perfectly. Her eyes teared up a little and we stopped.

Behind her, Delia went into robohump with pantomime blowjob, her own eyes rolling and delirious.

"I know," I purred. "But the other side of the equation is just as dangerous. Think about a dude who has no mommy to drive you batshit. Said guy could give half a fuck about voting, or even reading the newspaper. A sworn cat guy, swings a mighty dick at all hours. Will never eat fake food. Now, that dude may rock your sweet world, maybe take you to the kinds of places you never even knew were there, but company Christmas party material that man will not be. So you, delightful creature, are trapped between worlds. Maybe you should use that big-ass brain and make up your mind. Spring for a dousing wand. Send a postcard to the cosmos asking for directions to contentment. Find out which type is for the real you."

Mary looked thoughtful at my thinly veiled resume presentation. Alex looked on, face open with anticipation. Even the customers hung on the exchange. Delia ran her surprisingly long tongue around the outside of her lips in a rapid helicopter motion.

"You're right," Mary finally said, her voice just audible above a sonic eruption in Empire of Shit. "When I think about it, I guess Ronnie isn't asking too much. Maybe I'm just too much me me me. I try to control everything, and then I wonder why I have to do everything! I mean . . . he really is so sweet." It was there in her eyes, her expression, the artificial sweetener that was Ronnie.

Alex reeled back in disgust. Delia crowed softly and got back to work, smiling hugely from ear to ear, a smile so giant and tight and triumphant that it looked like it might explosively turn her head inside out with one more micron of glee. The customers looked briefly confused, but drifted back into stoicism when the machines opened up again. I nodded my agreement.

"If we only got more vacation time," she continued. "Ours never seems to match up."

"Vacation time," I repeated. I started tattooing again. Alex wiped his customer down, finished. He clearly couldn't stand to hear any more.

"Yeah. We went to Fiji once." She was dreamy at that point. "If only I could find a guy who had a good job and a nice home and liked the same things I do. That's what I kept thinking. And there he was, right in front of me. I just need to put in the work."

"Maybe try a dating service for free range—" Delia began.

"And that about does it," I said loudly, overriding her. "Just one more little bit of pokey pokey here and there and off to the races for you. Delia! Will you go in back and get me a tongue depressor?"

"Fuck that," she whined. But she got the message. The pout was instant.

A few people came and went, mostly lookers getting in out of the rain. I was far enough from the door to stay out of their conversations, so I learned all about Mary's Aunt Judith while we finished. By the time I was bandaging Mary I wanted to go over to her house and wear matching pajamas and watch TV. I wanted to rub some of the flavor of life off on her and ruin her for all time with color and bright, beautiful madness. I wanted her to lower and demean herself by making meatloaf and greens and cornbread. I wanted to go snow camping with her and talk about shit like artisan cheese. I wanted to feed her organic blueberries in bed and listen to her bitch about anything at all. It made me feel warm in the face. Sometimes I disgust myself. She was less than a minute out the door, on her way to a guilty post-tattoo cumber martini when my second appointment arrived. He was a likable enough guy, an entry-level something of some kind who had moved to Portland from Buffalo and was really into Brian Eno. We chatted about music, with Delia occasionally chiming in with all-important local band gossip. I was done in less than an hour. Alex went home a little early, which I'd been hoping for. When Nigel and Big Mike came in at six I made a 'wrap-it-up' motion and pointed at the back room.

"Gotta clear the station," Delia said. The union guy heaved a colossal sigh of exhausted relief. She'd been drilling on him for hours. I went into the back. Nigel and Big Mike looked up from their lockers.

"In the office," I said. "Time for a meeting of the senior staff."

I went into the lounge and sat down at my desk. Nigel came in a few minutes later, followed by Big Mike. They sat down and lit cigarettes.

"This about Bling?" Nigel asked. They both watched me with poker faces.

"Yep. He made some new friends."

They didn't have anything to say to that. We waited for Delia, who joined us moments later and settled into the chair across from me.

"I locked up and put up the BACK IN TEN, GETTING HEAD sign," she said. I nodded. Everyone looked at me, their expressions like those of convicts waiting in the chow line. I steepled my hands under my chin.

"Here's the story in a nutshell," I began. "About a year ago, I found out the Roland Norton flash was worth a serious amount of money. No earthly idea why. You've all seen it. Anyway, the buyer of the piece I tracked down lives in San Francisco. Bling must have discovered the same thing, which is why he stole all of it. I went down there and I kicked Bling's ass. He was still slinging pills, which I left"—Nigel rolled his eyes—"but he had money, which I took. And fuck you, Nige. Anyway, Obi tracked down Bling's boss, who by then I kinda sorta suspected might actually be the guy who put Bling up to the heist in the first place. I went to talk to him, but they ran some kind of low-grade whammy on me, and I had to split. But that's our dude. Name's Dong-ju." I paused to let that sink in. None of them said anything.

"The enforcer type I ran into was a monster with one bad eye, but he was smart enough to confuse the cops and put me on the red list down there, so my movements were slanted. On the way home, I busted the same guy following me. Bling knows where I am, who I am, all that, obviously. His boss does too. The only reason to follow me all the way back to Portland would be to dust me somewhere along the way. Make it look like a car wreck, or shoot me somewhere isolated enough to be able to get rid of the body and ditch my BMW. I was at the edge of just such a stretch when I caught sight of him on the security camera at a gas station."

Big Mike took in a breath. Nigel's angular mug hardened, but he smiled a little because I was still alive, so he knew the story was about to get good. Delia had heard the story already, but she was clearly prepared to enjoy herself.

"And . . ." Nigel said softly.

"I pulled into a truck stop just north of there, probably the last place with lights for a long ways. He waited out by some semis for me. I convinced some truck drivers to go fuck with him, maybe talk to him long enough for me to split, but he beat them into comas, so I broke my laundry room key off in his ignition and stranded him there. Cops got him after that."

All three of them began to talk. I raised my hand for silence.

"So this Dong-ju sent his monster to wax me. Fact. But any weirdo with that much dough has more than one of those guys on the payroll. And I picked one off all by myself. So I'm guessing more might be on the way, as in more than one." I let that hang.

"So we have a problem," Nigel summarized.

"Right."

"So, uh, so . . ." Big Mike looked at his hands and then up at me. "So what does that mean?"

I looked at Delia.

"If the floor is open, I think it means this," she began soberly. "No matter how we look at it, all four of us worked with Bling. All of us. So if they want Darby, I can't really see why they wouldn't like our heads too."

"I don't get it." Big Mike squinted. "Why?"

"The Norton flash," I said. "We can't figure out why the shit is valuable. But it is."

"Who cares?" Big Mike argued. "We don't have any. Bling stole all of 'em."

All eyes were on me.

"Not exactly. I still have two, in my storage space. The worst ones, real runts of the litter. I don't even know why I saved 'em. But I did."

"Does Bling know?" Big Mike looked worried. I shrugged.

"I'm betting he does, but he's hasn't said anything until now. It's possible, anyway. He was around for a while before we hired him, long enough to ask all kinds of questions. When I kicked his ass and followed his trail of bullshit back to the source, I think he got into trouble, and from what he said about this dude, that trouble was raw news. I think he used me as a chip to keep his skin, and also to get rid of me at the same time."

"He might be just smart enough to do that," Nigel mused, "but only if he was really fucking desperate."

"He was," I replied. "Told me they had pictures of his family. He wouldn't give Dong-ju up even when he thought I might kill him."

"And you might have," Delia added. "Might. He knows you're not really killing material, but you're nothing if not versatile, and he knows that too."

"Trapped in between a rock and a hard face," Nigel said slowly. "I can see how that could make a checkers man play chess."

"Yeah. So, I have an idea what we should do, but I want your ideas first."

Silence. They actually looked surprised. It was Big Mike who spoke first.

"Darby, I think I speak for all of us. You sort of got us into this. I mean, you hired him. If—"

"Mike!" Delia snapped. "Shut it."

Nigel looked at Big Mike and his jaw muscles pulsed, once.

"That's not what I meant!" Big Mike said heatedly. "What I mean is, look. You already got one of these guys. I don't do shit like break off keys in ignitions in some fucked-up town in California. I hit people. I kick them sometimes. Yes. I break shit. Yes. But any kind of clever bullshit is all you, dude. I got your back and I'm sure Nigel does too. I know Delia does. But maybe you should just tell us what we're supposed to do."

"He's got a point," Nigel said. "I also shoot people and occasionally poison them or steal their wives. But you had the whole rest of the drive back and all morning to think about this. We've had, like, no time at all. So where are you on this?"

"Let's vote," Delia said. "Who in this room wants to hide and who wants to go to the dark side because the Lucky is under attack. Vote." She raised her hand. "Kick some ass, get our shit, steal and rob and otherwise fuck shit up."

Nigel raised his hand. "All that."

"I'm in," Big Mike said. "But I don't want to go in blind. So spill. We know you have a plan of some kind."

"Okay," I said. I lit a smoke. After the first drag, I sat back and ran my hand over the arm of my chair. "My plan is this." I looked up. "First, we create a cloud in the street life. I've already started. Half the motherfuckers out there owe us favors and the other half want to. So we do this."

I turned to Delia. "Sweetheart, you research this Dong-ju Trust. The lid is off, so have your friends get in on it. Customers who have computer chops, all of it. Pull out all the stops. I want everything." Next I turned to Nigel.

"Nige. You're a scumbag and we all know it. Send your long sticky fingers out into your contact list. Any ripple, and I mean anything, I want us to know about it. The first wave could fly in, so anyone needing a shitload of cold guns and some limos needs to be flagged, and we need to know about it. Also hit up the MC reps and watch for muscle jobs, because those will be pointed at us. They won't hit us, but someone might ask them to. We want to know what those people look like. Names. Where they're staying, how they're paying, everything. Also, get the hookers riled up, and I'm talking way crazy. I want to see some greed, paranoia, and balls-out insanity. Except for Monique. Leave her to me." Nigel nodded.

"Mikey, you're my big-ass guard dog. You sleep here tonight. Flaco is already watching and putting the word out to the general wino and dime-bag population. Free rich dudes, all you can eat, plus one wish from the Lucky, so we have eyes on us outside. I also want you to deal with the day guys. I'm afraid those dudes are pussies. Keep their pulse rates low because I don't want any kind of disruption in the cash flow, and we have to project business as usual. The rest of us are going to be busy and they're going to notice."

"My chick is going to be so pissed," Big Mike said.

I shrugged. "She's always pissed." I raised the open palms of my hands, ready for questions.

"Fuck," Nigel announced into the silence.

"Why the hell did you ever hire Bling in the first place?" Big Mike asked. "And how did he fucking fool us?"

I shrugged. "He seemed all right, that's why. Look, we hit this snag every time. Take Alex and Dwight, for instance. They work hard and so they build a clientele, but do you think they really have the shit to hang in a street shop like the Lucky forever? I can't tell either, but my gut tells me they'll eventually farm out to some rosy boutique joint and turn into the tattoo equivalent of hairdressers or pro-level toenail painters."

"And make less money," Nigel pointed out.

"And make *different* money," I clarified. "But by then it's a status thing. They get big heads. I mean, who wants to work at some old shop in a broken-down part of town every day? When you can work at some fake-o little artsy place with recessed lighting, your own cubicle, and a receptionist?"

"I do," Delia said, clearly offended.

"Me too," Big Mike said, disgusted.

"Fuck those places," Nigel growled. "Like I'd ever work in a cubicle."

"So you see my point," I said. "And so did Bling. He really did. We were all waiting for him to become less of a tool and it never happened. So let's not feel bad, people. He made it about halfway to where everyone in this room sits. It's not our fault that he didn't make it across the finish line, and I think it reflects well on all of us that we even gave him the chance. I'm actually surprised he lasted as long as he did, considering what we know at this point. The street just gobbled him up, plain and simple. It happens."

"So what now?" Nigel asked. "You think this Dong-ju guy is going to be trouble, as in tonight, or in the next ten minutes?"

"I dunno, but it's a real possibility."

"The dude in the Lincoln is going to be bad news at some point," Big Mike said thoughtfully. "Though it sounds like he might be in jail for a while. You're a crafty fucker, boss. Laundry key in the ignition."

"Yeah." I scratched my head. It had bothered me a little when everyone cheered at that point in the story.

"I hate to even suggest it," Nigel said slowly, "but maybe you should call the cops."

"I was thinking the same thing," Delia said, surprising me even more. "I mean, it looks like the situation is a little more out of control than usual. We have no idea what'll happen next, except that if we do nothing, you'll never see that Roland Norton flash again, or the rest of what it's worth, and we all become game animals in some dipshit's human safari fantasy. Maybe we should just take the whole thing south as soon as I get all the research done."

"Shop field trip," Big Mike said, leaning back, warming to the idea. "Bring some of our more upstanding criminals."

"A half dozen gas cans," Nigel mused, looking inward. "Some of my homemade chemistry stuff . . ."

"Empire of Shit," Delia added brightly. "And Monique. And some ether."

"Nah." I shook my head. "Can't leave the shop unattended, plus a frontal attack means we have to leave our turf. It's better to fight here in familiar garbage."

"You stickin' around tonight?" Big Mike asked.

"Nope. Other than appointments, I think I'm gonna make myself scarce for a few days while I light some bonfires."

"What should we tell anyone who comes around looking for you in a mild-mannered way, like an actual new client or something?" Nigel asked.

"Get their name and number and tell them I'll call them back." I turned to Delia. "You done?"

"Yepper." She got up. "C'mon, I'll buy you a drink."

We went next door to the Rooster Rocket and sat down at a booth by the door. The place was mostly empty. Cherry, the head waitress, already knew what we wanted and brought us a round of Jameson's on the rocks and little Pabst beer backs. Delia waited until I'd downed half my whiskey before speaking.

"So you still don't have a gun." It was a statement. I shook my head.

"Nope."

Delia shook her head in disbelief. "Dudeboy. Those metal balls you carry around . . . ah shit. Lost my train of thought."

“Very clever.” I spun my drink and watched the ice cubes swirl.

“Maybe you should go to the coast or something. Get out of town for a few more days.” I could feel her eyes on my face as I studied my glass. “There was that little cabin you told me about, with the fireplace. The one you used to go to with that lesbian.”

I shook my head. “I can’t let anyone chase me out of Old Town.”

“Of course not,” she said sourly. “No one ever gets chased out of Old Town. It has never happened that advanced criminals from out of town came and made someone lie low for a few days.” She swirled the ice in her own tumbler, thinking. “So. The cops.”

“You can see how the police could complicate things.”

“Yeah.” She drained half of her beer. “You tell them a sanitized version of what you just told us and they might pick up on that. Not like they would believe you anyways, no matter what you say. This is a train wreck, Darby.”

A fresh round arrived. Delia paid for them again, tipping big to keep us to ourselves. Cherry left us alone.

“Well, as if all this wasn’t enough, it looks like we have a problem with Dmitri,” she continued. “I was waiting for a good time to tell you the whole story.”

“Shit,” I said, slumping.

“He came in yesterday looking for you. Dude looked like he hadn’t slept in a week. Smelled bad as fuck, too, like he’d been drinking bum piss white wine for breakfast and maybe had a dead foot tucked in his coat. I gave him the runaround, smiling and giggling like a toy bimbo machine, wiggled my boy butt, et cetera. You did pay the rent, didn't you?"

"Yeah, it's not that. Gomez is worried, too. So is Flaco."

"If we had to move . . ." She let that one dangle. Moving a street shop like the Lucky was a death sentence. It was bad for any tattoo shop. It basically meant you had to start all over again. An old place like the Lucky did well because it had been in the same place for more than thirty years. Even if people didn't know the name of the place, they knew it was a tattoo shop. The best advertising an alternative business could have was a big fat "X" on everyone's internal map. Even a move across the street would be disastrous. The phone book, the Internet, a year of ads in every paper, all were powerless to redraw our place on that map.

"Fuck," I said. "This week just keeps getting better and better. It's like we . . . it's like we got cursed by Gypsies or something."

"Just don't follow your instincts and we'll be fine," she said.

"What the hell is that supposed to mean?" I tried to look angry, but I could tell it projected as guilty evasion instead. I could feel it on my face. Delia considered for a moment before she replied, so something big was on the way.

"I'm going to use music to explain this. It's the difference between, say, Clapton and Hendrix. You listen and you wait for the moment you hear something masterful in Clapton, how close he can get to the edge of soulful fury without losing control. It's that moment when we measure the guy. Lacking in the end and probably only popular because he was white. Hendrix was of course black, and he had weird hair on top of it. But when you listened, there it was, a controlled raging beauty, precision deep soul fury navigation at its finest. He was like an astronaut flying with no computer and a blindfold through the fire part of reentry. Functional, genius-level insanity. It wasn't instinct. It was something else entirely, something so rare there isn't even a word for it."

She motioned to Cherry for another round and held up her glass to me.

"You're like that in a crisis, Darby. And sometimes it also happens spontaneously between drink number three and drink number nine."

So we clinked glasses and drank. And then we drank some more.

10

Dark, fat clouds were squatting on the toilet rim of the horizon as I drove home. The rest of the sky was one featureless mass of pot metal gray. The streetlights were flickering on and it was just starting to rain with promise when I pulled up in front of my house. I reached into the pocket of my bomber jacket and cupped the cold steel ball there as I got out and locked the car door. As the rain pounded on me, I looked the place over until I caught sight of Buttons sitting on the porch watching me. He was a shy cat for such a big boy, fond only of myself and Delia and the old Chinese lady who lived next door. He wouldn't be sitting there if a prowler had been around.

I went up the steps and let him in. His overlord and primary critic Chops greeted him with a beep and a few growls and then they went into wrestling mode, a random dance punctuated by grappling lunges and fits of licking. I couldn't help but smile as I watched. You can't trust people who don't like cats. Anyone who failed to notice how they brightened a place was empty.

I turned the lights on and changed into dry clothes, then popped a beer and went to the front window. Curtains of rain swept the street. A couple of cars sloshed past, a Jeep and a Ford Taurus. I sat down on the edge of the couch, drawing a blank as big as the rainy night. I didn't know what to do.

I didn't like sneaking up on my place and standing in the rain any more than I liked leaving the Lucky early. Part of being a good boss was playing the part well. I'd bailed Nigel out of jail once and loaned him my car a dozen times. I'd listened to his strange problems late into the night and bought him drinks while I did. I'd helped him exact revenge a few times, even when he was being purely spiteful.

Big Mike had crashed on the very couch I was sitting on many times, owing to his unfortunate taste for suburban women, who actually had no patience for him. When Mike's only family member, a cousin of his grandmother and the woman who had raised him since he was four years old, died suddenly of a stroke, I had spent many a night listening to the big man's stories of his "Memaw," as he called her, even though as an orphan myself I found his deep attachment to some stern old Croatian woman perfectly mystifying. Oddly enough, of all my long-time artists, only Delia had never leaned on me. But the fact of the matter was that I never really leaned on any of them, ever, no matter what. It would be a breach of trust, breaking into a piggy bank that was never supposed to be busted. Those people counted on me for their livelihoods, and their fates hinged on how well I held my shit together. And now I was leaning on them.

I sipped beer and thought about Roland Norton. Not the artist. The man. The man who had drawn a set of flash in Panama, 1955.

I'd bought the Lucky Supreme from Wally Langdon, my unstable non-mentor. He was the closest thing I had to family, which meant that he had given me a birthday present once or twice and I'd eaten dinner at his house on a handful of occasions, that kind of thing. We'd known each other for more than two decades. Wally would butcher anyone over pussy or a nickel, myself included, but he was sweet for such a terrible villain. When he'd finally retired at seventy-eight, the rain had gotten to him at long last and he and his obese wife had picked up and moved back to San Diego, where they'd grown up more than half a century before. Wally was eighty-two now and taught boxing part time at his local YMCA as a cover for his women and wine activities. After thirty years of working the night shift at the Lucky Supreme, he still kept late hours. It was a little after nine, so I decided to call him. His wife Maureen answered.

"Darby, you bad boy," she scolded. "You haven't called in months. We were wondering if you'd gotten married or you were finally convicted of something."

I smiled. "How's San Diego treating you?"

Maureen made an exasperated hiccup/burp/grunt. "Still sunny. I have to wear a hat whenever I go out, doctor's orders. My skin, you know. You're coming for Thanksgiving, aren't you?"

"You know me and free food." There was no way in hell.

"Oh goody. I have a couple of little jobs for you. The storm window in the living room is stuck and the downstairs toilet just keeps running after you flush it."

"I'll bring my tools." Maureen always thought of me as her personal handyman, her inept gardener and unpaid janitor. Her jiffy toilet repair guy. I was part of her humanitarian exploitation of the lost and damned, which also included three-legged dogs. A charity project to gloat about in the company of other, lesser old fat white ladies. I thought about her skin cancer. Her bad breathing. Her giant heart, bloated with cheese, straining with every beat, purple and taut.

"Let me get Wally." She put the phone down and whistled. "Papa, it's Darby!" Thirty seconds later I heard the phone clatter across the floor, followed by some muted curses and then rustling.

"Hey, boy! How the hell are ya?"

Wally's resilience never ceased to amaze me, nor the incredible volume of his voice, or the way he dropped every phone before he spoke into it. I'd once seen Wally eat a slice of pizza that fell wet-side-down on the floor of the tattoo shop after a busy night of really rock-bottom hookers, all getting his sloppy tattoos courtesy of a frat kid gone mad. Eating that fallen slice was like licking a scalpel in the medieval infirmary of a particularly nasty Haitian prison. It had shocked me mute at the time, and then he'd fucked the worst one in the group. I was silent for two days as a result. More than once during the long years we'd worked together I'd looked over to see him picking his nose with bloody gloves on while tattooing a horrifically bumpy, scab-pocked junkie's yellow neck. Either Wally had an immune system more advanced than a sewer rat's, or germs weren't all they were cracked up to be. I held the phone out and thumbed the volume down.

"I'm good, real good. Well, I mean okay. I guess. Actually, Wally, I have a small problem."

"I went down to the beach today and saw the cutest little number! These kids wear bathing suits like band aids! I remember when—"

And off he went. It was always that way with Wally. I could have called and told him a tulip had grown out of my belly button and the mysterious phenomenon had somehow resulted in leukemia, and he would have instantly launched into a story about whatever he was thinking about at the time, usually pussy or war, sometimes tits, and occasionally ass. Having a two-way conversation with him was like talking to a two-year-old at a theme park. His attention span was only seconds long and stuck in random. The three things that could make him focus were money, a woman who was seemingly impossible to attain, and the appearance of the children he had outside of his marriage. Then his scheming was eerie and alien, still out of focus but effective, like the war council consensus of the minds of a million clever rats.

"Wally," I interrupted. "Tell me about Roland Norton."

"Roland Norton? Didn't what's-his-name steal all that stuff from you? The kid with the fake name, what was it?" I could picture him squinting and rubbing his wiry gray hair. "Did you ever get any money out of that?"

"JB. Jason Bling."

"That's the guy! Whatever happened to him?"

"Nothing good," I replied shortly. "So, Roland Norton . . ."

"You know, I never met the guy. He worked with old Roy Bob down around Camp Pendleton. When I bought the Lucky from Roy, oh, in '76 or so, I found that Norton flash in a box with some other stuff. I think Roy Bob thought it was too ugly to hang up. I remember when—" and he was off again, tunneling down through the lengthy colon of his lies and memories.

"So who would know anything about him?" I interrupted quickly, before he got completely carried away again.

"Who? Roy Bob? That old redneck—"

"No, no, Roland Norton."

"Oh. Well, let's see. I think Red Avery's dad might have worked with him for a while. Right after the war. You could talk to him. Red's pretty . . . old, I guess they call it."

I had to make it fast. If I left any clues, I'd have the council of a million rat minds to deal with on top of everything else. "You don't have a number for Red, do you?"

An hour and many rambling, seamy stories later I hung up and looked at the number for Red Avery. Seattle area code. It was after ten, but I called it anyway. I got a scratchy eighties-era answering machine, full of condenser microphone static. A very old woman announced that no one was available to take my call. I left a polite message and my number, saying that I was a friend of Wally's and that he sent his best regards, though of course he hadn't.

It was getting late and I was tired after the last few days. I took off my shoes and socks and walked in my bare feet over the cold wood floor to the front window. There were no new cars on the street. The rain was steady and the drops were small. I lit up a smoke and went outside, flanked by

Chops and Buttons, who would guard me against malevolent night squirrels and errant raccoons.

Probing into Roland Norton, who was after all nothing more than a blurry memory in the minds of a few old-school con men, might amount to nothing. I was probably tracking a washed out scent down a dead-end alley, but that was pretty much all I'd been doing so far anyway.

In the morning, I worked out at sunrise and then walked around the corner to the G&G café for breakfast. I enjoyed the atmosphere of the little place and the food was better than good, plus it wasn't far to walk in the rain. The G&G had old brick walls, an exposed beam ceiling, and a few older but fine waitresses I flirted with outrageously at every opportunity. I took a seat at the counter and ordered two eggs with a side of biscuits and gravy. I was just settling back with a cup of coffee and my sketchbook, soaking in the morning vibe of clinking plates and the smell of bacon, when my cell phone rang. I looked at the screen. Seattle area code.

"Is this Darby Holland?" came a quavering, ancient voice.

"Yes, sir," I replied. "Thanks for getting back to me so soon."

"Not much . . . to do." Red Avery was a very sick man. His breath came in tiny, enervated sips between his almost inaudible words. I winced.

"Well, good to hear from you. Wally told me you used to know a man named Roland Norton. Do you remember him?"

I listened to the painful sound of Red Avery's breathing. "I do. Roland worked with my father. And Roy Bob. San Diego."

"Ah, good," I said brightly. "What was he like?"

Red Avery wheezed and then bubbled a small cough.

"You work for Wally?"

"No sir. Wally retired a few years ago. I own the Lucky Supreme now. I had some of Roland Norton's flash that went missing and I'm gathering information for the insurance."

Red Avery might have been a very sick old man, but he wasn't stupid. I listened to the labored patterns of his breath for over a minute before he replied.

"Insurance," he said finally. There was a note of skepticism in his whistly voice.

"I'm trying to file a claim, but I'm getting the run-around," I clarified. Every tattoo artist of Wally's generation had gotten stiffed by the system. We still did. Also, every one of the old guys always wanted money for anything, especially information. Wally had tried to shake me down a dozen times with various scams only just last night. "I thought if I knew a little more about Norton I could . . . I don't know." I left it there. Either he'd bite or he wouldn't.

"Roland Norton," Red whispered. "I knew him when I was . . . getting started. Thief. Crook." He took a moment to pant. It sounded like he was operating on one tiny black lung. "White drugs, whores. Beat a woman dead. Hated. Him."

"I see," I said, trying to politely fill in the next breathing episode.

"Went to Panama after the war. Tattooing service men. All we did." Pause. "Service men."

"Yes," I said. "The flash says Panama, 1955."

"About . . . right. Ever see . . . Basil Rathbone . . . movies?"

"Yes, sir."

"He was like him, but scummy." Pause. "Roy Bob . . . they went back."

"What happened to him? To Roland Norton?"

Red Avery wheezed for a moment. "Died. Black market. Jail. Panama. Mosquitoes." His breathing was terrible to hear. "That it?"

"Yes, sir," I said.

"How's Wally? We had . . . good times. Hear that? You . . . enjoy . . . your day, boy." He took a few whistling breaths and coughed up something big and thick as glue. "Don't come twice. Now money. The insurance. You—"

I hung up and grimaced at my phone. The smiling hippie waitress brought my breakfast with a bottle of my favorite hot sauce and set everything on the counter in front of me. She was a long haired, trim blonde in her late thirties, with glacier-blue eyes and deep smile lines around her mouth. I had a sudden, almost overpowering urge to lick those lines and then lick the inside of her smile, to suckle her sun-freckled eyelids.

"Bad news?" she asked, glancing at my phone. I ran my eyes over her and smacked my lips. She blushed and I grinned and watched her wonderful face, a work of lifespan art that told of dancing in cold mountains and drinking beer around bonfires after swimming naked in canyon lakes the color of her eyes. I was a regular there and we knew each other well enough to do a little visual groping without it getting too serious. Either way, I gave her a long, long look, and Red Avery went away.

"More of the same. Maybe I'll have some orange juice."

When I pulled up to the Lucky just after noon it was cold enough to see my breath. Monique was standing under the awning of the Korean mini-mart next door again, chewing the shit out of someone on her cell phone again. She was still wearing flip-flops.

The human body can exist, for some short years, on nothing more than Burger King's one dollar menu, desperation, whatever you can suck out of a glass pipe, and the bitter certainty that everyone dies, especially the people who fucked you over. At least that's what I understood about Monique, the little black hooker we let use the bathroom at the Lucky the most frequently.

She snapped her phone closed and glared at me. Other than the flip-flops, she was wearing three-quarter length bright blue spandex pants, a frilly red bra, and a big gray warm-up jacket that was hanging open. She must have been freezing, but you couldn't tell from looking at her.

"The fuck you want," she snarled.

I shrugged.

"Bitch stole my good boot," she fumed, stamping her sodden flip-flops on the wet sidewalk. I'd heard about it already, but it surprised me that she hadn't gotten the other boot back yet. Her toes were long and skinny. Monique had been around for a few years by then. Every year she lost a little more of the dreamy bubble butt she'd hit the streets with when she arrived, and her hair got shorter and thinner. Patches of her mottled scalp were finally showing. She rooted around in her giant purse and yanked out a single pink plastic boot. "What the fuck I'm supposed to do with this?" She threw it into the gutter. A brand new Old Town relic.

"Bitches," she spat.

"What happened to the other one?" I asked. Monique's nostrils flared in fury.

"That motherfucker got eight bitches in one room out on Interstate, so they's fightin' like cats in a fuckin' microwave oven. Some little white Alabama cunt took my boot! 'Scuze me, Darby, I know you'ze white. But I'mma slash that bitch's face."

"Right on," I said. It was getting even colder. Monique would be out until four a.m. She pranced and puffed on her cigarette, looking away. "What the hell are you going to do? About your feet."

"Right under the nose is where I'm gonna slash that 'Bama bitch. Never fuckin' smile at no one again. Bitch need a moustache I'm done."

"About your feet, Monique. The cold."

She fixed me with a hostile glare. "How the fuck I know?"

"C'mon." I said. I started walking.

"I ain't supposed to be off my run, white boy," Monique bitched, but she came alongside me and strutted.

"This will just take a second," I told her. "While we're walking I want to tell you something."

"What, you all in love? Got the warts? Turn faggot?"

"Nah. Got some bad heat on the Lucky. I've run up against some sort of shithead with a bank account."

"I fuck 'em up," she declared. "Mofucka fuckin' wif my bafroom what dat is."

"Just telling you. Put the word out. First come, first serve. They have deep pockets. But you be careful, okay? No crazy shit. You see anything, you call me."

We went around the corner and up two blocks to the Payless Shoe Store. They were having a going out of business sale, a spectacular event glaringly advertised by huge yellow and blue posters in every window. Soon they'd be replaced by some upscale Nordstrom's outlet or a bistro of some kind. When we walked in, Monique looked at me with a mixture of hope and sadness.

"Twenty bucks," I said. "Another five for socks."

She squished off down the six-and-a-half aisle as the lone attendant approached. I ignored him and watched as Monique picked out the first of the cheap boots for inspection. When the attendant started in her direction with his thin lips set in a scowl, I reached out and wrapped my hand around his flabby arm and jerked him to a halt.

"Can I help you?" I asked before he could ask me.

He gave me a sharp once-over and pulled his arm away. I cut him off once again, this time pointing at Monique.

"That woman is getting some boots. I'm buying them. Problem?" That kind of thing was part of the reason why I had so much trouble with the police. Some random little clerk, the sheriff of his tiny county, was a mouthful away from making me mad. Over cheap boots, for a broken down hooker wearing flip-flops in a rain so cold you could see your breath in it.

He huffed and walked back to the register. I watched Monique try on a pair of black plastic high-heeled boots that cost thirteen dollars and then pick out a three-pack of thick pink socks with cats on them. When I flicked a twenty on to the counter, the clerk didn't say anything or meet my eye as he made change. No lip whatsoever.

"Fuck you," I growled anyway. I couldn't help myself. He stared down at the register and stayed that way as we walked out.

"Thanks, white boy," Monique said when we were outside. She sat the bag down, tore the sock tags apart, and put on two pairs while standing on the pavement, using my shoulder to steady herself. The last pair went into her purse. She opened the shoebox and slipped the boots on one by one, standing on the box lid to keep her new socks dry. We left the flip-flops and the box and the bag on the pavement in front of the store.

"You hungry?" I asked. She looked up at me, then reached out and lightly touched my cheek. Her hand was cold and wrinkled and filthy, but I didn't flinch. A few weeks later that probably saved my life. A tiny bit of real human contact was more important to her than the boots. She looked a million miles away when she smiled.

"Naw, baby, naw. I gotta work and so do you. Maybe I stop by the Lucky later and put my grease down your commode. I know you was gonna get me dem boots cause you a sweet man in that crazy fuckin' head, but I watch my side of the street and I spread the word. Niggaz point they nappy heads at the white boy an' watch fo shit. Specially shit with money to get lost." She patted my cheek this time and sashayed off into the rain, tottering a little on her new heels. I lit up a cigarette and watched her walk, standing by an empty box and a pair of abandoned flip-flops. A block down, a car picked her up.

Big Mike had returned from his self-cleaning cycle and Delia and Alex were both working when I got back to the Lucky, half an hour late. We settled into an easy routine, Delia ribbing us, Alex smiling politely but more quiet than ever, almost certainly plotting a permanent exit solution, and me fielding phone calls and expertly steering Delia's rhapsodizing away from the X-rated or tabloid Bigfoot sightings. By the time six o'clock and the shift change came around, I was in an okay mood, ready for a drink.

Nigel arrived and started setting up after a quick round of greetings. Alex did his totals and went home without a word. Delia was on her cell phone planning an evening of unbridled debauchery with her two best friends, Cordy and Biji, two trashy cock-chasing lunatics we all adored. Both of them were computer nerds by day, so part of what Delia was planning was pure trickery. I was in the back at my desk looking over some indecipherable letter from the phone company when Big Mike peeked into the room.

"Customer," he said. "Wants to talk to you about a consultation. Iffy on the scumbagometer."

I got up and followed him out front. Standing at the tip wall was a power lifter with cropped black hair and a convict's handlebar moustache. His weathered black leather jacket hung open, revealing a massive chest in a tight wife beater tee. Some spidery, pencil-colored prison tattoos were drifting up out of his neckline.

"Howdy," I said. He nodded, and when he did his glaring, beady eyes stayed fixed on mine. A bad smile waited in his face.

"Hey, little buddy," he replied in a way-too-measured purr. "Wanted to talk to you about a tattoo."

"Sure," I replied. "What kind of thing you looking for?"

He shrugged and that smile spread open, a slash that was all wolf and rape. "Don't even care. Just know I want you to do it." The rictus held.

"Not much of a starting point," I said slowly. Out of the corner of my eye I could see both Nigel and Big Mike pause. Their heads swiveled in my direction.

"Yeah, I probably got enough ink. I wanted to get one last one from you, though. Heard they were gonna be a collector's item." He kept his long, yard-bully stare pointed straight into my face. "You know all about collector's items, right?"

"What the motherfucking hell are you talking about?" I asked, harsh. "Is that some kind of wussy talk?" I laughed. "Don't tell me. Some skank gave you a lap dance and some coke, then sent you in here to shoot your mouth off."

He shrugged his big shoulders. "Just heard you were the guy to talk to, little brother. Maybe you have a few things some people might want. Heard about a price tag. Heard you were gonna disappear." He made a poof noise and flicked his hands like an amateur magician. He reminded me of a TV wrestler working a kid's party

"Look, dudes," I said to Nigel and Mikey. "Test meat. The first assessment of our defenses." I turned back to him and gave him my sad face.

"Fuck you," I said evenly. "Pussy." He laughed and made a "bring it on" gesture with his hands.

I plowed through the gate in the tip wall. The guy reached into his jacket pocket and pulled out a seven-inch angel blade, one of those Italian jobs. He flicked it and the gleaming double-sided sticker glinted in his hand. He dropped into a fighting crouch with a wide grin and had an instant to glance to the side as the chair Delia had thrown crashed into his big head.

I kicked him viciously in the small ribs as he went down. Big Mike vaulted the tip wall and stomped on his knife hand with his size thirteen boot, breaking it horribly, then kicked the loose blade away. Nigel winged in behind me an instant later and kicked him square in the forehead, envisioning a field goal. He stayed down, moaning. A wet McFart bubbled up out of the back of his leather pants.

"Get this piece of shit out of here," I spat. I almost kicked him again, but Nigel stopped me with a hand on my shoulder. Big Mike pulled his wide leather belt off and started whipping the guy on his ass and legs with long, powerful strokes. The whipping continued as the guy half crawled and half dragged himself out the door and a few feet down the sidewalk, clutching his broken hand to his chest, pushing his face along the pavement at points. Eventually he climbed to his feet using the side of the building and staggered off, holding his side. A few cars had slowed and then sped away while Big Mike kept whaling away, breathing like a bellows. Across the street a small cluster of homies cheered and toasted with their paper-bagged forties, but other than that the sidewalk was ominously clear of pedestrians.

Big Mike came back in thirty seconds after they'd rounded the corner and put his belt back on, panting. I could hear sirens in the distance. I took the ball bearing out of my pocket and gave it to Nigel, who dropped it into a jar in Delia's station.

"Guess I'll be talking to the cops after all," I said. "I goddamned knew this fucking day was going to end this way."

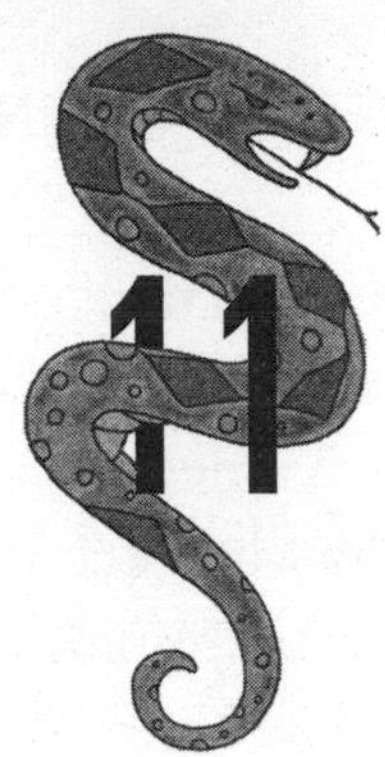

11

"I'll handle this," I said firmly as the first police car swept up, lights flashing.

"Jesus." Delia groaned loudly, throwing up her arms in disgust and spinning around. She stormed into the back of the shop and slammed the door behind her. Big Mike and Nigel looked at each other and exchanged mute shrugs. A second police car pulled up behind the first, and then another one across the street. In less than a minute there were two more. Must be a slow night, I reasoned. All the cars were carrying single officers. The five of them had a brief conversation out front while looking up and down the street, then they came in.

"What's the story," the lead officer said, totally flat. He was a tall older guy with a chiseled face and close-cropped gray hair. They were all big, in fact, the new breed of Old Town monster cops, with code-bursting chest walkie-talkies and guns, tasers, mace, beating flashlights, batons, and multiple cuffs, plus a ton of other crap velcroed and buckled all over them. "Who's in charge." Neither were questions.

"That would be me," I said. "Darby Holland. I own this place. Some big convict jackass just pulled a knife on me a few minutes ago. The knife is right over there." I pointed to where it lay in the corner. "I hit him with that broken chair and got in a lucky shot. I'll never get that chair glued back together. Then I took my belt off and beat his ass out of here. It seemed like the responsible thing to do." I shrugged and smiled. "He was pretty big. Like you guys."

The lead officer glanced at the knife and then gestured offhandedly, practically stoned with who-cares. Another officer bagged it without any clinical TV enthusiasm.

"These witnesses?" the lead officer asked, motioning with his head at Nigel and Big Mike. Delia had walked back out and was surveying the entire ensemble before her with open disgust.

"They were hiding in back, the worthless pussies," I replied. I turned to them. "So no one gets a Christmas card this year." Big Mike shrugged and made a face. Nigel rolled his eyes. Delia scowled and crossed her skinny arms, one hundred percent negative sassy.

The lead officer pursed his lips. The rest of them stared at me with ten-mile eyes. Not one of them believed even for a second that I was capable of telling the truth, but judging from their tired expressions, it didn't matter.

"Let's step outside," the lead officer said. He was a foot taller than me.

I held my hands up, biting back a remark about Batman or Dick Tracy.

"So what'd this guy look like?" the lead officer asked, once we were all out in the rain. I looked at his badge. Sergeant James Yeary.

"Big. Dyed black hair, cheesy moustache, black leather jacket, leather pants. Prison tattoos."

He nodded at one of the other officers, who got back in his car and rolled out to make a halfhearted attempt at rounding the guy up. He was gone and they knew it.

"Any idea why he pulled a knife on you?" He squinted at me, prepared for a lie. I sighed.

"Better get your notepad out," I replied. He didn't. Instead he just stared at me.

"A few years ago someone stole some art from the shop. Old stuff we'd had for decades. A few days ago I found out some douche in San Francisco had it. The stuff is valuable and I want it back, so I went down to talk to him. His people strong-armed me, so I left. But now he's evidently pissed. He probably sent the fuck-up with the knife."

"Did you file a police report?" the officer asked. He looked sorry to be standing there at that point, but he did take his pad out and click a ballpoint pen.

"I was just getting around to it."

"So you think this guy who pulled the knife on you works for . . ."

"Nicholas Dong-ju." I gave him everything I had, even dug the napkin address for Dong-ju Trust out of my wallet and handed it over. He scribbled his notes, occasionally looking up and shaking his head, as if he wanted me to just stop talking so he could get on with the rest of his night. He didn't want to be taking down notes about some out-of-town mutant any more than I wanted to be telling him about one. But when another one of Dong-ju's goons showed up, I'd have it on file that I felt threatened. I never placed much faith in the law, but they did keep records.

When I was finished, Sergeant Yeary went back to his car and typed on his computer. The other cop cars pulled out one by one until I was left standing on the sidewalk alone. I looked over at Flaco, who waved, enjoying the show. He gave me the double thumbs-up, ostensibly to indicate that I should keep going with his evening entertainment, maybe even make it more festive. One remaining officer was still inside the Lucky taking statements from the crew.

It was beginning to look like I might not get arrested after all. None of the other cars came howling back and no higher-ups came screaming in. No fire department showed. I watched as the police sergeant typed, and then unfortunately he sat up straight and looked at me, giving me a long, appraising stare. Then his cell phone rang. He talked on it for less than a minute. Halfway through he looked me over again and gave a description. His eyes went from my feet to my face, slow and wordy. Then to the neon Lucky Supreme sign, and finally to the beaming, jovial Flaco, who waved again.

Shit.

The officer got out of his car and cinched up his belt. He walked back to me slowly, with the deliberation of a superior but modest gunfighter.

"You're not under arrest," he began, "but you better come with me. Some people want to talk to you right now, and if you don't they'll whip up a warrant in less than half an hour." He'd seen my record and he knew I understood him.

"God damn it," I complained.

"You can ride up front." He said it in a conciliatory way.

We walked together back across the street to the car and got in. I looked back at the shop. Big Mike watched me through the window, stone-faced, the equally blank Nigel beside him. Delia was animatedly describing something to the remaining cop, gesturing forcefully with her arms. Probably lecturing him on the Constitution, a document every punk kid beat the police with at every opportunity.

We rode in silence to the downtown cop station, a place I unfortunately knew all too well, and then . . . past it. When we came to a stop in front of the Federal Building, Sergeant Yeary looked over at me and his overall demeanor was almost apologetic.

"What the fuck are we doing here?" I asked.

"Watch the mouth from here on out, Holland. Free advice. These boys don't fuck around."

I could feel my face turning red and the sweat taps in my armpits opened to maximum flow. When I got out of the car, my knees felt weak. I was experiencing the prelude to a high-powered, pig-induced panic attack.

"Fuck this," I announced, too loud. I turned on Yeary and my hands folded into slippery fists. "If I'm not under arrest, I'm walking."

"Don't," Yeary said. It wasn't a command. More of a suggestion. "Just don't." He sighed. "Listen. Your story popped some big red flags. These boys are just looking for intel, avenues of association, that kind of thing. Talk to them. If you walk or lawyer up, it'll look suspicious, and that's not what you need right now. Just get it over with. Considering the nature of the flags, you might actually want to make friends with these guys. It looks like you stumbled into a bee hive, Holland. It says something that they wanted to talk to you right away."

"I fucking hate this kind of thing," I said. Feds were way out of my comfort zone. Entering the Federal Building was like desecrating a coffin. It would contaminate me on a spiritual level. My hands and feet felt like they were covered in frost and ant poison.

"Can't blame you. You ready?"

The ROCN offices were on the second floor. Sergeant Yeary escorted me through the ground floor metal detectors, after which my photograph was taken by a uniformed fat woman with long fingernails and an attitude. Then I was issued a security pass I had to hang around my neck on a red leash. Yeary got the same routine, and he seemed equally impressed. We rode the elevator up in silence.

The doors opened on a short, wide, silent hallway that ended in a single door. It looked like something out of a horror movie shot in an insane asylum. I could just picture a pale gibbering eater of doll heads beyond the door, buffing the old linoleum municipal floors all night while he thought about silent cartoons and puppy meat.

"Now comes the really fun part," Yeary said grimly. I scowled up at him.

"Don't," I said. "Just don't try to lighten the mood."

"I always encourage cooperation," he said, "but these particular guys? I'm not saying . . ." He trailed off. "Fuck it."

Now I was both confused and acutely paranoid. We walked side by side down the hallway to the door at the end, two sworn enemies approaching the Gateway to Hell together at last. Yeary glanced down at me and then opened the door. The sudden wash of light and sound almost gave me a heart attack. I took a step back.

"I know," Yeary said. He gestured for me to enter.

The place was alive with activity, even though it was past ten. And the room was huge. Yeary and I waited in a surprisingly modern lobby after he gave some information to the receptionist. The doors to all the offices beyond the main desk were open, and I could hear dozens of voices, printers chattering, the clatter of heels on tile, two fighting radios. I took a seat and a moment later Sergeant Yeary sat down next to me, ramrod straight with his eyes forward. We waited, Yeary sitting at attention. I slouched and worried the laminate on my visitor's pass with my thumbnail.

"Sergeant Yeary, Darby Holland?"

I looked up. A scuzzy version of Doogie Howser had appeared in the hallway behind the receptionist's desk. He was wearing most of a shitty blue J.C. Penney's suit and scuffed dress shoes, and looked like he'd been boning low-end whores and snorting speedy coke for the last three days.

"Here," Yeary said crisply, rising. I reluctantly rose as well.

"This way." The fed led us down the hall to a room straight out of a low-budget thriller, with a one-way mirror on one wall, a long fake wood table with plastic chairs, and a video camera on a tripod. Another man was sitting at the far end of the table, drinking black coffee out of a Styrofoam cup. He was older, with a sagging gut, pock-marked face, and sleepy eyes. I pegged him as a wife-beating closet boozer or a born-again Christian, maybe both.

"I'm Agent Dessel," the Doogie Howser kid said. "This is Agent Pressman. We just have a few questions, and then you can go."

"Sergeant James Yeary," Agent Pressman said, picking up the clipboard in front of him. "Thanks for the escort. You may leave."

Sergeant Yeary gave me a blank look and walked out. He closed the door a little hard.

"Have a seat, Mr. Holland," Pressman continued. I sat down in one of the plastic chairs. Dessel remained standing, hovering and animated. Pressman looked over his notes for what seemed like a long time before he cleared his throat.

"I have your record here, Mr. Holland. Eleven counts of assault with no convictions. Amazing. Some minor drug shit, a suspected connection with . . . well, just about everything we have a law for." He tossed the clipboard on the table like he didn't want to touch it for another instant. "So why don't you tell me what you're doing with Nicky Dong-ju." There was no sleepiness in his eyes now. They glittered like the eyes of a weasel studying a nest of unguarded eggs.

"Lawyer," I said.

"Fine, fine. We'll get you one right now." Pressman crossed his arms, but made no other move.

"Wait a minute!" Agent Dessel said, making smearing motions in the air with both hands and smiling. "Everybody just settle down." Dessel spun a chair around and straddled it across from me. "Listen, Holland, you're strictly small time. We know that." He winked and then his face went grave. "Nicholas Dong-ju isn't. So let's trade. You tell us everything we want to know and we'll be so happy with you that you'll walk, guaranteed. We'll even owe you a favor. We'll be that happy. How's that sound?"

"Or you get a lawyer and we get permanently irritated," Agent Pressman added.

"We just want information," Dessel continued in an exasperated voice. He shook a cigarette out of a pack from the breast pocket of his wrinkled shirt and fired it up. "Not supposed to smoke in here, but fuck it. Crack that window, Bob?"

Pressman got up and opened a window, then lit a cigarette of his own, a bent-up generic.

"So," Dessel said warmly, smiling again. He really did have a big personality. "Take it from the top."

I wanted to know what they knew, and there was only one way to find out. So I talked. Sort of.

I went through the whole thing again. Pressman watched me like a human lie-detector while Dessel took notes and asked questions. I gave them a little more than I'd given Sergeant Yeary, including the truck stop incident this time. Pressman snorted with amusement when I got to the part about snapping off my laundry key in the Town Car's ignition. Just like everyone at the Lucky had. Dessel actually laughed out loud, a braying, boyish thing that was embarrassing to hear. When I was finished I fired up a cigarette of my own. It was well past midnight.

"I'm a little sketchy on how you found Dong-ju in the first place," Dessel said, looking over his notes. "Tell me more about that."

"The shithead who stole the stuff was spotted by a friend of mine."

"Right. The shithead being one . . . Rick Deckard, the old buddy one . . . Emilio Gutierrez? Those real names?"

I shrugged. Even after all Bling had done, I wasn't about to rat him out to the feds, and of course I'd go to prison or an unmarked grave with any secret involving Obi.

"That's a yes or no question," Pressman said.

"Then yes," I replied.

"Why would you want to protect someone who stole"—Dessel glanced at his notes—"this *flash* from you?" He seemed genuinely curious. I shrugged again and Dessel nodded.

"Okay. Let's move on. How did 'Rick' and 'Emilio' come up with Dong-ju?"

"Something Rick said when I asked him where my flash was made me think he worked for whoever had it. The trail led back to Dong-ju."

"This Rick Deckard," Pressman said, his eyes bright on mine. "He wouldn't be dead, would he?"

"If he is, I'm afraid all deals are off," Dessel said soberly.

I met Pressman's probing headlights. "He was alive the last time I saw him. I'm not going to kill some idiot over old flash. Especially not Roland Norton's." I held Pressman's look until he seemed satisfied.

"Okay. Back to Dong-ju Trust. Describe the building again. Try to remember everything you saw inside this time."

That went on for another hour, then they asked several questions about the Lucky Supreme, if I'd noticed any new people in the neighborhood, if there was any chance my apartment had been gone through. It seemed like they were fishing, until around four a.m. I realized with a cold shock that they were developing a detailed picture of my life and habits, to make it easier to unravel had what happened to me when I was finally killed, which they evidently assumed would happen shortly. They were building the framework for a very tidy conviction. All they would need is for Dong-ju to kill me and they could wrap him up.

"Quite a cast of characters you have working for you," Dessel went on. "Nigel Hurston. Registered to carry a concealed weapon. You bailed him out of jail a few years ago. Expunged. Nice of you. Michael Tayman. Seems like an okay guy. Drives too fast, I see here. Dwight Garnett. Sort of dumbass, don't you think? Dropped out of UNM after one semester . . . picked up for drunk driving in Boise a year later. Alex Chin. Couple years at Brown for him, eh? I see he did a little time in juvie in Montana. And finally Cordelia Evelyn Ashmore. Daddy's a big time LA mover and shaker. Private school, picked up a degree at Cal Arts. Owns a condo up on the west side. Slumming. Fine quality in a young woman." He put his clipboard down and grinned. "Ever see that movie, the one with all the minor scumbags who crossed some really big scumbag . . . I forget." He snapped his fingers at Pressman.

"*The Usual Suspects*," Pressman said.

"That's the one!" Dessel chirped. His grin ramped up a few dozen watts. "Dong-ju's like the gimpy guy, ah . . ." He snapped his fingers.

"Kevin Spacey," Pressman intoned.

"Right! The smart one. Plays people like fucking bongos, Holland. I'm not trying to insult you when I say he's probably ten times smarter than you are. Ever think any of your little circus clowns might be involved in all of this? I mean, you actually *trust* these people?"

"That's it," I said, rising. "Fuck you guys."

Pressman and Dessel had smoked a pack of cigarettes between them. Neither of them looked ready to stop.

"Just a few more questions," Dessel said, picking up his notes again. It was a fat sheaf of paper by that point. "I'll even trade you for something."

"Trade?" Lame.

"Trade." He glanced over at Pressman, then back. "Let me ask you something, Mr. Holland. This handlebar moustache man with the knife? Consider. Think really hard. Does this seem like the kind of guy Dong-ju would hire? And does the whole nature of the confrontation seem in keeping with his style?"

"No." It didn't.

"Because it isn't. And that can only mean one thing. Dong-ju is close to you now. Very close. He's moving around you, he and his people. And someone who knows what Dong-ju does, someone very like him, has noticed."

"And so the trade is . . ."

"Would you like to know who that someone is?" Dessel's eyes burned. I didn't say anything. He leaned forward.

"Work with us, Holland. Work with us, and we can find out together."

"Nope." I stood up. "You guys know where to find me. If anything else happens and I'm still alive, I'll try to call you."

Dessel took a card out of his wallet and slid it across the table. "My cell's on the back. Any time, day or night."

I put the card in my jacket pocket.

"Luck," Pressman said, smiling sourly.

Agent Pressman was a hard old cop and he'd been watching me for hours. I'd been watching him, too. He was an inquisitor, looking for a simple true or false, trolling for half-truths he might be able to button up. His scope was limited by his training, his instincts muted, a retarded predator. As a tattoo artist, I'd learned much more about faces and the language of the body than he would ever know, probing as I had to into the deeper realm of dreams and vague visions, every day reading the descriptions of images only half-formed. I knew what Agent Pressman was thinking when he wished me luck. I could see it in the narrow shape of his baggy eyes and the pre–car crash set of his shoulders.

Agent Pressman was watching a dead man.

Agent Dessel was smiling at me.

"You know," I said softly, "when you're sitting in the electric chair? And you're all strapped in and ready to go? You can smell the hot in the wires, and feel the last guy's fingernail marks under your hands. The overhead light has chicken wire wrapped around it in case the bulb explodes. People are watching and smiling, just like you're smiling right now. Or they're just watching, bored, waiting for show time. And then some state-appointed killer with a big enough god to forgive him asks you . . . what the hell does he ask?"

They looked at each other. Agent Dessel cleared his throat.

"They ask if you have a statement, Mr. Holland."

"Bingo," I whispered. I snapped my fingers and it echoed. "A statement. See, right then, sitting in that chair, I'd say the most confusing amount of shit I possibly could, so that everyone was going down into the dark with me. So my statement would be a kind of curse, so that nothing I ever did, nothing I ever said, would be admissible. Don't bother asking me to sign anything, because I can't put my name on any of that without seeing some money. Fiction is way more expensive than poetry."

They looked at each other again, and then back at me. Agent Dessel cocked his head, his grin gone blank. Agent Pressman narrowed his eyes. It was my turn to smile.

"See ya." I winked and then I left.

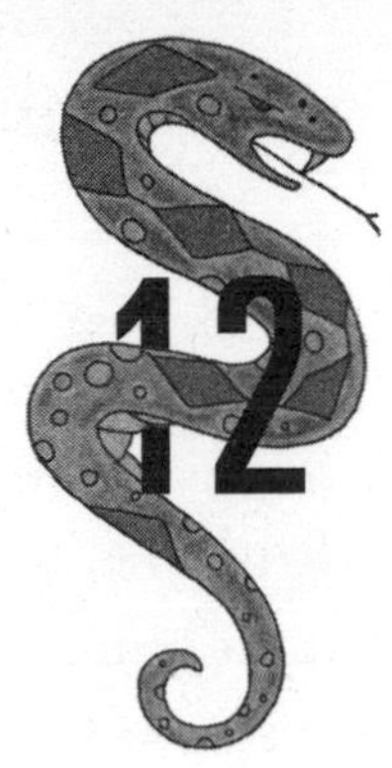

I walked through downtown feeling wasted and vile. The cigarette and urine stink of the chat room clung to me like a huge wino ghost diaper. My spontaneous parting insult had an accidentally revelatory element of truth to it that would have pissed me off at any time of day. It was just before dawn and the courthouse region of the damned city was already awake. People in business suits and service uniforms of every description scurried down the sidewalks, their heads down against the misting rain. I walked slower than everyone else, with my head up and my eyes blinking, a lost man rinsing his eyes.

My senses were blasted. The sound of wet cab tires on the street grated up my back, electrical shivers radiating from my spine. The flashes of light from passing cars left jagged red trailers over my retinas. My feet were soaked and my right ankle was throbbing, like it always did when I was cold and wet. A vague, all-over headache was emanating from my scalp like the first stage of radiation exposure. The inside of my mouth tasted like I'd been chewing on old cigarette butts scavenged from the lobby of a casino full of white wine drinkers.

I ducked under the awning of a coffee stand and ordered one, noticing as I paid that my hands were astonishingly white, like I was dead already. I stood off to one side sipping it and lit a cigarette with one shaking hand. The coffee guy, a skinny kid with a floppy Jamaican hat and a scraggly hipster moustache, scowled at me, but the look on my face when I glared at him with a mute willingness to hurl my steaming cup into his face shut him down. As the sky went from black to slate in the east, the mist grew in strength into an earnest drizzle. The awning protected me from the knees up, but the rain gusted in sideways and froze my already drenched feet.

I sighed and felt my ribs crack. It was shaping up to be a shitty day.

"Hey man," the coffee guy said, totally out of the blue. I couldn't believe it. I glared at him again.

"What."

"You just get out of court?" There was no one else around. He must have been seriously bored to try and strike up a conversation. He leaned on the counter of the cart on his elbows and gave me a knowing look.

"Did I just *what*?" He was scaring me.

"This time of the morning . . . usually court. Maybe county. Hooper, that kind of thing." He glanced at my cigarette.

"Oh my God," I said. My stomach turned and a burning line of bile and acid rose up through my chest. The flesh under my right eye started to tic. He cocked his head, at once wise and knowing beyond his years.

"Sleep it off," he suggested, "and seriously about the cigarette, dude. Secondhand smoke is rude. Sorry. It's just way super rude."

"Oh my God," I said again.

"Yeah man," he went on. "Kinda sorta see ya." He made a shooing motion with one skinny hand.

"You just filled me with the worst sort of terror," I confessed. He looked parentally admonishing. I continued. "See, it's like this, Pussy. I just got grilled all night by some wack-job feds over my impending, grisly-ass murder. So I'm standing here wondering if I can hammer my way out of it, if I can just go stone cold fucking crazy and still come back. Because evidently I have to. So when some hippie cretin at the first coffee stand I hit post-interrogation gives me shit of any kind, it makes me wonder at my game. Don't I look scary? Don't I look like the kind of guy who might just freak out and bash your idiot skull flat and light your fucking corpse on fire? Because I know I did about six hours ago. You want to do me a big favor? A really big super solid?"

He was backing away fast, ready to run. I put my cup down on the counter and stared into his cringe.

"Give me a fucking refill."

He couldn't move. I reached over the counter and squeezed two shots of coffee out of the big thermos into my cup. He remained frozen.

"You know what brave is, dummy?" I took a sip and scalded my tongue. He made a tiny shake of his head. "I'll tell you what it is because I know. All that John Wayne shit? James Bond? The *Mission Impossible* guy? Those dudes can suck my dick. They're not even real. No, hipster pusswad. Brave is a mental illness you get when you're desperate. Sometimes it lasts for less than a minute. Sometimes it sticks with you forever, like leprosy or TB. It all depends on how many times you have to carry the condition around in your head. Think I could flip this level of shit to . . . I dunno. A Cambodian dishwasher? Works all night all year for peanuts? No fuckin' way. We'd be rolling around in the gutter trying to bite each other's fingers off."

I took one more sip of coffee and dropped the half-full cup in the trashcan, flicked my cigarette butt into the swollen gutter, and started walking again. I couldn't decide what to do, so I headed for Old Town, my brain rambling through the fog inside of it at the same defeated pace my wooden legs chewed up sidewalk. Bitching out the hipster had been a so-so idea, but I did feel a little better. I wanted to go take back the stuff about John Wayne, but that would have made him call the police.

By the time I got to the Lucky I was shivering. I went in and locked the door behind me and headed straight to the back. After I stripped off my jacket and shirt, I dried off with a beach towel and then grabbed a Lucky Supreme T-shirt and hoodie from the merch cabinet and put them on. In the bottom drawer of my desk was a bottle of single-cask bourbon, a tip from a bartender customer, probably stolen. I opened it and sloshed three fingers into a paper cup. We had ice in the mini-fridge, but I was too cold and too tired to get up again. I looked at the cup for a solid thirty seconds, studying the floral print on the waxed paper lip.

If the mind is a basin for memory, then the stuff in the paper cup before me was definitely Drano, and I sure as hell needed to clear some hairy wads of scum out of my head. The final judgment on Pressman's face, Dessel's hungry smile, the charting of my life for a conviction against some kind of errant investment specialist the cosmos had appointed as my digestee . . . the new convict-knife-guy variable . . . bitching out that coffee kid . . . my wet feet, again . . .

I drained the little cup and poured another in the same motion. By the third, my spirits had lifted somewhat and I was warm, though black specks flitted around the edges of my vision. I put the bottle back in the drawer and prowled the dark shop, my thoughts sufficiently lubricated. I took a ball bearing out of the top drawer of my desk and rolled it around in my palm and paced some more.

I had four options, as I understood things. One: go back to San Francisco and really get out of control in a bad way. Take the whole gang and some really hard-hitting scumbags with me. Things could resolve fast in fast-moving situations. I didn't like the idea of hitting the gas like that and I'd disregarded the idea once already, but I had to reconsider it. Two: come clean to the feds and actually work with them. If I did that I would definitely get into trouble of some kind. I didn't know for what, but there was every certainty of it. I'd already done too many bad things, and I was definitely going to do more. Three: somehow communicate with Dong-ju and back off of the Roland Norton flash, then just wash my hands of the entire thing. That was clearly the most sensible idea, but the one I dismissed first. It was too late, and it meant I was playing along with the system and letting myself get crushed by the hammer of the dollar. There was no way I was walking down that dead-end dirt road. I never had and I never would. And four: stall for time until I found a sweet spot, an opening of some kind to maneuver through. Take my time and look for a window. Keep beating down whoever Dong-ju sent. Maybe see what Delia turned up. Keep the street on fire and pour more gas on it. Score some dope and have Nigel run it as a reward system. That idea had some merit, but it was likely that whoever Dong-ju sent next would have a gun, and there might be more than one of them. I'd lose eventually, and possibly soon if Agent Pressman was right. Those were house odds. The biker-without-a-motorcycle knife-guy had been curiously amateur, either a solo operator who knew someone on Dong-ju's payroll, or a playful, sacrificial warning from one of Dong-ju's enemies. In either scenario, it confirmed the feds' theory that Dong-ju had me under a microscope.

Whatever I eventually decided, I was exhausted and one of my cats had been out all night. I locked up the shop and drove home, keeping an eye on the rearview. The gray streets were empty.

When I got home I called Buttons as I walked up the steps, but he didn't come. When he finally did get home he was going to be pissed, I thought. Out all day and all night. An angry cat could really hurt your feelings. I checked the porch for signs of little wet paw prints, but there were none. No massive boot prints either.

On opening the door I knew immediately that someone was in my apartment. I silently closed the door again and took the steel ball out of my pocket. It was warm and slippery in my suddenly sweaty hand. The hammering of my heart swept my exhaustion aside, at least for the moment, and I felt my face twist into a mask of violated rage. That was it. I took a deep breath and felt my chest crackle with life. I could taste blood in my mouth.

I gently pushed the door back open and went in low, my right hand cocked to deliver a speedball to someone's face as a prelude to barehanded strangulation. The apartment was dark, but my eyes adjusted in three rapid blinks. I closed the door and quietly locked everyone inside with me. Then I stood.

Cordelia Evelyn Ashmore was asleep on the couch, breathing softly. There were six Sierra Nevada Pale Ale bottles on the coffee table next to her. Her sketchbook and a pencil lay in the mix. Both cats were sprawled out over her legs, regarding me suspiciously. Buttons yawned and lowered his head. Chops snorted like a baby hog and rooted into the warmth at Delia's side. She stirred slightly and quieted.

Her mouth was slightly open. I stood over her and studied her face. Asleep, she looked like a forest pixie from a fantasy movie, Lord of the Rings without the pointy ears. She seemed almost frail without her personality blazing from her compact body. I pulled the blanket she had stolen from my bed over her leg and her bony shoulder and studied her peaceful face again. Amazing, I thought, the things that came out of that mouth when she was awake. Cordelia Evelyn Ashmore. Another mystery. I walked through the dining room and found a note she'd left on the table.

"Let myself in to check on Pinky and Dillson since you were in jail. Again. You're really racking up some debt. I have better things to do. You better give good head, loser. —D. PS if I'm asleep don't wake me up or I'll barf. I drank all your beer."

I took a shower, checked on Delia again, and finally climbed into bed. The house was quiet. I turned out the light, and as tired as I was sleep didn't come. Eventually I lit up a cigarette and smoked in the dark, then finally sat up and turned on the light.

I got up and opened the bottom drawer of my dresser, moved the clothes out of the way. In the back was an old cigar box. I carefully lifted it out and set it on top of the dresser. It was layered with old tape and bad memories. It was one of the very first things I'd bought when I first got to Portland, for two bucks at a junk store that had vanished from Old Town two decades ago. I opened it.

Inside was a skull ring. Tin, the kind of thing that cost five dollars at a head shop in Denver in 1989. There was a deck of playing cards from a Vegas casino, all the aces missing. And a small framed picture. The three oldest things I had, that I'd somehow kept with me against all odds. I took the picture out and held it under the lamplight.

The glass was cracked. The frame was bent and old, but nowhere near as old as the photo. It was a picture of me and my brother. He was sitting on the floor, maybe all of four years old, a worried kid with big eyes. He had his arm around me. I was standing in a trash bag, smiling, curly hair. Some kind of juice had stained my mouth. My eyes were going to look just like his in a few more years, but I was too young right then to know. I often wondered what I'd been thinking, what he'd been thinking, who had taken the picture, where we were. That kind of thing. I always felt a singular variety of sad's emotional cousin when I looked at it, something I never felt at any other time, but knowing I still had it made me feel something, too. Maybe I'd tell Delia about it someday.

I put it back in the cigar box and put the box away, rearranged the clothes to hide it, and closed the drawer. Then I got back in bed and turned out the light again. Maybe someday, I thought, I should try to find that dude, if he was still alive. Find him before I died or he did. Some kind of clock had started ticking around the time that picture was taken, and the ticking sound was louder now. Dmitri had talked about destiny like it was something proud he could cling to, which only meant that he had no idea what he was talking about. Chaos was his destiny, same as mine, same as everyone's. I closed my eyes and I was asleep in seconds, holding my ball bearing like a talisman.

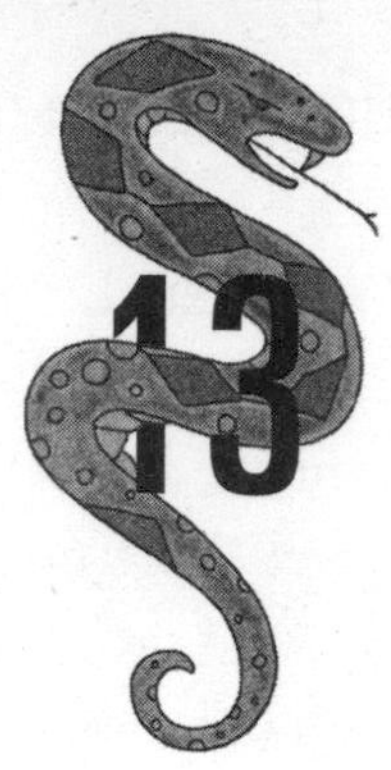

When I woke up at noon I felt like a pile of shit squeezed into a human-shaped cheesecloth. Sweaty and loose. My back hurt in a stinging way, like I'd scraped my spine on something rather than the digging-with-shovel ache. I'd slept for five hours.

The smell of coffee hit me, and close behind it the sound of humming. It was a Stooges tune, "No Fun." I sat up and rubbed my face. My eyeballs made squeaking sounds. I groaned.

"Oh goody goody wakey wakey," Delia called, singsong.

"What the hell are you doing here?" I called back in a hoarse voice. She padded into my bedroom with a steaming cup of coffee and set it on the nightstand. She was barefoot, wearing one of my black T-shirts and a pair of skintight, ripped-up jeans with white yarn Frankenstein stitching. It was the first time I'd ever seen her without makeup, in broad daylight no less, and her skin looked like milk, the skin around her eyes very tight, almost pulling at the lids of her large green eyes. Curiously healthy for a woman who had blacked out on my sofa, every bit the forest pixie I'd studied the night before. She patted my cheek and wrinkled her pug nose.

"You stink," she said sweetly. She turned and padded back into the kitchen.

I took a sip of the coffee. It was pure rocket fuel, thick and black. I took another sip and fired up a smoke. From the kitchen came the sound of running water.

I got up, stretched, and put some pants on. The water stopped and Delia's humming came through again, a bebop version of "I Wanna Be Your Dog."

"Brekkie," she called.

I followed her into the dining room, where she set down two plates of cantaloupe, oranges, and buttered slices of baguette. I settled in front of a plate and she sat down across from me. Her sketchbook was by the ashtray, and it made me wonder how long she'd been awake, if she'd peeked in on me and seen my sleeping face. I watched as she picked up a piece of orange and popped it into her mouth. She watched me back.

"You didn't molest me in my sleep, did you?" I asked. She shook her head and wiggled in her chair, obviously pleased.

"Good." I sipped my coffee and picked up a piece of cantaloupe. "So what happened after the cops carted me off?"

"They asked us a bunch of questions. Standard stuff." She took a big bite of bread and then talked around it with bulging cheeks. "Nigel and Big Mike were happy you took them out of the scene. And thanks for not telling them I threw that chair."

I shrugged.

"We all told them the same thing. Scumbag comes in, says something to you and whips out a knife, you kick his ass, blah blah blah. They asked if you were some kind of psycho. They pulled your record, I guess. We said no, just slow and sort of unstable."

"Huh. Good. They can add slow and unstable to the rest of the shit. I wonder what that will cancel out." I ate some orange and then launched into a detailed account of what had happened with the feds. By the time I was done Delia had a serious look on her face.

"Holy fucking shit," she summarized.

"Yep."

"Strange about the scumbag. I almost wonder . . . It sounds plausible that it was a warning from one of Dong-ju's competitors, but what if it really was Dong-ju? Even the feds said it wasn't his style, but what if that was deliberate? What if Dong-ju is trying to confuse the feds? Make them ease up on him so he can move around while they look for another player? Darby, what if Dong-ju drove you out of town just to see where you would go? Just to follow you all the way to where you hide all your shit? Which you might want to check on at this point?"

"Interesting . . ."

"It would be just like a guy like that, to kill so many birds with one stone." She looked worried. "So many possibilities."

We thought about that for a moment.

"It figures that they assume this Nicholas Dong-ju is going to butcher you," she said eventually. "I lamped the shit out of his ass on my lap top. My whore posse helped out too. Cashed in some favors and now we owe some."

"What'd you guys find?"

"Mostly the kind of bad shit that backs up the feds' butchering theory. He has a pretty low Internet profile—suspiciously low, considering—but no one can entirely escape the web. First, he's some kind of Kung Fu dork, tournament level. Kendo too, same deal. Fought and won in China, Japan, Korea, you name it. Kendo is where these dudes dress up in bamboo and hit each other with sticks, in case you were wondering. Rich as hell, as in on the board of directors for someplace called the June Yacht Club, so he might have bought the trophies, but I somehow doubt it."

"Great."

"That is great, when you think about it. The man isn't a scrapper, but he sure as fuck wants to be."

"Meaning?"

"Meaning he'd probably be surprised if you pulled one of your classic Darby Holland moves. The fake stumble followed by the eye poke. The surprising face bite. The good old-fashioned dick punch. Even your totally original ball bearing speedball to the sternum is uniquely effective against any kind of fighter who actually knows what he's doing. There's no defense against that kind of flat-out chicanery."

"I can't believe I'm hearing this. You just threw a chair into some dude's head. Yesterday."

She wiggled around, pleased again. "I'm tiny. You're . . . you. Kind of like Batman, but uneducated and broke. And your costume is perfect, because it looks just like street clothes."

"Are you flirting with me? Batman? And is this all we're eating? I'm fucking starving."

Delia snorted in disgust and sashayed into the kitchen, returning with the coffee pot.

"Don't even flatter yourself, you messy-haired weirdo. My kind does not flirt with yours except out of habit. I know the kind of wretched yuppie poon you slobber yourself to sleep dreaming about and no way am I putting on a power suit and carrying lube in a briefcase so you can blow your load in my ass in a fancy boardroom, plus you don't even—"

"Change of subject. Back to Dong-ju and breakfast." I finished the bread and the fruit and pushed the plate back. "That made me hungry."

"Mexican?" She cocked her hip, standing in the kitchen doorway. I shrugged.

"Okay then. And quit looking at my ass." She went back into the kitchen and got eggs out of the refrigerator. I watched as she started cracking them and lit another smoke.

"So to continue," she said as she worked, "this rich martial artist, art collecting, temperamental boss of Bling also seems to have pissed off the feds, but you already knew that. He was also mentioned in a *Chronicle* article a few years ago, and it might have started there. Bigi found that by the way, says you owe her a bare-bottom spanking, but in the article he was in some hot water over shady investment activity. It was never mentioned again, so he probably got off."

"Did it say what?" I didn't really care.

"You don't really care," Delia said. She finished cracking eggs and started whisking. "I read the entire article and even I had a hard time figuring it out, but it seems like he had provenance issues based on undated materials sold at a Sotheby's auction."

"What a total fucker," I said.

"I know. Douchbag, right?" She disappeared from view and I heard one of the burners fire, followed by the clang of a sauté pan. "So not much else. His house was mentioned in an architecture magazine, but only in passing. No photos of him, which was weird. But he really does seem to be an art collector. He has a few pieces out for show from time to time. Mostly industrial crap. Big. He likes glass and metal and red."

"Huh. So no pictures of him? Not even a blurry one? Harvard yearbook?"

"Nope, but I was thinking Obi could get one of his loopier clients to go after him with a camera. You have a little money to spread around after robbing Bling."

"True." I smoked and thought about it while Delia chopped a yellow onion and opened a can of green chilies. "I guess I'd rather keep Obi out of it. He'd just do it himself and refuse to charge me. He has that kid now."

"Your call, but you're right." She disappeared again and I heard the sizzle of chilies and onions hitting a hot buttery pan. "I bet we won't need a picture though. I already know what he looks like."

"Really."

She popped her head around the corner. "Yep. A rich bad-ass. Korean, but probably only half, hence the Nicholas.

Lives in that mansion of course, but wears Kung Fu pants around the house, athletic suits when he's out. Except when he's doing business, and then our boy is this year's tailored Italian, always black. Real white teeth. Ponytail. Interesting eyes. Strong hands. Abs like yours, but without the scars." She disappeared again.

"Draw a picture of that for Nige and Mikey," I suggested. "I'll give Monique a complete description to drop into the gutter, too. Be on the lookout for white-tooth karate-pants guy with a stick and boat shoes, possible gym clothes. Rob to death on sight, caution advised. Just in case he wants to make friends."

"Use your imagination, Darby," she scolded. "You wouldn't even see him coming."

I stubbed my cigarette out. She appeared in the kitchen doorway, a giant knife in one hand. She gestured with it.

"But I see everything," she purred. She stood like that, staring at me with an unreadable smile, knife poised. I felt a sudden, powerful pulse of love for her, and I realized how different the look on her face was from Pressman's or Dessel's, or anyone else's. Delia really would use the knife in her hand. She'd use her fingernails. But most importantly, she would use her mind. For me. Some of the lead shifted around inside of me, old metal that had all but rusted into a fixed wad in a different age.

"I love you, Cordelia," I said. It was the first time I'd ever used her full name. Maybe that was why she blinked.

"And I of course love you," she replied. She gestured again with the knife, pointing at the bathroom. "Now go take a shower while I finish the migas. You have four minutes, so just hose off the big chunks."

I went into my bedroom and stripped. I peeked out the door and scampered past into the bathroom when her back was turned.

"I saw that," she called. "I wasn't kidding about seeing everything, dude. Naked savage, early morning, super bad hangover with eggs in my face. I'm getting the pukes."

I cranked the water and waited until steam started to roll. Four minutes later I emerged red and vibrant, ready to be butchered after a suitably vicious display of the combat techniques Delia was so fond of making fun of. She didn't look up as I walked past with the towel around my waist. I though about snapping her one, but she still had the knife. When I got back to the dining room table she was already sitting, a steaming plate of *migas*, basically a green chili omelet with fried strips of corn tortilla, waiting for me. She'd given herself a tiny portion in comparison. I dug in.

"So what's next?" She watched me closely, enjoying my poor manners. "You learn anything when you talked to Wally? You never told me."

"No," I said. "Not really. I had to be pretty vague about what I was looking for so he wouldn't smell money."

"Darby, he owes you." Delia put her fork down. "I mean, money? Really? *Again?* You helped that old bastard get his mommy's inheritance back after he spent it all on pussy and trips to Hawaii. You helped him pay off his house as part of the price tag for the Lucky, which wound up being way too fucking much and we all know it. He lied to you and cheated you for years, and now that all this is happening, you're afraid to tell that shitty old man the truth? Even when it might save your life?"

"That's about the size of it," I confirmed. "I did managed to get him to talk briefly about Roland Norton, but he passed the buck, so to speak."

"Isn't that, like, totally suspicious?"

"Not really." I sighed. It was time for a tattoo history lesson. "See, it's like this. We can all agree that most of the tattoo artists in Wally's generation were just garden variety carnies running a cartoon scam, right? Midway cabbage people next to the Ferris wheel, sell you a discount midget kind of guys? Small-time P. T. Barnums?"

"Midgets? What the—"

I shook my head. "What I mean is that by and large they were the kind of people you couldn't trust. They didn't trust each other either. For them it was all about the cash, but also the equally important poon. Crank, too. None of them could draw very well and they knew it. It . . . it's just . . ."

"Slow down," Delia said calmly. "Think."

"Okay. Let me offer a string of examples. Wally and those guys, they were filthy. Like, dangerously, biologically dirty. Before Wally hung up his machines, I saw him do shit all the time that put his customers in mortal danger. Them and everyone around him. I couldn't fire him because he was my boss, and if I left . . . if I left. All those customers would have never stood a chance. It was like he was a germ dispensary, a friendly helping hand to bacteria and viruses everywhere. Now, Wally knew better. So why did he do it, time and time again? Because he didn't care."

"So . . ."

"Wally would also screw any woman who would have him. Fat, skinny, junkies, vomiting drunks, it didn't matter. He even fucked his wife Maureen, and she weighs so much she has breathing problems. He would recklessly put a stranger's life on the line for twenty bucks a dozen times a day and I bet he still collects empty rum bottles. He's that sort of dude, Delia."

"I almost get it. But keep going. Add it up." She cocked her head, fork paused.

"See. A guy can lie to his wife every day. And then he can go to work and lie to his customers. But no one can do that kind of shit forever."

"Wall Street. K Street. The EPA. The—"

"Fine," I interrupted. "But those are groups, sweetie. They have mutual daily reinforcement. Like-minded villains to lean on in times of weakness. But Wally and his so-called pals, well, no such luck because of the internal trust issues. No way were they going to have support group meetings. Fucking place they had the meeting would have been struck by lightning if they survived the initial bombing."

"So they needed something different."

"Bingo." I frowned. "And they found it. Lots of people have found the same thing, I guess. See, Wally can sleep at night for one reason. He learned how to lie to himself. Convincingly. He actually believes anything that comes out of his mouth, just because he said it. It's at the heart of his rambling."

Delia didn't have anything to say, but she looked both alarmed and disgusted.

"People wonder what evil is, and that's my guess in a nutshell. But even if a guy like that isn't a war criminal or a serial killer, even if he's just a Wally, it also means something else."

Delia arched an eyebrow. I nodded.

"You guessed it. I wouldn't believe anything he said, because he himself would have absolutely no idea if it was fact or fabrication. Since he believes both, or neither, depending on how you look at it."

"Jesus." She shook her head.

"Yeah. I did get the number for some guy who tried to pump me with the cash-for-old-news boomerang, but . . . maybe Norton died of a mosquito bite in a Panamanian prison. He might have been a drug smuggler. And then the guy I talked to might have made it up looking for an angle. Maybe Wally even got to him first."

"So back to your plan." Delia loved it when I talked shit about the old guys, but now she was focusing. I forked up some migas before it got cold.

"I thought it over," I said, chewing, "and I have limited options. Central theme has to be surprise. I'm leaning toward going back down there and going crazy on the fucker. Hit the fast forward button. Make some chaos and then hope I can find the back door faster than anyone else when the shit hits the fan." I spun my fork around and chewed. "You know . . . cops all freaked out because of anonymous call . . . bomb squad . . . Aryan Nation looking for their lost meth lab at the same time. Fire department . . . Chicano gang all riled up about prostitutes, maybe a few dozen rattlesnakes let loose in the grass to light the fuse . . . all kinds of terrible shit could happen right then."

"Hmn," Delia murmured. "That's kind of what I was expecting. Making things up as you go along is sort of your default setting. It gives you an advantage because it comes so naturally to you. Almost everyone else tries to avoid it."

I kept eating. Delia was a fabulous cook. The eggs were at the perfect point between too loose and rubbery, right in the butter zone seldom nailed by anyone except for grizzly old short order cooks. The tortilla strips were crispy and she'd added a dash of crunchy cumin seeds.

"Whatever. The feds are going to leave me out there dangling like shark bait. I'm just a big piece of chum as far as they're concerned, and knowing I have that kind of value gives me an advantage. The next shithead Dong-ju sends out will probably shoot me after what happened to the last two, and maybe shoot you and whoever else is around for good measure. Fuck that. So on to my default setting, as you call it, the sooner the better. I'm officially pissed at this point anyway. I don't give half a shit what Bling got himself into. I want this over with. I have you and the guys to consider. And the cats."

Delia tucked her legs under her and took a tiny bite. She chewed it while watching me, swallowed.

"Weeelll," she said, trailing off. She leaned across the table and plucked a cigarette out of my pack. "Sounds like a small slice of a vague plan, anyway. It's a dramatic start."

"I know," I agreed. She fired the smoke with an impressive thumb switch off the matchbook. I watched her smoke tendril up to the ceiling to avoid her gaze. "I got a day or two to fill in the details. A day, anyway. Hours, for sure."

"Everyone at the Lucky is on high alert," Delia said. She set her smoke down in the ashtray and carried her plate into the kitchen. "Alex and Dwight are totally freaked out, but it turns out Dwight is a gun nut, so . . ."

"Wait," I said. "Why the hell aren't you at work?"

"It's my day off, genius. Jesus Christ, that isn't the same brain you're planning on using to figure our way out of this shit, is it?"

She washed the breakfast dishes in silence. I finished the migas and added my plate to the sink, then went into the living room and peeked through the blinds. Patches of blue were visible between low, dark clouds. The streets were wet and clear. No one had slashed the tires on my car or bashed the windows in. I could feel the gears in my head click and grab. The coffee was digging in.

"There was one other thing," I said. "Kind of a little weird." I sat back down at the table. Delia refilled our cups and picked up her cigarette, settling like a bird across from me.

"Please continue."

"They asked about all of you. Everyone at the Lucky. It looks like we have files now. I mean, I've always had one, and of course Nigel, but you . . . Cordelia Evelyn Ashmore?" I raised an eyebrow. "Private school. Graduated from Cal Arts. Daughter of some LA big shot? What the hell are you doing working at a tattoo shop in Old Town? How come you never told me about any of this?"

Delia's face warped into a kabuki mask of barely contained fury. Her lips peeled back from her white teeth and she hissed cigarette smoke. I'd apparently just made a huge mistake. "Those cops tell you all that?" Her eyes drilled into mine.

"Well, yeah," I said defensively. I turned my attention to my coffee cup.

"Hey. Look at me, asshole," she said quietly. I slowly raised my head.

"You never talk about your family, Darby. Why is that?"

I shrugged. "I don't have one."

"Lies. And in the three years we've known each other, did I ever pry into that? Did I ever ask how they died, or if they even died at all? Even one time? No, I didn't, did I?"

"Ah, no." I squirmed a little.

"And do you know why I never asked?" She leaned forward. I could smell her shampoo and something like blueberries. "Do you? Can you even fucking guess?"

"Well." I paused. "No."

"Because I don't fucking care," she spat. She sat back and crossed her arms.

I was stunned. And somehow hurt. Deeply. Her anger cut me to the bone. After all that had happened in the last week, that was by far the worst. More awful than beating on Bling, more terrible than being hassled by the feds. I fumbled a cigarette out of my pack and stared at it.

"I was talking to you," Delia whispered. I looked up and met her smoldering gaze.

"You really mean that? Delia, I thought we were friends. Way more than that. You mean you never even wondered about, I don't know . . . me?"

She shook her head in disgust and smashed her cigarette out, then plucked a new one from my pack. When she lit it, she slapped the matches down on the table and blew twin jets of smoke through her nostrils.

"Darby, I know you as well as I've ever known anybody. Better. Who you are today hasn't got a damn thing to do with your past and you know it. Free will and all that shit." She brushed the air. "Everybody gets to decide who they are. You did. You actually embody that concept, which is why you seem so crazy. Everything else is just a shitty excuse, or worse, it's destiny. So don't you sit there and mouth off to me about some idiot profile the cops fed you. In fact, don't you do anything like that to me ever again. Ever."

We sat in silence, Delia smoking and looking at the nail on her index finger, me mentally kicking myself and afraid to speak.

"I went to an all-girls private school for twelve years. In upstate New York. So did my two sisters."

"Delia," I interrupted, shaking my head, "you don't have to tell me this."

Her eyes snapped up, glittering. "You asked, Darby. Didn't you?"

I closed my mouth.

"We went home to LA for the summers and the holidays. It was all very, very dull. My mother likes to start the day with a martini, but she's not really a drunk, if you can understand that. My father is a tall, wimpy pussy of a gentleman who enjoys spending his free time on his boat. When I graduated from the long-distance finishing school mill I went on to Cal Arts, because all the Ashmore kids go to college. And that was a pretty stale experience, too. Somewhere along the line I learned how to be myself, who

I actually was. Just like you did. But all of that, that . . . life. That was my fate. I was programmed to be . . . them."

I took a deep breath, let it out. I didn't know what to say.

"My older sister Margaret lives in Tulsa. She runs a law firm, the best one in the city. My younger sister Marie is married to an accountant and lives in Delaware. She likes to fuck around with boats, too. Real Daddy's girl. We exchange Christmas cards. My mom gets elective surgery every January."

I raised my hand for her to stop.

"No, damn it," she snarled. "I've seen those scars you have, Darby. Don't think I haven't been watching every time you change your shirt, and you're not even wearing one right now. I know you know how to hotwire a car. You scare people sometimes when you go to the dark side, even Big Mike and Nigel. So you know why I never told you about my dry little sterile childhood, with all the ponies and lawn parties and piñatas?"

I shook my head. Her eyes were moist when I met them, and her voice almost cracked.

"Because I was afraid you would think I was boring. My history can be just as confusing to other people as yours is."

I took a sip of coffee. A kind of hurt broke inside of me, a wave that crashed on the rocks and sprayed and took my breath in its explosion. I closed my eyes, and when I set the cup down I was grinning. And then I laughed. I couldn't help it. Great waves of gulping hysteria almost crippled me. I reached out and grabbed one of her hands, gradually steadying myself.

"Oh sweetie," I gasped, wiping tears from my eyes with my free hand. "That's just about the most fucked-up thing I've ever heard."

Delia snatched her hand back, but she smiled a little.

"You," I continued, "are just about the most interesting person I've ever known."

"Don't you fucking forget it, either," she said, and laughed a little herself. "And if you tell Nigel or Mike about any of this, I swear to you, Darby Holland, that you'll regret it for a short few seconds after I hear about it."

I held up my hands. I could almost feel the rare October sunlight touching my bones.

"I got things to do," Delia said, rising. I turned around and watched as she walked to the door and slipped her boots on, then tugged her jacket over the shirt she had stolen from me. She gave Chops a kiss on the head where he was draped on the back of the couch and then fixed me with a firm look.

"Thanks," I said. "Sometime soon, when all this is over, maybe we can . . . I don't know. I owe you a story."

She looked at me and a slow progression of things went through her eyes. It finally settled and became unreadable.

"Get your shit together," she said finally, opening the door. A fresh breeze gusted in, rippling through her maroon hair. "Don't plan the massacre trip until we go through it all again. I'm going to lamp these feds, too. And you better go see Dmitri."

I did sit-ups and pull-ups until I was breathing hard and my abs ached and my hands felt like sweaty metal hooks, then took a second shower and got dressed all over again. The exercise was how I fought off the hangovers, and it made my clothes fit better. Plus, morning endorphins were a terrific buzz. While I was lacing my boots, I did a mental inventory. I too ostensibly had the day off, but it never worked out that way, and with everything else going on actual work would have been a relief.

When Wally had run the Lucky Supreme, I'd been free to tattoo all day without a care in the world, except for disease, chemical-related poisoning, death by gunfire for fucking up, and of course getting ripped off by Wally. There were other low-grade concerns, like getting ink in my eyes, the chemclave blowing and taking a finger, that kind of thing, but not too many. Those were good times and I knew it. Now I watched as my employees got all the choice jobs. While Nigel was tattooing the crotch of some giggling, nubile coed with two of her friends waiting, I was hammering away with a monkey wrench in the bathroom, fixing the toilet. While Big Mike worked on a sleeve with a lush gambling theme, I was at the bank, standing in line, being eyed by security. While Delia was brushing in the delicate grays of one of her truly enormous and masterful ongoing pieces, full of wind and light and elements, I was replacing floor tiles or patching the roof for the millionth time. And most galling of all, when the new guys were soaking up the super-easy money that came off of the constant flow of names and kanji symbols, I was often preoccupied with issues like tracking down thieves, maintaining diplomatic relations with the nightworld, and dealing with bummers like Dmitri.

I'd known Dmitri for almost twenty years, from way back to when Wally owned the Lucky Supreme. Dmitri was an eccentric even back then, and Wally's way of dealing with him had been to leave him alone as much as possible, and out-crazy him when he couldn't. Over the years Dmitri had gotten worse until he'd finally deteriorated into his potently wretched present state. Ignoring him or out-crazying him hadn't been an option for a few years. I had to take both barrels in the face every time I dealt with him.

To begin with, Dmitri was a consummate fatalist, always depressed about something, and always amazingly stubborn about it. The very topic of depression was one of the few things that could inspire him into lucidity. In addition to the sagging brick building that housed the Lucky, Gomez's bar to our left, and the Korean convenience store to our right, he owned a small four-story tenement down the street where he ran "mitri's izza," his personal brainchild masterstroke of innate business acumen, designed to springboard him into the world of pizza so he could destroy Domino's, an outfit that had righteously pissed him off one too many times. It was on the west corner of the ground floor and it was almost always open.

Dmitri was the cheapest man I'd ever known. He'd inherited the two buildings from his father, Foti, and it was rumored a sizable chunk of money in the single digit millions as well, but to look at him you'd think he was just another old street lunatic who'd lost his shopping cart. His big, curly hair had grayed and gone wild over the years, and he wore the worst clothes the Goodwill had to offer, garments so awful that they were almost certainly given away for free. He eschewed showering in favor of Dollar Store cologne, and proudly claimed to have never purchased toilet paper.

I tolerated Dmitri because I had to, and evidently the sentiment was mutual, but in recent years I'd found myself in the uncomfortable and reliably volatile position of being his squeamish confidant, as had Gomez to a lesser degree. Gomez had his uninspiring ten-mile stare and I didn't. Dmitri had been looking for me for a week, so it was time to play shrink. It was just what I needed for my fragile sense of well-being, which was on an upswing after the migas.

I drove downtown, checking the vital signs on the street life as I went. A potbellied old dude rocking a hockey mullet was holding up a cardboard sign that read "UFO broken, need money to get home." Points for originality. The sky was still a mixed bag of Concord clouds and patches of gauze and blue, omen-free as far as I could tell. I parked in front of the Lucky and looked through the windows. Alex was tattooing the tiny foot of a big girl with big hair, and Dwight was sitting at the desk reading a comic book. It was Dwight's day off so he was there supporting his buddy, the other new guy. It smacked of mutiny.

I waved at Flaco as I passed on the walk down to "mitri's izza." Above the fabled headquarters/pizzeria of my landlord were three floors of apartments, and some of them were occupied. The D and the P on the neon sign in the window had burned out years ago, so it had read "mitri's izza" for as long as anyone could remember. He claimed to have done it on purpose, and sadly he may have. The windows were filmed with years of accumulated soot and grease and the front door needed a new coat of paint a decade ago. I pushed the door open and a little bell tinkled.

Dmitri was slouched behind the counter next to his ancient push button cash register, staring without visible interest at a crossword puzzle. He wasn't holding a pen. There were three slices of pizza in the heated glass cabinet next to him, two red-slicked pepperoni and a dried-out cheese that looked a few days old. The sticky Formica tables were empty. A few of them boasted paper plates with petrified crusts and hanks of napkins. It was anyone's guess as to how long they'd been there.

"Lucky boy," Dmitri murmured, looking up. His eyes were dark and glassy, the whites yellowed with morning booze and weeks of bad food, all on top of nights of no sleep and bouts of hysteria. His giant oily wigwam of curly gray hair was listing off to one side. He was wearing a red and black checkered polyester coat and lime-green pants, and the overall impression was that of a small-town rodeo clown too fucked up to find his face paint. "I been lookin' for you. Where you been?"

"California," I replied. Dmitri pointed at the pizza case with a long gray finger and I shook my head. "So what's up, man? How you doing?"

Dmitri sighed and looked out the grimy windows, a lost, pitiful look on his face. I waited.

"Oh, you know," he said finally. "I don't have good dreams anymore, Darby. I never did, but now I don't even sleep."

I pulled up a stool and sat.

"Tell me about it," I said. He focused on me and gave me a sad, boyish frown.

"The world is changing, Darby, and I'm too old to change with it." He shook his head and gave me the expressive two-handed Greek shrug. "Old Town is going to be New Town in a few years. Maybe sooner. Have you noticed what's going on?"

It had never occurred to me to wonder how gentrification looked from Dmitri's point of view. His childhood had its roots here. He'd been brought up in Old Town, back when it was simply the immigrant section. He'd even fucked Monique more than a few times, I knew, so his experiences were current. "Has someone been leaning on you, Dmitri?"

"Nah." He waved the idea away like a bad smell. I'd never seen a gesture so filled with lies. The new landlord class had been pouring in like piranhas all around his hemorrhaging idiocy. "The city wants to give me a zero-interest loan to 'upgrade.'" He said the last with something close to a snarl. I sat back and zeroed in on an old, cluttered fly strip dangling behind him. I was beginning to get a glimpse of the bigger picture.

The fastest way to get Dmitri to throw an awesome, Chimpanzee-style tantrum was to report that something was broken in one of his buildings. As tenants, we'd all learned that long ago. If a toilet broke, you fixed it and said nothing. Same with a broken heater, a leak in the roof, electrical problems, basically everything. It didn't matter that most of the pipes in the building that housed the Lucky were over sixty years old and the roof had never been replaced, that the wiring had been chewed on by generations of rats and was probably substandard to begin with.

Dmitri took all those things personally in a very weird way. If some part of the building broke that it was technically his responsibility to maintain, he would fly into an inhuman rage when confronted with it, because in his mind it meant you were accusing him or his departed father Foti of putting low-grade ghetto junk into the building in the first place, that he was too stupid to know what was built to last, and finally that a toilet distributor or a bent window man had ripped him off thirty years ago because he was gullible.

It didn't matter that his buildings *were* actually falling apart, that everything was held together with layers of crazy glue and bent screws and the amateur repairs of the occupants. Having the city point it out to Dmitri had aged him visibly, I realized. It was eating him alive from the inside, like he'd finally swallowed a bat bug hive that had been breeding on his breakfast table his entire life.

Dmitri desperately needed me to lie to him. So of course I did.

"Fuck those assholes," I said. "Why does everything have to be new and plastic? You know something these buildings have that no prefab mini mall ever will? Style. Old World charm."

"That's exactly what I said," Dmitri said, perking up a little, his eyes widening.

"It's the difference between a beat-up hood rat with a nasty pussy rash and an elegant lady with a bottle of fine champagne," I continued. Dmitri slammed his hand down on the counter.

"Exactly!" he roared.

I had to be careful not to overdo it. If I got him too stoked up, he was liable to do something reckless, like march over to City Hall and freak out, maybe even take his green golf pants off and wave them around like the flag of Atlantis. His underwear alone would bring the wrath of God down on all of us.

"Just ignore 'em," I advised, slyly moving to a different tactic. If I could get him to roll out his condescending wise man routine, it would make him feel satisfied that he'd made his case, even though I ultimately viewed all of his opinions as horseshit and he knew it. It had worked before. He just needed to vent. "They'll come around once they understand the concept of architectural character."

Dmitri narrowed his eyes at me, rising to the occasion, even though he knew what I was doing. He sighed in a maudlin way as a prelude.

"Darby, I will tell you something about yourself, and you should listen. You aren't a smart man. Don't be insulted. Just don't bother. I'm already tired." His face firmed up and then went slack. His eyes took on a profound distance. It was working.

"You, your little Delia, poor, doomed Gomez, the Cho Family Circus, all of you are outsiders. Almost everyone in Old Town is. It's why you're all here in the first place." He paused to dump some white wine into a paper cup from a half-gallon jug. He didn't offer me any, so I couldn't refuse. After a big gulp and a vaudeville flourish he continued.

"As spectators of the admittedly obscure state of social affairs, you're far more lost in your opinions than most people, which is why I pointed out your intellect. You personally bear two crosses, Darby."

I shifted, but said nothing. It was imperative to keep him flowing until the tap went dry. He confused my attention for tacit agreement. I suppressed a smile, which would have only confused him.

"The landlord class, well, we are different. We have a responsibility to a greater cause, a cause that imbues us all with a heightened clarity. We are all akin to spiritual miniature mayors in that way."

"Spiritual miniature mayors," I repeated.

"Council members, with a charter that defies description. It's much more than a birthright or a lifestyle choice. It is a destiny."

"Destiny . . ." I breathed it.

"Correct. This change? This change occurs in every aspect of the social body. Psychology? Sociology? Those are infant French pseudosciences engineered to comfort the masses. The only accurate mechanism for understanding our fellow man is economics. Numbers don't lie, and as a species we generate them by the trillions, individually and collectively."

"I see." I did, unfortunately. It was horribly cynical to the point of being partly blind, but I did see. Change in the tattoo world was driven by numbers these days. Dong-ju with a tattoo shop in a mall, a rich weirdo so entitled that the whole Norton affair wasn't theft so much as an investment decision. Money had driven the art in the beginning, and then the art had driven itself for a while, until the blossoming of a period of robust development had, naturally, attracted people interested primarily in money.

"Now consider," Dmitri continued patiently. "I am like a zoo keeper. You are all my animals. So it's like a carnival, or a game preserve. The new landlords are corporations, and they behave like prison wardens. The numbers will bear me out."

"A spiritual miniature mayoral zookeeper," I said, putting it all together.

"Don't mock me," he scolded with an indulgent, professorial smile. I held up my hands.

"The wardens don't like outsiders. You represent a variable in their tidy equation. They actually don't like me either, but for entirely different reasons . . ." He trailed off.

I couldn't stand another minute of it, so when it looked like his meditative state of self-doubt was going to hold I stood up, mission accomplished. It was an improvement from drunk and cornered. His thoughts had been organized. I took my wallet out and nodded at the pizza rack. "Gimme a slice of that pepperoni to go."

"You got it," he said. A measure of life and enthusiasm had flowed back into Dmitri for the moment, but just enough for him to work on a solid buzz and a nap. He used a crusty spatula to slide the greasy slice onto a paper plate and beamed Buddha at me. I flicked three bucks out on the counter, and he rang up the sale on the cash register as I walked out.

I went straight to Gomez's bar, dumping the pizza slice into a bus stop trashcan as I passed. The inside of the Rooster Rocket was dark and mostly empty at that hour. Gomez was wiping down the taps and talking to the new waitress.

"Darby," he called. "Christian thimble or a real one?"

"Vodka rocks," I replied, "and pour one for yourself, my treat. I just talked to Dmitri."

Gomez raised an eyebrow and then tossed his head at the booth all the way in the back. I crashed into the old Naugahyde bench on one side of it and lit up a cigarette. A minute later he joined me with two glasses.

"What did he say?" Gomez asked, and then raised his hand. "Wait!" He picked up his glass and drained half of it, sucked at his black moustache. "Okay. Now I'm ready for anything."

"The city has apparently been hassling Dmitri about the state of his buildings. They went so far as to offer him an interest-free loan to upgrade. And I get the feeling that the new real estate moguls buying up everything around us might be leaning on him to sell and the city is their way of depleting his resources to make him desperate. He's pretty much freestyling on the outer edge of sanity at this point. Described himself as a spiritual mini mayor with a destiny."

Gomez's eyes went wide and he leaned back, then forward again to hunch over his drink. "Well," he said, with strange Mexican calm. "We appear to be fucked, my friend."

"Yep. You know how that crazy fucker gets. He's not going to take the loan or fix anything, that goes without saying. It won't be long before we get visitors of our own. City visitors. Inspectors. And they're going to be extra nosy."

Gomez gulped down the rest of his drink and reached out for mine. I slapped his hand away and picked up my glass.

"Madre de Dios," he said softly. "They'll bypass Dmitri and fuck with us directly. When was your last fire inspection?"

"Last year. I derailed the guy by talking about boxing. No way we would pass."

"I did the same thing. Fishing, which I know nothing about. Liability insurance?"

"Up to date. I'm wondering about electrical codes and that kind of thing. When Wally owned the place, he made the most utterly half-assed repairs imaginable, and of course he didn't pay for them, so I don't even have the names of the repair people to find out who did what. I'm probably supposed to hide from them anyway. It's that fucked. One building inspector would sink me."

Gomez's eyes went blank as he conducted a mental inventory of everything he'd done to his bar over the last fifteen years. When he was done he shuddered. "What the hell are we going to do? Did you tell the old lady at the mini-mart?"

"You tell her," I said. "Maybe try sign language." I gunned my drink. "I have no idea what to do. Only thing I can think of is to clean up the front of our places. Maybe sneak over to Dmitri's at night and wash the windows and paint the fucking door, fix his idiot pizza sign."

"Right . . . a little paint, sweep the sidewalks. That'll hold 'em off for a few minutes."

I sat there thinking. Gomez was silent as well, staring at his big hands.

"So you said your lease is up in five years?" he asked finally.

"Four years and change," I replied. "I just re-signed less than a year ago."

Gomez shook his head. "We must have rights of some kind. I'll look into it."

"Good idea. I've got some customers who're contractors. Maybe I can convince one of them to come down and give the building a once-over on the down-low, just to give us an idea how bad it is."

"Right. Good. What was up with the cops at your place last night?"

I shrugged. "Some asshole pulled a knife on me, so I spent the night in jail getting interrogated."

"Again?" He looked surprised and amused.

"C'mon, Gomez. I get enough shit from Delia."

"I haven't been to county in almost a year," he bragged.

"I remember. I was in the fucking Federal Building, which brings me to one more thing. Personal."

"We need another round."

"Don't look so glum, but it is bad news. The Lucky has another problem. I do."

Gomez switched gears from aging Mexican bar owner to the other Gomez, the seventies East LA cholo who left with his girlfriend when she got pregnant. I never knew what he did in those years, other than from the brief snatches of the stories I overheard at the Gomez family picnics, and from the way his face could go from hard to diamond. The old gangster was on line behind his eyes.

"You can tell me anything, Darby," he said in a low voice. "My guns are yours."

"Thanks, brother. I might need 'em. That kid Bling who worked for me?" Gomez nodded. "He stirred up some shit in the form of a rich guy named Dong-ju. So we're on red alert. He's out of San Francisco."

Gomez looked down at his glass, then raised his hand and gestured at the new waitress for another round. When he looked back at me his eyes were black holes in his head.

"San Francisco . . . I know people in LA. People who are in . . . you know, crisis management. They have cars, but traveling is very, very hard for them."

"I can dig it. For right now, anyone asking the wrong kind of questions, that kind of thing?"

"I'll keep 'em here in the bathroom until you sort them out." He smiled, but his eyes stayed the same. I nodded.

The drinks arrived and we sipped them in silence. Eventually I clapped my hands together.

"I'm out of here. Thanks on the extra eyes. Call me on my cell if Dmitri flips out, or tell Delia. And call me the minute you hear anything about the lease rights, but let's keep this to ourselves for now. Things are tense at the shop already."

Gomez silently gestured at me with his glass, then to himself. His eyes went to the new girl and the rest of the bar. Silence for his people too.

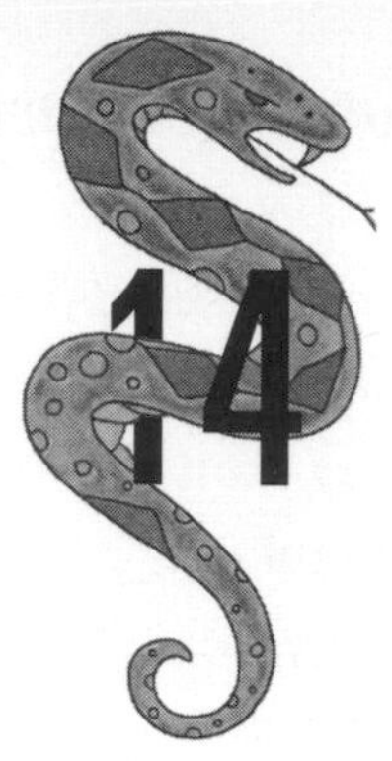

14

I walked next door to the Lucky Supreme and found Nigel prowling the lobby. He looked away from the windows at me with a carefully neutral expression, which betrayed an inner landscape of alarm and the immediate potential for violence. Everyone was talking with their face and it was all bad news.

"You're early," I said. It was a little after four.

"Alex had to go pick up his kid," he replied sourly. "Or so he says. Dwight went with him." He looked out the windows again and gestured with his head. "Check out that ride."

I followed his gaze. A maroon Oldsmobile was parked across the street. The windows were tinted, but I could make out the silhouettes of two figures inside. Great big ones.

"Alex said they've been there too long. Freaked him out. Dwight was hanging with him. Those two chickenshits know something is going down and they aren't stepping up."

"Hm."

It was Monday, so Nigel would be working alone until Mikey showed up just before closing. I had forbidden guns in the shop, but everyone was breaking the rules. I couldn't blame them.

"Think they're feds?" I asked. Nigel looked at me like I was insane.

"In an Olds?"

"Right. Keep an eye on 'em."

I went into the back and sat down at my desk. Bling's box of cash had arrived and it was sitting in the center of my desk. I put it in the bottom of one of the filing cabinets. After a moment I opened the top desk drawer and rummaged around until I found the matchbook with Monique's phone number inside. She picked up on the first ring.

"Hey baby," she purred.

"It's Darby."

"Damn!" She was instantly furious. "Thought you might be a man with money and a load. Nobody calls this fuckin' phone for pussy anymore. Always some other shit. Monique you late, Monique gimme the money, Monique where my fuckin' wig. I don't even know why I bother to answer this fuckin' thing."

"Where are you?" I asked.

"Hangin' out front of Murray's up on Twelfth. Got me an ice tea. Cold as fuck out here, don't know what the fuck I was thinkin'. I tell you what though, I scratch up that 'Bama cunt's eye last night, sure as fuck did. The pink boot bitch. Dumbass Okie—"

"Monique," I interrupted. "I want you to do something for me."

"'Bout damn time," she replied. "I's figurin' you for queer."

"No no. There's a maroon Olds parked across from the Lucky. I need you to scope them out. They might be feds, might be the scumbags I was looking for. So be careful. It's what we talked about. Call me as soon as you're done, but don't come in the shop."

"Cost you twenty bucks, white boy. I get in trouble you come out and help my ass, hear? I'm talkin' guns blazin'."

"I'll be watching," I replied. "So will Nigel. Just don't get in the car."

"Don't you boss me!" she yelled. "Not me, white boy! You think I'm stupid? Fuck you!" She hung up.

Damn.

I went back out and stood at the tip wall next to Nigel. We watched the car in silence.

"Maybe I should just go over there and see who they are," he said eventually. Right then I knew he had a gun.

"I don't think it's a good idea for either of us to approach that car," I replied. "We do need to know who's in there, though. Let's just watch for a minute. I think I got it covered."

"You sent a spy?" Nigel turned to me and raised an eyebrow.

"We'll see."

Monique strutted around the corner onto Sixth on cue, decked out in a gray plastic mini, a tiny sky-blue halter top, and an oversized peacoat that hung open, revealing her dark abdomen. Her tiny outie belly button stuck out like a cold cork. She wobbled past the Olds with her iced tea in her hand and then turned around, as if noticing the car for the first time. She was great at playing a hooker.

She swished her hips and sauntered up to the Olds and rapped the bottom of her bottle on the passenger side window. Nigel and I watched as the window slid down and Monique leaned in, cocking her butt out.

"Don't tell me," Nigel said in a tone of wonder, "that you sicced Monique on them."

I watched, ready to move if they pulled her in.

"Sometimes . . ." he shook his head. "You definitely have a signature style, dude."

Monique abruptly staggered back from the car, her face twisted in epic, biblical rage. She screamed something and flipped them the bird, then took a big slug of her iced tea, which was at least half cheap gin, and spit it through the open window. Then she staggered back and gave a mock laugh, her face expressive enough for a dozen enraged people. After one more violent middle finger display she got moving.

"That's our gal," Nigel said. "Masterful, Darby. Simply brilliant."

Monique hobbled off at top speed, a bowlegged fast walk, hurling insults over her shoulder, eyes on fire, her face wild with primal mobility. When she reached the corner she turned back and chucked the bottle with all her might. It fell mercifully short, shattering on the pavement twenty feet in front of the Olds. She screamed something, flipped them off one last time with both hands and rounded the corner.

"This has the benefit of originality," I said.

"I agree. Keep them off balance. Hurl crazy hookers at the enemy at every opportunity. Sun Tzu said that, didn't he?"

"I believe he did."

The Olds remained in place. A moment later the shop phone rang. Nigel picked it up and handed it to me without taking his eyes off the car.

"Lucky Supreme Tattoo," I answered. "This is Darby."

"You owe me fifty bucks, white boy!" Monique thundered.

"What happened?" I held the phone just away from my ear. Nigel leaned in.

"I did what you asked and now you owe me fifty fuckin' dollars s'what happened! Muthafucka!"

"Calm down," I said. "I have your money. Just tell me what you saw."

"Two big ol' fuckin' white boys. Strapped. Suits, but they ain't no fuckin' feds, oh no no no! Told me they wouldn't spit on my asshole if I was the last nigger bitch in prison. Pole smokin' faggots. An' that car stink, too. Them men been up in there all damn day. Wrappers and shit everywhere."

"Okay. Stay off of Sixth for a few hours."

"I want my money!"

"Fine. I'll get it to you later tonight."

Monique hung up.

Steeling myself, I called Obi on my cell phone as I walked back to my office, leaving Nigel to stand guard. He answered on the first ring.

"Hey boss, what's up?" The ever chipper Obi.

"I need a little favor, bro, and fast like a motherfucker. I need you to go to a pay phone and call the number for Dong-ju Trust. Book an appointment for me to meet him tomorrow afternoon. Do it fast, man, and don't use a phone too close to you. This dude is even worse than we thought. It looks like I'm minutes away from a badass gun fight and fucking Nigel only brought the one gun."

"Done." Obi hung up, no questions asked. I was gambling that a meeting might put the brakes on the situation for the moment. I also wanted to let Dong-ju know that I had people in his area that I could trust, to encourage him to consider a pause. Plus, a little extra confusion never hurt. If the Oldsmobile was his, and I was sure it was, then they had to know that their cover was blown after what just happened.

I took a ball bearing out of my pocket and rolled it around in my hand. The front door chime sounded and I was on my feet in an instant, gliding swiftly through the room. Two Goth chicks had just come in. From where I stood in the doorway, I could see the Oldsmobile. They were still just sitting there, maybe waiting for me to be in the Lucky alone. Maybe waiting for the Goths to leave. Maybe taking a nap. Maybe checking their clips.

I went back to my desk and sat down again. My heart was beating a little faster and my palms were getting sweaty. I rolled the steel ball back and forth in my right hand. When my cell phone rang five minutes later, I jumped. Obi.

"Done deal, boss," he said quickly. "But real weird. Some woman answered, said they'd been expecting you. You have an appointment tomorrow at two. It was almost like you already had one and you forgot."

"Great," I said flatly. They'd been expecting me. Dong-ju was one move ahead of me again. All it had taken to prompt me to confirm the appointment he had made for me was a sinister car parked in front of my shop, and all I'd managed to deploy on my end in retaliation was my crazy street-walker. I sighed.

"I should tag along this time." Obi sounded worried.

"No way, dude, but thanks. I'll catch an early flight. If I have to stay overnight I'll give you a call. Thanks, Obi. I owe you a big one."

"You'll never owe me one, boss."

I hung up and walked out to stand next to Nigel at the tip wall. The two girls were sitting in the lobby looking through portfolios. Nigel was outwardly calm, but I knew he was ready to rock with no preamble. His only sign of tension was a minute tell; a rhythmic flexing of his trigger finger. In some part of his mind, he was already shooting.

There was motion inside the car and Nigel and I both tensed. His hand went to his side and mine to my pocket. Exhaust plumed from the tailpipe of the Olds, and it rolled slowly down the street and turned. Nigel let out the breath he'd been holding. So did I.

"Who was that on your cell phone?" he asked quietly.

"Obi. I had him book an appointment for me to meet with Dong-ju. Tomorrow at two."

"Huh." He shook his head, worried. "I have a strange feeling Obi made that call right on schedule, boss. We're getting home schooled."

He was right. I patted him on the shoulder. Nigel was the kind of guy you weren't inclined to touch like that, but I did it anyway.

"We're always getting schooled, Nige. And I might be a little behind in the game, but the tardy student takes the widest path."

I called around and got a seven a.m. flight to San Francisco for a reasonable price. Then I called Delia.

"I need you to watch my cats again. Obi set up a meeting with this Dong-ju dude for tomorrow afternoon. My flight is at seven a.m." I told her about the Olds.

"A meeting," Delia said, clearly pondering. "This is good. Much better that the purely psycho plan you were entertaining earlier. Way to go, Darby." I shook my head. "You finally talk to Dmitri?"

"Oh yeah."

"That bad?"

"Probably worse than you can imagine. He says the city wants to renovate. I sort of threw a hypnotism on him, but it won't last."

Delia was quiet, a rarity.

"I told Gomez earlier. I don't think there's any need to bother any of the guys yet. Nigel had a shitty afternoon already. He thinks the new guys are fixing to pull their rip cords."

"What the hell are we gonna do?" she asked.

"I dunno. For now, I'm going back to San Francisco. We'll see what happens."

"What do I do if a building inspector shows up?"

"Wing it. Stall. Kill him. Run. Hire that big tranny with the beer can trick and say she's in charge. Borrow my default setting. Right now I have a one track mind until I'm done with Bling's crazy boss. Fucker's playing me like a puppet."

"That's not hard to imagine," Delia said. "You can talk to me."

"I know." I blew out a big breath.

"You're trying to be a good person. Remember?"

"Bad timing, I guess."

"Darby," she snapped, suddenly angry. I was pissing off every woman I knew anymore. "You know what I admire about you the most?"

I didn't know what to say, so I didn't say anything.

"Think about it, moron," she spat. Then she hung up.

I stared at the wall for a few minutes, thinking about it. Then I took two extra ball bearings out of my desk and drove home to pack. I gave Nigel three twenties from my wallet on the way out. Monique would be in soon to collect. The ten bucks extra was a good faith gesture to women in general.

I never slept well before a trip, and that night was no exception. Between fits of tossing and turning, I had disjointed David Lynchian nightmares about Dmitri weeping and frisbeeing pizzas out into Sixth Street, fiery plane crashes, and San Francisco hoodlums in ski masks. Delia stabbing me with a fork, slashes of lipstick all over her snarling face. Monique dead in the gutter in front of the Lucky with one pink boot clutched in her stiff, chalky arms like a teddy bear. I was glad to be awake.

I made coffee in the dark kitchen and tossed a few last-minute items in my bag. The house was cloaked in that early morning quiet, which normally seemed so peaceful to me. Instead it felt tense and uncomfortable, even depressing. I found myself trying to stay in the moment, tiptoeing around, a whisper inside of an echo of the shadow of the ghost I was fast becoming. I didn't even wake up the cats.

At five thirty, I locked up and caught a bus over to the Max line. The redline train was the fastest way to the airport and the trains themselves were bright and new. It wasn't raining, so I stood downwind of the shelter smoking until the redline arrived. By the time I got to the airport, the dream cobwebs had melted away and I felt angry rather than simply bleak. Because of the ball bearings, I checked my bag with some sleepy-eyed, overworked old lady at the terminal. After that I went through security with nothing but my sketchbook, got a second cup of coffee while I waited for boarding. When I took a seat at the gate, everyone around me seemed tired and distracted, all of them deep in their personal shells. Almost everyone was staring at a laptop. I drew sketches of their sad, puffy faces.

Airports had changed in the last few years. The Portland International Airport was a reasonably big one, with coffee shops, a decent steak house with a bar, a surprisingly good bookstore, and then the usual junk outlets. It even had sushi. Piano music wafted through the air. Distant stands of Douglas fir were visible from any of the banks of rain-spattered windows. I used to enjoy the once festive vibe there, and after 9/11 it faded to zero. I was surprised as anyone when it bounced back. The creepy militarism that had ruined American air travel and had all the airlines whining about lost revenue didn't stick. The pussies won the day and they thought they could keep it, handing over their rights and their much more "important" comfort for nothing, but no. The fearmongers lost and no one gave a shit anymore. It was a strange, even unique thing in American culture. The average passenger had become immune to the checkpoints and the Homeland Security people. "Terror" as a tool lost its bite. It was a small triumph that I didn't find as glorious as I normally did.

I took a sip of coffee and surveyed the other waiting passengers, casually trolling for something nice to look at, my mind still drifting, my sketching pencil still. Opening myself to memory.

Once, when I was a little kid, I'd gone to Lake Havasu with the foster mother of the month and her boyfriend. The episode bubbled up to the surface unbidden as I sat there people watching.

Lake Havasu is a foul, greenish body of polluted sludge in the California desert, perpetually fogged with the exhaust of speedboats and the orange smog rolling in from LA. Sunburned drunks with money ruled that weekend kingdom with a complete suspension of common sense, and it was to my child mind a nightmarish place of car wrecks, bikinis, broken sunglasses, withering heat. That first morning, I'd wandered around in the blazing sun until I found a quiet, filthy little lagoon. A crumbling slab of foundation cement jutted out into the oily water, so I'd walked out onto it and sat down. The light off the water was so bright I could see patterns when I blinked. It smelled like a mixture of summer morning dumpster and boiled dog.

A duck appeared, followed by a line of five ducklings. I laid down flat on my stomach on the hot gray slab and watched them, as still as a boy mannequin. They scooted by me and as they did the duckling at the end suddenly panicked and jumped the line. At first I thought it was me, but it wasn't.

A big fish rose up through the dark, still green, its mouth an obscene, distended circle. The water dimpled as it sucked at the round belly of the next duckling. The tiny bird made a desperate leap and the giant, prehistoric monster sank back down into the darkness. Its bulging eyes were the size of quarters, centered with disks of mindless utter midnight. An hour later I saw the mother duck again. There were three ducklings.

I drew.

I was the little bird I was sketching right then, I knew, with hungry things roiling around in the scum below me, sitting in a hostile airport with a thin veneer of humanity over it. Ready to make a desperate jump to cruising altitude.

I was thinking about this and doodling a picture of a yawning fish mouth when the stewardess announced over the loudspeaker that it was time to board.

It always amazed me that a city the size of San Francisco couldn't manage to run an airport. I eventually got my bag and took a shuttle to the Hertz rental lot, where I picked up another anonymous white Camry. I pulled out of the lot just after ten a.m. I had time to kill, so I went to an old oyster house I knew of down by the bay and killed an hour and two dozen plump, juicy Kumamotos. I enjoyed eating off of the newspaper, and when I went to take a leak, the filthy bathroom was wallpapered with trashy seventies pin-ups from *Hustler*. A good oyster place really needed a certain *je ne sais quoi* and those folks had nailed it decades ago with sniper-like precision. After noon, I headed out for my meeting with Nicky.

The warehouse looked abandoned when I pulled up with fifteen minutes to spare. No light shone through the grubby windows this time. The fenced parking lot was empty except for the tin shed and the street was blank.

The Lincoln was evidently still in an impound lot with my laundry key. I got out of the Camry and lit up a cigarette.

At exactly two o'clock, a new white Mercedes slid out of the fog and rolled to a stop in front of me. I regarded it calmly, smoking.

The tinted driver's window rolled down. The driver was another goon, a big, Slavic-looking guy with a flat face and slicked-back hair. Sort of like the driver of the Lincoln. Nicky was consistent with his messenger service.

"Get in," the driver said. He tossed a thumb at the backseat.

"No."

He seemed genuinely surprised.

"Now," he said firmly, an incredulous smile warping his lantern jaw.

"Nah."

He sighed. "I'm taking you to meet Mr. Dong-ju, asshole. Just get in the fucking car."

I flicked my cigarette away and gave him my coldest look, a real frostbite-on-the-nuts piercer.

"I'll follow you," I said. I patted the hood of the Camry. "Car's a rental and I don't want to leave it in this shitty neighborhood. Take me months to straighten out the paperwork if some scumbag jacked the stereo or fucked with the ignition."

He muttered a string of insults and rolled up the window.

I stretched, checked my phone, and then leisurely climbed into the Camry, taking my time just to piss him off. When I finally started the engine, I flashed the high beams at him to let him know I was ready, and also to see who else was in the Mercedes. It was just the driver, flipping me off.

We got on the freeway and drove northeast for about forty-five minutes, then got off somewhere around San Rafael. I followed the Mercedes up into a hilly residential area, resisting the impulse to fiddle with the radio. The houses were all expensive McMansions, a mixed bag of everything from sprawling Victorians to Spanish Colonials. The road wound up and narrowed and the Mercedes finally stopped in front of a glass and steel postmodern nightmare perched forty feet above the road. Jutting from the fog and lit from within, it looked like the fortress of some awful techno goblin prince. I already didn't like Dong-ju. Looking up at the place, I was prepared to hate him.

I parked behind the Mercedes and got out. The driver climbed out slowly, the new car rocking on its suspension. He had the build of a pro linebacker who had gone on to a barstool. He straightened his suit coat with his massive, bent hands and scowled at me. I had a ball bearing in my hand with the car key.

"Arms out," he said, approaching me on stiff legs.

"Nope."

He closed the distance between us and glared down at me. He was a good foot taller than me and at least one hundred-plus pounds heavier, most of it hard old gut muscle.

"Remember your little stunt at that truck stop in Northern California? Yeah? Well, that was my brother, you cocky little shithead, and now he's sitting in some weed grower's hippie nigger faggot spic migrant prison in NoCal looking at seven years. So either I frisk you or I beat the shit out of you and then I frisk you. *Ponyat?*"

I held my arms out and he roughly patted me down. When he was done he grunted and started up the stairs. The scrawny legs under his tailored slacks wobbled a little as he pushed his massive upper body up the steep stairs. He moved like a man who suffered from constipation and hemorrhoids. I followed him at his pace, slipping the steel ball and the rental car key into the front right pocket of my loose black cords.

The big guy was breathing heavily by the third flight of stairs. As we climbed, I marveled at the hideously sculpted landscape. The terraced levels were dotted with exotic shrubs and miniature trees, all tortured into bizarre shapes. Nature as a surgical exercise, my least favorite motif. When I considered that the creature who lived there was connected to the theft of the most remedial art in my personal collection, I almost laughed out loud.

We finally arrived at the front door, a huge reinforced glass affair that looked like it had been pried off the front of a Denny's. The panting driver tapped a sequence of numbers into a keypad, shielding it from my view with his broad back. There was a camera above the door pointed right at me. My gaze trailed up to it and I stared into it without expression.

The driver pushed the door open.

I followed him in and instantly cringed. The entire tableau was transparently designed for a breathless entrance after the flight of steep stairs. The entryway was the white of skim milk, almost watery. Bleached tile buffed to mirror reflectivity stretched across the floor to meet with emergency room, bone colored walls, all under the jagged glass sculpture of a chaotically lit chandelier. On the far wall opposite the door was a huge painting done in shades of red that ranged from bright arterial to dried scab, a splattery fever dream that might have been the last work of a tribe of wrecked howler monkeys stolen from a pharmaceutical test facility.

The driver looked at me and harrumphed, mistaking my expression for impressed. He smiled with satisfaction and sucked in his stomach, empowered to be a part of such imposing surroundings. My hand closed around my lighter instead of the steel ball bearing as I glanced away from the horrifying canvas.

This will not go well, I thought.

I followed him into what might have passed as a waiting room in a sterilized, futuristic hospice for CEOs. Several low white couches were clustered around a massive glass table that rose to about knee height. A jumbo plasma TV on the far wall silently spooled stock data below a muted commentator. The floor-to-ceiling windows along two walls had a panoramic view of other people's rooftops.

Thankfully, there was a bar in the far corner. I wandered over to it under the watchful eye of the driver and inspected the constellation of bottles. A predictable range of spendy scotch, cognac, single-cask bourbons and some high-end vodkas. Expensive vodka was a waste of money, but it showed bar status in the same ignorant way as the painting in the entryway showed an undisguised misinterpretation of value. I poured three fingers of Lagavulin 21 into a crystal glass and plopped in a couple of ice cubes.

"Quite a view," I commented to the driver, gesturing broadly at the fog-soaked windows and rooftops. He shook his head.

"I can't believe the size of your mouth, little guy," he growled.

"Great big dick, too." I sipped the scotch. Amazingly good.

I could hear the driver's teeth grinding as I sat down and focused on the TV, where I studied the ticker tape and pretended to know what I was looking at. Two sips later there was a buzz somewhere behind me. I turned a little and watched the reflection of the big guy in one of the windows as he answered an intercom box and nodded a few times.

"Mr. Dong-ju is on his way down," he announced. He actually stood at attention, hands behind him, his big jaw jutting forward.

I swirled my scotch, and then with the perfect timing that has often graced my existence, I leaned to the side and farted. Then I fired up a smoke.

16

Nicky Dong-ju swept into the room flanked by two tall, skeletal blondes who both wore skimpy black dresses and extra heavy jewelry. Dong-ju himself was slightly less than six feet tall, barefoot and wearing worn karate pants and a white linen shirt that was unbuttoned to reveal a hairless, muscled chest and the six-pack abs that came from long hours at the gym. Most men with his build were slightly off balance, but Dong-ju was not. His tanned bare feet gripped the ground over his center of gravity with the hard-won grace of a seasoned fighter. He was Asian around the eyes, but his hair was long and curly, almost permed, and brownish rather than black, held back in a high knot tied off with a strip of leather. He was holding a martini glass in one blunt, callused hand.

"Darby Holland," he boomed, beaming at me with giant white horse teeth. "We meet at last!"

I raised my glass to him and his smile widened. I could almost see his one-pound molars.

"You found the bar. Good." He winked at me. "How was your flight?"

I wondered if he knew the names of my cats.

"Short," I replied.

Dong-ju settled across the acre of glass he used as a coffee table on one of the albino couches and instantly struck a pose of total relaxation.

"How do you like my home?" he asked, making an encompassing gesture with his free hand. He had very bright, attentive eyes that wandered over my face with what appeared to be genuine curiosity.

"I'd love to meet the designer," I replied.

He cocked his head in a quizzical way, his grin almost imperceptibly morphing into a smile as ambiguous as a wordless business card. Curious.

"That would be a very expensive lunch. But then you do have money, don't you? I've researched you, Mr. Holland, I'm sure you don't mind. You're not like our mutual acquaintance, Mr. Bling. No, no, you're a working artist and a man of principles." The word "artist" rolled off his tongue with an almost undetectable sarcasm, so subtle it might have been imaginary, as did the word "principles." He snapped his fingers.

"Ashtray for Mr. Holland," he directed to no one in particular. His eyes and the smile returned to me. "An artist. That's why I ask you about this place. For your impressions."

I cleared my throat. "I didn't fly down here to give you some kind of free tutorial, dudeboy. Frankly, I wouldn't even know where to begin. So how about you give me my shit back and quit fucking with me. Then we can forget all about each other."

Dong-ju was delighted. "Ah, of course. But let's talk first. You flew all this way!"

Dong-ju gestured at my glass with his. An instant later one of the Prada women poured another two fingers of Lagavulin into my glass and plopped in another ice cube with a pair of stainless steel tongs. I looked up at her and she licked her ruby lips.

"I could never trust a man who didn't have the sense to properly bloom a fine scotch," Dong-ju said pleasantly. "Rare hooch deserves a rare cup to drink it from. That crystal is from Prague, the Iron Prague. Might have too much lead in it, but the cubes are distilled water. So, balance of a sort."

"Yummy." I took a big pull and nodded my appreciation. His look of amusement never wavered.

"It all comes back to Jason Bling, doesn't it," Dong-ju said, still watching me closely. "You're angry and I don't blame you, so let's start there. Jason is a poor liar, and of course a tragically inept businessman. He owed an acquaintance of mine a sizable sum of money, and as a favor I assumed the debt. It's as simple as that. I honestly had no idea he'd stolen the Roland Norton flash art from you, but now that I am aware of their provenance, I can assure you that they will be returned to you before you leave."

I sipped my drink. The chemical smell of the place was beginning to sink into my clothes. If I actually walked out, I'd smell like new car for days.

"Why Roland Norton?" I asked. "He was a nobody. A turn-and-burn hack. OG, as in original gutter."

Dong-ju shrugged with his martini glass. "To be candid, I've been buying tattoo art and memorabilia for investment purposes for a few years now, ever since my broker discovered the emerging market potential. Art is never a bad investment, Mr. Holland, as I'm sure you know, and tattoo art is certainly no exception, especially considering how popular your trade has become. There is a finite amount of work from Norton's era and other collectors have been gobbling it up in recent years. I can appreciate your enthusiasm for getting it back. Once Jason turned his—or rather your—collection over to me, I found another Norton piece in England and a third in San Diego. It's become one of my many hobbies." He took a minute sip from his glass and then uncrossed and recrossed his legs, watching my every expression.

"What about Bling?" I asked.

Dong-ju pursed his lips. "Jason and I will work this out. He was a bad boy, but that just means he has to work for me for another few years. It's actually a plus for him in the long run. He's artistically maturing now that the stakes are high. I run a little operation of my own, you see. Nothing like your venerable Lucky Supreme. It just happened. One of the many small businesses I own that I've never even set foot in. My personnel department, advertising, it's all run from the warehouse you visited."

"Huh." It was pointless to point out that "maturing" for a tattooer like Bling meant perfecting his turnstile, herpes-cannon business ethic, or that the profoundly artless splatter in Dong-ju's entryway exempted him from anything approaching art criticism. He continued before I could interject anyway.

"So back to Roland Norton and our little boy Bling. How in the world did you find him? I assume he was hiding in some way. The tattoo world can't be all that big. I'm curious. A rumor mill alert? A 'Tattoo Industry APB'?"

"It doesn't matter. He stole something, I'm getting it back. He had to lie low for a few years and I sort of kicked his ass a little bit. He's been punished enough as far as I'm concerned. Once I get home safe and sound—" I shrugged. "I call it all good."

Dong-ju nodded. He sipped his martini before continuing.

"The way it works in situations like this is that I return your property to you and take up the dispute with the party who sold it to me, which has been done. You in turn stop any legal grievance filed against me and it's like we never even knew each other, just as you suggested. I've had provenance issues before. Never again." He still seemed at ease, reclining with great leisure, but his crossed leg was bobbing a little.

So the feds had been there already, I realized, bringing up a potential provenance grievance as a subtext for their bigger agenda, namely bringing the hammer down on him. Probably right after I'd been grilled by them. Amazing. Things were moving faster than I'd imagined.

"Why'd you send your people after me?" I asked.

"I'm sorry!" he exclaimed, sitting up so fast that some of his martini sloshed out of his glass. "I thought you were some kind of baby criminal associate of Bling's! I had no idea you were his former boss or that he'd stolen anything, though I shouldn't have been surprised. Believe me, it was all a mistake. Calling the police on you seemed like the responsible thing to do. My spare driver was instructed to follow you to the state border and return home. Keep in mind, that was before we had a clear picture of your identity or your intentions. I don't know how the truck stop episode unfolded, but I'm tempted to believe he was being threatened as he claimed. I hope you can forgive me." He set his dripping glass down in front of him and put his iron hands together in prayer.

"I guess I can see that," I said diplomatically. He really was a fantastic liar.

"Of course you can," Dong-ju replied, gushing a little. "You're a businessman. And as far as business goes, I'll gladly repurchase the Roland Norton flash from you for an equitable price, plus any more of his work you may have come across as well, after your provenance has been re-established and all this has settled down. If you're interested, an agent of mine will contact you in a month or two. Take everything home for now and hang it up, do whatever you want with it, but I'd like to make you an offer."

Too easy. Some kind of new angle was in play, I was sure of it, but I couldn't fathom what it might be. Dong-ju had been too slippery thus far for the storybook ending he was trying to sell me, but I decided to put the brakes on my inner asshole, at least for the moment. Dong-ju nodded. He held his drink up and one of the women replaced it with a fresh one. I lit another cigarette.

"Have you . . . Are you familiar with the term tulipomania, Mr. Holland?"

"Nope." Delia had told me all about it.

"*Tulpenwoede*. A form of . . . madness. I engineer modern variations on that classic theme. I do this with a variety of commodities. Watches. Automobiles. Market guidance, through the Invisible Hand. I won't bore you with all of the details, but consider. The value of old tattoo flash art is in a speculative phase. No baseline value has been established. An early market example of solid baseline formation is the work of Sailor Jerry. Now Ed Hardy. These are names you know well. Now, the merits of the art itself don't exactly matter to me. But the consumer value does. You see, if, for instance, I buy all of Roland Norton's work from various places, I can actually establish a baseline value by how much I pay for it. As an investment strategy, it's impossibly simple and it almost always works. 'It takes money to make money' is the phrase attributed to this kind of market manipulation."

"And it's legal," I said. He nodded enthusiastically.

"It most certainly is. Now, I suggest you call England and find out what I paid for the Norton piece I located there. You see, I've already started. Once I got those first pieces from Jason, I saw the opportunity and I took it. I'll pay the same price for yours once the provenance is clear, or . . ." He shrugged and sipped. "Or you can hang them back up, but their value will decrease rapidly. My two purchases were not enough to establish the baseline, and to force a correction, I'll have my broker lower the opening bid on the next one we locate to ten dollars, or dump the ones I have for pennies on Ebay. It's not blackmail I'm talking about, Mr. Holland. It's just business. I'm sorry, but I don't make the rules. So, you see . . ." He let it dangle.

It was depressingly plausible. If everything he'd said was true, or even half true, then he really was an art critic after all. I sighed. OPEC, the diamond trade, Mexican drug cartels, wine . . . so much of what people bought was based on the illusion of value he was talking about creating. All he really wanted was to eat more numbers than other people.

"C'mon, Mr. Holland," he whispered softly, urging me, watching me think. "Play with me."

"Fair enough," I said in a neutral tone. I was so disgusted that it made me tired. Dong-ju clapped his hands in delight. He looked like a painted robot.

"Excellent!" he cried. "I love business! Jessica, bring the coke! Lizelle, why don't you make yourself useful and bend over that couch, just like I taught you. Let's see if Mr. Holland here can drive two hard bargains in one day. I have a feeling he might surprise us."

One of the blondes materialized at my side bearing a platter-sized onyx slab in both hands, a mountain of pure white snow in the center. The pile was so deep that paper straws stuck out of it, freestanding. She set it gently on the plane of glass before me, her focus totally on the coke, her mouth almost watering at the sight of it. The second woman climbed on to the sofa beside me and lifted her skirt, stuck her pudenda in my face, and then glared back at me with mean, freezing eyes. Her tongue was candy pink when she slowly ran it over her collagened upper lip. I looked from her empty face to her ass. She wasn't wearing panties. I was sure that at that same moment Bling had done a fat rail of nearly pure coke and then mounted up for a long public workout on one of those creatures, pumping away with his drippy dick like a rodeo windup toy. The whole scene had an undercurrent of replay, an every Friday night kind of feel. I looked at the seemingly pristine butt and shook my head.

"I better get," I said, but I did give the blonde a playful slap on her skinny rump. I couldn't help it. It was hard and cool and plasticky.

"Milo," Dong-ju snapped. "Get Mr. Holland his case. And move it!"

Dong-ju was suddenly, instantly enraged. A light sheen of sweat bloomed over his upper lip and across his forehead, giving him a shine. Without a backward glance, the blonde in front of me pulled her skirt down and walked over to the bar. The coke was whisked away by her counterpart, and the two of them fell on the pile like starving wolves tucking into ground beef. Dong-ju didn't spare them a single glance. Instead, he took a tiny sip of his martini, watching me intently. His face was red and his leg was really pumping.

Milo the driver appeared with an expensive portfolio case moments later, the treated leather kind used to transport maps or blueprints. He set it down at my side, panting quietly.

"About time, you motherfucking sloth," Dong-ju spat at him. "Get your big ass back on the treadmill for fuck sake. What the hell do I pay you for?" Dong-ju looked back at me and rolled his eyes.

I opened the case. All fifteen pieces were there. I started to take them out when Dong-ju tutted.

"Take the case. You'll need it at the airport." He studied me with a forced politeness, visibly trying to control himself. I nodded and zipped the case closed.

“Thanks,” I said, rising. “I’ll consider your offer. And sorry about the dude at the truck stop.”

Dong-ju waved dismissively. Milo the driver stiffened at this and his jaw muscles stood out.

“Later days,” I said. Dong-ju paused before answering, and when he did he had a predatory light in his eyes.

“And better lays,” he said. My neighbor Flaco’s reply. I kept my face carefully blank. Nicky Dong-ju had been watching me closely all week, maybe longer if he knew little details like that. It was chilling to think that I hadn’t noticed.

Milo escorted me back to my rental car. The trip down the stairs was even worse for him than the trip up. He worked the stairs like he was wearing stilts, his knees clearly shot. I followed him, watching his meaty hand sweep beads of the fog’s moisture from the handrail. When we got to the bottom, he gestured at my rental and leaned up against the Mercedes, lit up a Nat Sherman.

“Your boss is a dick,” I said.

He grunted. “Tell me about it.”

My hand wrapped around the steel ball in my pocket. I watched him closely.

“Sorry about your brother,” I said.

He stared at me and then nodded, once.

“You think Dong-ju’s going to keep fucking with me? He seemed pretty pissed when I wouldn’t snort his coke or play live porno with his . . . whatever she was.”

He shrugged. “Nicky does what he does. He didn’t buy that house with food stamps, dumbass. He’s the best there is at whatever he feels like doing.” He squinted at me through a curl of smoke. “You play chess, little man?”

"Don't even play checkers, dude."

"Nicky plays eight games at a time. In his head. He doesn't even have a board. Just calls people and tells them his next move. He never loses."

"Gnarly."

Milo shook his head. "You're too stupid to understand what I'm saying."

"I'm sure that's true." I smiled. "So exactly what does he do? Other than manipulate art, I mean."

The driver peeled off the car. "I don't like you. But I will give you one free piece of fact." He looked up at the mad tangle of light and glass that was Dong-ju's house. "Once you walk through that door, Nicky owns you. You do what he says and maybe you come out again. But he always keeps one finger on you. He's somewhere in your head right now, and to him, you aren't anything but a little tiny piece in a game your eyes are too small to see. That's what he does."

We stared at each other appraisingly. Eventually, I cleared my throat.

"Sucky," I observed. "To be you, I mean." I heard his hands crunch into old hammers.

"I better never see you again, kid," he said evenly. I returned his flat gaze.

"It's good to have hope."

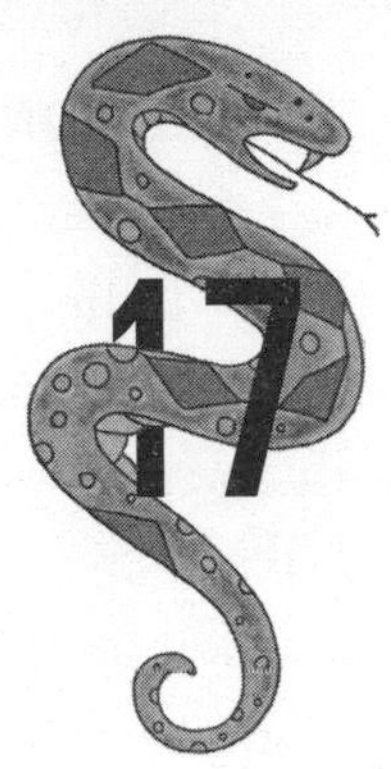

17

Whenever something is too easy, it makes me paranoid, and on a scale of one to ten I was hovering somewhere high up in the heartburn region around eight point five, especially after the conversation with Milo the driver. Every alarm bell was ringing and smoke and flashes of lightning filled me. My nostrils burned with ozone and phantom coke. My dick felt ichy. The scotch had left a bad cave-dirt taste in my mouth.

I had a white-knuckle grip on the wheel as I wound the Camry out of the foggy hills. It didn't look like I was being followed, but I drove fast anyway. When I hit the freeway, I headed back toward the city, still eyeing the rearview mirror. The paranoia was going up instead of down as I got further away, so Milo the driver was right; Nicky was in my head. Nicky Dong-ju was clearly crazy. Not groovy crazy, but ticking time bomb, way fucked up nuts. I was totally certain that I hadn't seen the last of him. It was like some part of him was sticking to me, and I wondered if Dong-ju had told Milo to tell people that story as a parting fear tool, if the creepy lecture had been scripted. If it was, then Milo needed a raise, because I was freaking out. Either way, the big question was when Dong-ju would surface again, and if I'd be lucky enough to catch it in time.

It was a bad time to be dealing with a situation like that, but then again there never seemed to be a good one. I couldn't let myself be distracted by Dmitri and his brewing feud with the city, or the increasing pace of the demise of Old Town and the new, harder edge of the nightscape. I had to focus on Dong-ju for the present, as much as I could, without letting everything else go down the drain while I did. Eight games of chess in his head. Jesus. I hadn't been kidding about the checkers.

The part about Dong-ju owning people after he interacted with them, in particular, had left me cold. It was almost like he was describing a one-man credit card company. There was something medieval in the vision of Dong-ju as some kind of wizardly investment guru that somehow fit together with everything else, like the snug pieces of a children's puzzle depicting a flat plain of featureless brown. Billions of people were converted into cash every day, but in this case there weren't even any shareholders to spread the blame around. That made Nicky Dong-ju sort of like the devil.

I blew out a long sigh and cracked the windows, then lit up a smoke, rental policy be damned. Maybe I was just worn out, I thought. Tired and stretched thin and hung over, harried by bullshit from every side into a state of general nervousness. He had given me the Roland Norton flash back and offered to purchase it legitimately, after all. He'd even apologized. The feds had evidently been to visit him, and nobody really wanted to screw around with them, no matter how many games of chess they played in their head at one time. Every criminal relied on heavy case loads and quickly diminishing interest, but they all knew that once the federal badge man got a good bite out of you, he wasn't going to stop eating until dinner was finished, the silverware was licked clean and ready for auction, and the table was stolen from impound.

I shook my head. After twenty years of tattooing, I'd learned to read people well enough, I reminded myself again. Pressman and his morgue face, Dessel and his cheery death wish. Delia and her deep worry. Mikey's coward side. Nigel's inner sociopath. Gomez and the lost flowers. Dong-ju hadn't liked that I'd found him, but he somehow hadn't seemed too surprised, so complex fakery was conceivable. There was something too playful about him, a menacing variety of smoldering interest in the way he watched my every action, mapping my face with his eyes, like a hyper version of Agent Pressman, but with a new and troubling dimension. Dong-ju had the aura of a killer, the type of man who had poured boiling water on small animals as a boy. And the sudden snap between moods, the freakish whores. That was more than enough for me.

I took an off-ramp at random and checked the rearview again for any signs of a tail. No one exited after me and I soon realized why. I'd found my way into some awful California suburb that reminded me of a miniature Orange County, one of the nation's most expensive urban blights and a place so close to hell that I'd never visit it again unless I stumbled upon a stray nuke. It did nothing to improve my mood, which was finally moving past panic into the edge of fury. I forced myself to relax my shoulders and something popped in my lower back.

I surveyed the darkening streets and what I saw somehow enabled me to take a rare detour on the road to anger. The exit to depression. No wonder people were decorating what was under their clothes. One look at where they had to live spelled it out. It was all of it the same, and the sameness had touched the dark side of the moon in the sleepers inside of it.

I wondered what this area had looked like back in Roland Norton's day. The densely packed, middle-class ghetto of fast food chains and cheesy plastic restaurants, of barn-like houses plopped down on tiny wedges of lifeless Martian soil, had probably been low hills back then, with a few groves of fruit trees, maybe some grapes. Clean wind had played through long grass. Families might have had picnics there, driving out from the city in their DeSotos and good-time Sunday Chevys. Picnic baskets. Lemonade.

I shouldn't have smacked that woman's ass, I thought. If I'd been half a man, I would have crushed Dong-ju's forehead right then, just buried a metal ball in his brain, frisbeed the coke slab into the driver's ruined knees, burned the whole entire shithole of a mansion to the ground, and then peed on the smoking foundation. Taken those women straight to an airport and given them enough Bling dough to make a go of it somewhere, anywhere. Maybe robbed Dong-ju's palace before the arson and given them that, too. I swore and smacked my forehead. At the next stoplight I took the ball bearing out of my pocket and looked at it, then held it as I drove.

The ridiculous metal ball was a symbol of something I believed in, perhaps one of the only things I knew to be true. That metal ball was what Delia had tried to remind me of, even though as a symbol she found it lacking. I'd resolved a long time ago to make my own rules, and it was a more complicated resolution than was easily realized. I would not carry a gun just because everyone else did. I hated the things and viewed them as one of America's most flagrant pusswad atrocities. I wasn't going to shoot someone just because they shot at me. I might, but it wasn't part of any kind of "plan" I had. In many other ways as well, I tried to never let the world around me tell me what I was going to do next, to force me to mirror behavior good or bad, confusing or terrible. Maybe that made me a dick sometimes.

All my adult life I'd tried to live that way, first because I had no choice and then later because of pure cussedness mixed with other, darker, more lonesome things. I decided what it was to be a boss, a friend, a neighbor. Other people could believe what they wanted and do what they would, but there was some kind of priceless freedom in being alone enough to decide every time to do what you, the individual, should do. I often failed in that regard, but I was generally going to do what I felt like I could live with, and a lot of the time it barely made any sense at all.

So many things were changing, as poor Dmitri had said, and I was in the middle of a situation where I didn't know any of the rules I was supposed to break, least of all my own. I glanced at the ball in my hand and felt a ripple of doubt. It was entirely possible that my philosophy was a little too fortune cookie. Maybe Milo had been right. Maybe my eyes were too small to see the big picture.

Fuck it, I thought. It was absolutely the wrong time to reexamine my life and have deep and harmonious choir practice with the universe. I clicked on the radio and settled on a Mexican pop music station. I'd always been able to convince myself that they were going on about something cheery, since I couldn't understand the lyrics. After a few more turns, I found my way out of the hellish suburb and into something different and oddly soothing, an older area with slices of ocean occasionally visible in the distance through patches of wind-gathered fog. I followed the streets down to the coast and eventually onto a wide boulevard that ran into a tourist strip. There was a Best Western right on the beach, so I pulled in and checked it out. A room with a balcony overlooking the beach: two hundred and seventy bucks, once again courtesy of Bling and the pharmaceutical industry. I paid in cash.

I needed to unwind, so after I tossed my bag and the portfolio into the room I walked down to the strip and stretched, then went in search of a bar. I found a promising one a block down, in the front half of an old, weathered steak house called Jimmie's. It was dark inside, a solid wood and brass type of place, and the atmosphere settled around me like a comfortable old coat. It smelled like steak, oyster shells, old beer, and Lysol—my kind of place. I thought about calling Obi or Carina, but I decided not to. They were both more than an hour away and there was a chance some asshole would attack me that night, plus I was in too weird a mood to bother anyone without feeling guilty about it later. I nursed a beer and a Jameson's on the rocks and ordered the prime rib plate with salad.

"Where you from?" the bartender asked, after I'd ordered dinner and it looked like I was going to be there for a while. I squinted at his nametag. Mike.

"Up the coast a little," I replied. "Just in town for the night."

"Fog, huh?"

I nodded. He accepted the chatter pass and wandered down the bar, doing bartender things.

Some rowdy surfer guys and gals came in and sat down. I turned on my stool a little and watched them. I'd always had a thing for surfer chicks—they qualified as a cousin to my athletic librarian dream bride. The evening was firming up, so to speak. It was soothing to listen to them talk about waves and secret breaks. After a while they segued into a lengthy discourse about some kind of new rack one of them was thinking of getting for a van. I knew there were people out there in the world, especially in America, who led carefree lives like theirs. I hadn't been designed to be one of them, but it was nice to eavesdrop on them now and again.

My food came and I tore into it. I hadn't eaten since the oysters that morning and I'd been driving around fueled by nothing more than a stomach full of Dong-ju's cave water and the steam power of mean. I finished the prime rib and the salad and pushed the empty plate back, sated but still light. I could and maybe should have eaten another entire round, because sometimes I felt the hunger behind the hunger, when I'd been burning for too long, but I needed the room for booze. The cheery group of surfers evidently knew Mike the bartender and maintained a friendly banter with him. They gave him standing instructions to bring a pitcher of margaritas every five minutes until one of them fell out of a chair, which he obliged.

"I made it," one of them said. Adorable, with a sunburned face, wide set eyes, and long, clean limbs. She looked healthy, hard, and full of sky and sails. She was talking about a BBQ grill.

"Let's take it to the point," her boyfriend suggested. "Scrambled duck eggs at dawn." He was lean and fit, L. L. Bean. I was in too good a mood to dislike him for having what I might have had in a different life. For some reason that made me go internal. That woman had made a BBQ with her own hands, with the express purpose of taking it to the beach, and that dream realized had been expanded to duck eggs at dawn. I needed that. I needed that more than I needed any of this other shit, and it was possible. Unlikely, but we were all going somewhere. Maybe it was the hooch; Nicky Dong-ju eased back out of my head a little. I more watched than listened at that point. By drink number four I had a secondhand surfer buzz.

I left before any of them wiped out, feeling okay for the first time that day, emotionally smeared. The fog was a little thicker as I walked back to the hotel, but it seemed less menacing, less like something full of hidden danger and more like something I could hide in. I waved at the little Lebanese clerk at the front desk of the Best Western and took the two flights of stairs up to my room. Before I slid the pass card through the electronic door lock, I put my hand around the ball bearing in my pocket.

The room was empty. I shot the bolt on the door and went to the balcony, pulled the curtain aside, and opened the sliding door. The heavy night air that rolled in smelled like ocean and wet street. I added some cigarette smoke to it as I reviewed the day.

On impulse, I went to the portfolio Dong-ju had given me and took out all the Roland Norton flash, spread it over the bed. I picked up each one in turn and inspected it closely.

They were definitely the originals. Flash from that period was generally done on a type of pressboard, which was essentially several sheets of paper glued back to back. Thick, sturdy stuff. They had the manufacturer's faded green stamp on the back and all the water damage was consistent with what I remembered.

Still, the sheets had been tampered with. Restored, I guess is the word. The edges had been faced with a nonreactive tape I recognized from other old collections, but which I didn't use myself, and the new facing held in place a thin sheet of UV acetate to protect the surface from exposure to light and moisture. An expensive job had been worked on the pieces, very professional.

I put them back in the rich leather case and went back out on the balcony. My return flight was in the morning unless I wanted to change it, and I couldn't see any reason to. I sat down in one of the white plastic patio chairs and fired up another smoke, listened to the surf I couldn't see through the thickening fog. I was essentially blind to the world around me right then. Also half drunk in a city I didn't particularly like, and I'd just met with a killer who was always right in front of me. But I'd managed to hit my emotional reset button, so it was the perfect time and place for a little late-night reflection.

I took in a big breath of ocean air. The distant Pacific tide pulsed like a giant heartbeat, scraping across the sand and rocks in the darkness. Tomorrow the planet would rotate around to the sun again, and my little late-night puzzles would seem different to me. No matter how I played the hand I'd been dealt, no matter what I decided, for better or for worse, I'd be out of that fog by noon.

I got up and went to the minibar, poured myself a drink, then went back to the patio chair to smoke with it as I listened to my train of thought. Roland Norton. I'd looked him up on the Internet and so had Delia. There was nothing, not even a whisper of a digital rumor that he had ever walked the Earth. Roland Norton might have left a trail, even as an alias, but he hadn't. Delia had taken it personally and spent hours and hours before she finally gave up. Red Avery had mentioned the black market, and Dong-ju had smelled like it. He'd reeked of it. The feds, the weirdo games. The coke and the disturbing whore women. That terrible painting. The feds had never actually seen the flash. They didn't realize how shitty it was, how it had to be part of a bigger picture in some way. I put my smoke out, went back in and poured two more fingers of whiskey, then pocketed the room key and my smokes and took the stairs down to the lobby.

It was still quiet. The lone desk clerk was sitting in front of the computer at check in, fighting off the sleepy jazz drone Muzak with a jumbo coffee. He looked up and smiled. I tossed my head at the guest center computer.

"Okay if I use that for a few minutes?"

"Go ahead. Need help just let me know." He looked back down.

I carried my drink over to the little computer station. It wouldn't take more than a minute. I typed "Panama 1955" into Google search. Remon-Eisenhower Treaty. I didn't even bother reading it. Instead I sipped and scrolled down. A dude named Jose Antonio Remon Cantera had died. Sad news, but I didn't do it. There were images for Panama 1955. A treaty was signed. The president was slain.

I considered reading all of it. I was tired and a little drunk, past tipsy. It was the kind of research that might not lead anywhere, but there was a possibility of finding something. I yawned and then scrolled back up to the search bar. "Panama Black Market Crime 1955." The sound of my fingers on the keyboard echoed with déjà vu.

I hissed. Then I sat down.

Two hours later I went back into my hotel room and poured myself another drink, tossed my notes on the dresser. After I gulped it down I poured another and then spread the Norton flash back over the bed again, this time face down.

The backs all had a code stamped into them in faded green, right under the paper manufacturer's stamp. It was the same set of numbers in two of the sheets. I wrote them all down and then carefully studied each one again. The coffee stains and random pen and pencil marks, the smudges and signs of wear were all consistent with flash that had seen active duty for a few years, then been stored in a box in a forgotten corner of a storeroom in a tattoo shop in a rainy city. I rearranged them a few times to see if an impressionistic code image emerged. None did. Then I turned them back over and studied them ugly side up.

There was no kind of hidden map in the wobbly lines, the third-rate shading, no meaning in the color schemes. The randomness of the lettering didn't spell anything. Norton could barely write. I turned them all upside down and unfocused my eyes a little. Nothing, just a different kind of Z list. I frowned, then studied them all sideways.

It was an hour before dawn when I put them all back into the case and crashed into the bed. Nothing. Not even a clue. But every detail of the flash was successfully uploaded into my memory, so there was no telling what might emerge in my dreams. As I drifted off my thoughts flicked back to the machine gun death of the Panamanian President. A rape case. Machine guns at the racetrack. Handing over the canal. Railroads. Flags. Lots of flags. It was like the pieces of Dong-ju's brown puzzle, where nothing fit together easily, and there was no way some two-bit con man with a lame trick bag could have done anything more spectacular in 1955 Panama than dying of a mosquito bite in prison. None that I could imagine, anyway. It had to be some kind of seemingly ignorant investment scheme that would somehow pan out, and the only reason I couldn't see it was that I was too jaded, too ignorant, too pissed off. Who knew what rich people were thinking when they stared at all those numbers. My last thought as I fell asleep was that maybe dreaming wasn't a great idea after all.

The flight back to Portland amazingly left on time, the pleasant people at Hertz didn't give me any shit about smoking in their car, and I scored an awesome extra-small Shuckins Taxidermy T-shirt for Delia on the drive in. She called twice, both times I couldn't pick up, but she didn't leave a message either time, which I interpreted as a good sign. The tenor of the week was changing. Even my hangover had a soft, fuzzy quality. My dreamscape had revealed nothing about my far-ranging research and examination, but it was all still sitting in the front row of the all the stuff in the back of my mind. It made me feel curiously well equipped.

I slept for most of the flight and took a cab home. It was raining in a serious way when I arrived and I didn't want the Norton flash to get any more water-stained than it already was. Even with the fancy new facing and riding in the expensive new case, the pieces were still vulnerable, plus it was too damned cold to stand around waiting for a train. Fall was approaching dead center.

The cab pulled up in front of my dark house, and I paid the driver and hauled my stuff up the slippery stairs. Buttons was waiting by the door, his thick red fur soaking wet, purring and ready for snack time. He was the only cat

I'd ever met who didn't in the least mind being wet, though his next move would be to go and lie down on my pillow. I slapped his soggy back and let him in.

The house was warm and quiet. The heater was on and the place smelled like lavender and furniture polish. There was a note from Delia on the dining room table.

"Since you didn't call, you're either dead or you got your stuff back. You're out of whiskey and mayo. —D."

I turned on a few lights and called down to the shop. Dwight answered.

"What's rockin'?" I asked.

"Oh dude," he said with a partly suppressed giggle. "Is this the first time you called since you left?"

"I've been gone for about thirty hours," I replied with a sinking feeling. "What happened?"

"There was a fight in front of the Rooster Rocket last night. Some hipster kid got two of his teeth knocked out. And get this: Delia went out and found one of the teeth in the gutter. She autoclaved it and used the tools in the back soldering station to make a fuckin' earring. She was wearing it this morning when she came in to check supplies."

"Barfo." I walked over to the refrigerator and opened it. Nothing caught my eye. She had left the empty mayo jar on the top rack, upside down as a reminder.

"Oh yeah, dude, it's nasty. You can tell it's a real human tooth too, like roots and all."

"Jesus," I said. "I leave for one fucking day. Any sign of Dmitri?"

"No, but Gomez came by an hour ago, drunk as shit. He left a message, here . . . let's see. Come or call by ASAP. Kinda sorta doesn't make sense, but you get it."

"Great." I lit a cigarette and opened the front door. Gomez had apparently gotten day drunk enough to lose my cell phone number. It was a good thing I'd taken a nap on the plane. Gomez was the kind of drinker who never went deep by accident. "I'll be down in a few. I gotta rinse the airport off."

I took a quick shower and put on clean clothes. Then I slipped a couple of steel balls into my bomber jacket and drove down to the shop.

Monique was on the corner, staring with a raptor's gaze at the passing cars, making sucking faces at them. I waved at her but she ignored me. Dwight's red pickup was parked out front, but there was no sign of Delia's Falcon. I waved at him and then ducked into Gomez's. Flaco was in his cubby and looked like he wanted to say something, but I brushed past him. I'd save him for on the way out.

Gomez was sitting alone at his own bar, still drinking in the morose pose of the lost, staring down into a tumbler. Cherry was behind the stick unloading a box of assorted bottles. Her look when she met my eye was grim.

"What's up?" I asked, settling on the bar stool next to him. He raised his shaggy head and stared at me. His face was puffy and red and his thick mestizo hair was wild from repeatedly running his hands through it. His eyes were past hard and slightly out of focus, like he was looking at someone he wanted to kill who was standing right behind me.

I held up a finger at Cherry, summoning the drink I knew I'd need.

"Building inspector was waiting for me when I got here," Gomez said quietly. "He looked around for a long time, *vato*. Took lots of notes. Pictures with his little camera. I kept him away from the worst of it, but he will return."

"Shit. He say anything? Leave a note or a notice or whatever?"

Cherry set my drink down and quickly backed away.

"You got to calm that mad Greek fucker down," Gomez said forcefully. A little fleck of his spit hit me right under the eye. Gomez didn't notice. I held up my hands.

"What the hell is wrong with you?" he snarled. "Off in California, fucking around? This is a crisis! Out landlord, our landlord! Your landlord! He's a lunatic!"

"I know, I know," I replied calmly. "I was away on that business I told you about, but it looks like it's done for now. At least I won't be going south again anytime soon. What did this inspector say?"

Gomez shook his head. "Nothing, but that is very bad." His swollen eyes were slow to focus. I'd known Gomez for fifteen years and I'd never seen him like that. "Darby, for years we have kept this building together ourselves. YouTube videos and those how-to books you got at the Salvation Army. There is smoke coming out of my fuse box on some nights. The plumbing looks like a puzzle and there's duct tape involved. You have to talk to Dmitri. He has to finally do something right. We did not deal with his shit for all these years just to have it end like this. He listens to you, God knows why."

I nodded. Another inspector would be coming my way soon. Disaster. I thought about the calls I'd missed from Delia and my scrotum tightened.

"Later," I said. "I'm on this like a motherfucker. And have Cherry get you a cab before she has to mop you up, homie."

"Fuck that," he replied thickly. "I own this fucking booze. I say who drinks in cabs, not you."

I gave Cherry the throat cut motion and she shrugged helplessly, apologizing with her face. As soon as I was outside, I took my phone out and dialed Delia.

"People were taking pictures of the building, Darby," Flaco said, leaning out his window. "Where were you? Delia tried to call you. Dmitri tried to tell me my horoscope but he has lost the power of speech. Gomez is drinking. Delia has a new tooth. I—"

Delia picked up on the third ring. I kept walking.

"Bad news," she said shortly. "Some dorks in business suits came in right after we opened yesterday. S'why I called. They smelled like talcum powder and Old Spice."

"You could actually smell them? Through the cloud of your personal birthday cake explosion?"

"I'm immune to my own fragrance, dumbass. You are too, apparently. Anyway, they wandered around in the lobby for a while like penguins in the Sahara and then one of them took out a little digital camera and started snapping pictures."

"Shit. The old flash? No possible way."

"Nope. The floor, and a few choice shots of the ceiling and the heater vents."

"Inspectors. They got Gomez too."

"Big Mike was there, the grumpy piece of shit, so we took the camera away and described how it was illegal to take pictures in the shop without the permission of the owner because of the art content. Mike deleted the shots and gave them their camera back, but dudeboy, they were super not happy."

"Christ." My forehead felt sweaty. "What were they driving?"

"A white Prius. No writing on the doors. When I went out to spy on their ride they were taking pictures of Flaco."

"He just told me. Apparently Gomez let them in and they really went through the place with a fine tooth comb. He steered them away from the flagrant violations, but he won't be able to pull that off a second time."

"Oh no. What happened?"

"Well, he's as drunk as he can get and still talk, in his own bar. Cherry might eighty-six him."

"Fuck." She sighed. "Welcome home, I guess. I almost don't want to ask, but did you get the Norton flash back?"

"I did. Some . . . something is seriously wrong with this whole picture. Dude claims it was some kind of investment thing. He told me all that shit about Dutch tulips. He's interested in using the Norton flash as an investment tool. Transmute shit into gold dust."

"Clever," she said. "And the cop trap? The ambush in the middle of nowhere?"

"He says he called the cops because he thought I might be an associate of Bling's, who he's come to realize was a scumbag."

"Unfortunately all true. He's good."

"He sure is. He claims the ambush was for the same reason. The Russian guy was supposed to follow me far enough to make sure I was gone for good, then turn around."

"Thin."

"Thin but plausible if the Russian was the kind of guy whose range of employment skills are restricted to grunting, wandering around in the rain calling the same number over and over, and doing a crappy job following someone."

"What about the pro wrestler with the knife?"

"Didn't come up, actually. It was weird, but the whole time I got the feeling that he was trying to read my mind, like everything I said spoke volumes. If my theory about the meat spaz being a kind of messenger from a third player was true, I didn't want him to know. If you were right that the guy was sent to distract the feds, which seems more and more likely, then I super don't want him to know that it probably worked."

"Hmm. I see your point. So you think there's even a remote possibility that this guy is on the up and up?"

"In no way do I think that. He whipped out some coke and these two really strange stick women. The whole thing was mental. His driver slash lackey says I hawked my soul when I took the flash back, so we'll see. But yes, I have it, so next bummer up for the time being."

"A therapy session with Dmitri."

"You know it. No way out."

"I'm shaking my head right now. I'm so proud of you for not completely losing it. So, maybe the motivational speaker angle, touch of nostalgia to distract him from—"

"I'm going to beat him with a garden hose."

I looked up at the Rooster Rocket sign and blinked. Then I looked some more and blinked again. I wanted to tell her about my sketchbook for some reason. About the boat. I wanted to be sitting in that park again, maybe with Delia and Obi, doing nothing more troubling than sketching a BBQ we were going to build.

"Darby," she called.

"Right," I said, snapping out of it. "We're all so paranoid about the art on the walls. I mean, being saved by paranoia happens just often enough to us to make it seem productive. Miserable, isn't it? Tell the boys to watch for official haircuts and cameras of any kind, even cell phones. I gotta figure out how to . . . well, shit. What are you doing tonight?"

"Me and the girls are going out for sushi, then we'll probably go to Indierobo and do some dick watching. Why?"

I blew out a breath. "I dunno. I have shit to do, but I still owe you that story."

"Well I'll be." She tittered. "Darby Holland, are you asking me out on a . . ."

"A date?"

"A date. Yes."

I thought about it. I didn't think I was. But then I didn't know.

"Well," I began, "I'm pretty sure I'm not. But it's possible that the evening will have date-like qualities. Booze, maybe a snack, the whole story time. But that in itself is not necessarily the kind of thing—I mean, given our history. Well, let's put it this way, if you're wondering if it will involve, you know, the—"

She hung up.

I hung up, too. Then I took a deep breath and went over to Flaco's window. He was staring at me with a tight, pissy expression.

"What?" I asked. He shook his head in disgust.

"You have all the whores in Old Town looking for something. The Negros are closer and pick-picking, looking for a big man's wallet, for a score big enough to buy a boat. Gomez is drunk and Dmitri is crazy, crazy, crazy. And you ask what. You tell me, Lucky Boy. You're right in the center, so you should know."

"Flaco, do you have something important to tell me? Or are you just another one of these problems you're telling me about?"

Flaco shrugged and stared back out at the rain.

An hour later and half drunk, I walked through the rain down to "mitri's izza." It seemed a little more inviting in a downpour. At least the windows looked cleaner, and thus the interior had the remote possibility of being different than last time. Dmitri was slumped at the counter as usual, this time wearing his only coat, a greasy down hiking parka circa 1979. He looked up in alarm at the sound of the door chime.

"Lucky boy," he croaked in a dead voice.

"Dmitri!" I shouted. "What the hell have you done, and why is it so damn cold in here?"

He shrugged. "City shut off my heat, and the heat upstairs, too. Nothing's up to code." He looked out the windows, his mouth twisted down at the concept of safety standards.

"Did you do something to make them fuck with us? Like go down to City Hall and start accusing people of oh, I dunno, maybe being Soviet agents or Armenians? Gomez got a visit this morning." I crossed my arms. "The Lucky did too. They took pictures of the inside of the Rooster Rocket, Dmitri. Of all the shit you let wear down and all the dumb shit we did to fix it."

Dmitri shrugged indifferently and a petulance slowly came across his face. He didn't like any interruption in his pitiful wallowing.

"So what happens now?" I continued. "The city shuts your buildings down because you never kept them up and the Lucky has to move? Do you have any idea what that's going to do to me, Dmitri? To Gomez? After twenty fucking years I have to start from scratch?" I was yelling. "Are you going to at least try to fix this?"

Normally, Dmitri would have screamed back at me and possibly kicked over several tables, but he just stared at me, his mouth slightly open, revealing his stained lower teeth.

"You backed the wrong horse, tattoo boy," he said eventually. He cocked his head to the side. "Are you okay?"

"Fuck no," I spat. I took a deep breath and sank down into one of the sticky chairs. "I got problems, Dmitri, not the least of which is you. You're a slumlord, but you're so pathetic about it I can't seem to hate you the way I should. What the fuck is wrong with me?"

"Tell me," he prompted in a soft voice. He looked old in the gray light and he knew it. Dmitri's attempt at a paternal change of the subject. For whatever reason, I obliged him.

"Some fucking goon might be after me for God knows what at this point, a pure psycho with bad taste, way too much money, and nothing better to do. Gomez got lamped by the city and so did you, so heads are getting ready to roll. I'm next, and rat-mind Wally left me a cherry legacy of super half-assed shit I can't even begin to fix in time. And you've finally gone . . . whatever this is."

"Ah, whatever. Such a feminine word. You sound like a woman when you complain."

"Fuck you."

Dmitri shrugged again. There was no getting a rise out of him when he was this far gone.

"Listen, man," I said firmly, reverting back to therapist. I sat up and lamely held my hands out, sculpting the air between us, trying to convey everything with genuine sincerity. "We can get through this. I'll help you, but we're not going to just give up. Understand?"

"The sharks are circling, Darby. Learn how to walk on water. Then you can carry me."

He turned away and I watched him stare out at the rain with a hangdog expression for a moment. Nothing I could say was going to make any difference. Dmitri wasn't depressed or confused. He was defeated. I threw up my hands. He didn't say anything as I walked out and headed back to the shop.

Dwight took one look at my face and wordlessly went back to tinkering with his tattoo machine. I don't know what my expression was, but a defeated Dmitri was too much to bear at the moment. It shook my faith in the concept of crazy, for one thing. I went straight into the back and crashed down into the chair at my desk. When I felt a little more centered, I opened the top drawer and took out Agent Dessel's card. I dialed and he answered on the second ring.

"Dessel."

"Darby Holland from Lucky Supreme. I just wanted to call and tell you I got all my stuff back. Had to brag to someone. I'm in a questionable mood and I thought it might make me feel better."

"What happened?" I could hear the clatter of federal industry in the background.

"I made an appointment with Dong-ju and explained everything. He gave my shit back. We drank some scotch. I came home. End of story."

"Sounds easy."

I didn't say anything. I knew he wanted me to come in and tell him the entire story. He knew I wasn't going to.

"You meet with him at his house?"

"If you could call it that."

Agent Dessel laughed. "I've seen pictures. We have some limited surveillance stock, but there was a photo spread in *Architectural Digest*."

I snorted.

"He whipped out the Matterhorn of cocaine, didn't he?" Dessel almost sounded wistful. "Maybe offered up one of his half-sisters? You knew they were his sisters, right?"

I had no reply.

"Something we think he picked up in Russia. At least they do the same thing over there, anyway. Did you man up and blister the ass of one of them? Maybe both? Get all gacked out on Nicky's fancy blow and do the public cowboy dance? Hoedown corn porn?"

"Up yours, Dessel," I growled.

"They probably have just about every disease know to modern medical science," Dessel said before I could hang up, "but no condoms allowed, am I right?"

"I didn't . . . shit, man. I have style. Are you out of your fucking mind?"

"You're damned either way, Holland. If you didn't play Dong-ju's little game it makes you a pussy in his eyes, and therefore sympathetic to pigs like yours truly. If you did . . . well, I'm just glad I'm not the doctor that's going to be holding your rotting dick in my hand in a few weeks. I'd have to commit suicide. If you'd have called me first, I might have advised you to have Dong-ju mail your stuff back to you. Actually going down there was borderline . . . I mean, I have no idea what that was. You're lucky we aren't tweezering little pieces of you out of a carpet right now."

"It's over," I replied. "The guy was nuts, but I'm out of it."

"I doubt it. I guess"—he interrupted himself with a boyish laugh—"I guess I'm just surprised to be talking to you, Mr. Holland. People have this amazing way of changing forever after meeting Nicky in his home. But he's probably never met anyone like you, because there can't be any more of you. I bet you made him laugh."

"I was high comedy, you creepy—"

"You know," Dessel interrupted, playing at thinking out loud, "we have no idea how he travels. Master of slipping a tail. He's in one place and then, like magic, he's somewhere else. Are you calling from home? Peek under the bed for me."

I admit I leaned forward and peered out at the front door.

"This man never misses a beat, Holland," Dessel continued. "I have it all right here. Last year he bought a vintage Aston Martin in Saudi Arabia, had it transported to Italy. Five days later it was found off the coast in one hundred meters of water, as in dumped off a boat. Two days after that he deposits three million yen into a bank in Switzerland. Now what do you make of that?"

"Why are you telling me any of this?"

There was a long pause at the other end of the line. He finally cleared his throat.

"I'm sure you've come across your share of pathological liars, Mr. Holland. But I doubt you've come across a hyper-logical one. Dong-ju toys with codes inside of riddles at the core of doublespeak as a warm-up exercise. Think about it, as it were. Did his driver tell you anything? It would have been at the very end of the night. This is key to understanding exactly how fucked you are. It's a certain kind of speech, but there are variations. If he did, then—"

I hung up.

At times like that, and there were many of them, I thought about splitting town for good. I had Bling's money and some savings of my own. I could hole up in Belize for a few years, eat beans and rice, maybe take up spear fishing.

Sell weed or flip-flops on the beach, something harmless and stupid. Embrace my inner cretin, who was sitting in the corner these days, lonesome and ignored because no one had invited him to the party this month. Find some rich Eurotrash bimbo and learn the secret language of her bikini. Do some laughing. Learn how to tango and get good at it. It was a fantasy I had a few times a year, but it was the second time that week.

So I let myself dream for a few minutes.

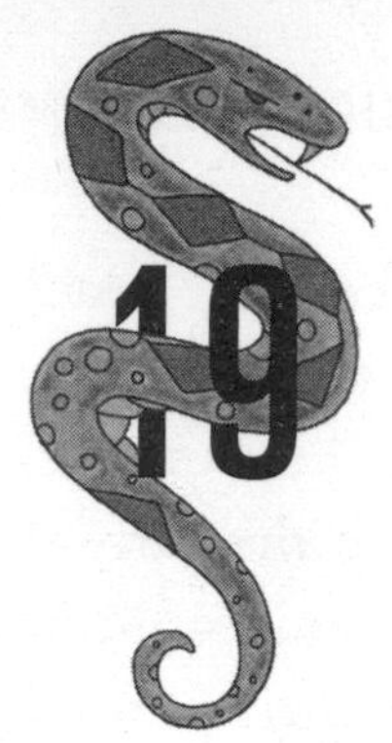

I drove home from the Lucky once Dwight had packed it in and Nigel had finally arrived, early once again, and presumably armed. We put up the BACK IN TEN, GETTING HEAD sign and went into the back room.

"Delia told me you got the Norton crap back. Dude as psycho as she said?"

"Worse. You had to be there. Even the feds think the guy is going to kill me."

"Shoot your mouth off?"

"Big time." I shook my head, darkness in my eyes. "I couldn't help it, Nige. I guess Bling's dick is going to fall off soon, and that's pretty much the bright side."

"That is one yucky grande of a bright side, boss. I take it we're still on red alert? Me and my gun are . . . okay hanging out during office hours?"

"Just don't tell me about it, dude. No harm, no foul, but just so you know I was already aware that you're packing. Of course you are, because everything is totally out of control, so why wouldn't you be? Jesus."

He looked almost apologetic. Almost.

"The red alert has moved up to spurting red, dudeboy. Plus, Dmitri has gone downhill and we have inspector issues. The city. So, ah, crisis."

Nigel sat and rubbed his face. "We should move to fuckin' Mexico. Start a tattoo shop in Cabo and change our names. Dibs on Coug, and I'm thinking I'll go for the permanent aviator glasses look. You can be Little Bob Barracuda, ride a Ducati. Carry a sword. Delia can get a bunch of Communion dresses and pretend like she's your autistic sister. Mikey can finally be a drag queen." He sighed and kept rubbing. "But I'm probably the only one of us with a solid fake ID."

"Think again. Belize, but I still have to check on the extradition, mostly because all the crime we'll have to do to get out of this shit. Frito pie and BBQ joint, I run the kitchen with Delia, you take the bar, Big Mikey is the waitress. We can tattoo Europeans in the bathroom, lie low in style." I sniffed. "What the fuck stinks in here?" It smelled like a locker room mixed with extra feet and Febreeze.

"Mikey. He's been sleeping back here for the last two nights. He drinks beer, farts, snores between burps, farts, and eats pork rinds with hot sauce and sour cream and onions." Nigel shook his head. "I sent him home until midnight to burn his clothes and rub himself down with turpentine."

"Super. So one more bad. I need you to score some bags off of Lenny. Twenties, maybe five of them. Tell Lenny to put the word out that we're expecting a robbery of some kind and we want his people one block closer and watching. First one who sees something and gives us a heads up gets the bags. They're already looking, but this will bring it up a notch."

"Why not just give Lenny a bill?" Perplexing Nigel with a mutant variation of Three Card Monte would normally make me smile. He looked like a convict taking an algebra test.

I shook my head. "He'd just keep it. But five bags is a convincing hard cash illusion. We have a slice of his pie, so we're a repository worth guarding. We need to be a bank with credit cards for the next little while."

Nigel nodded. "A bank with credits cards . . . Genius. This is on par with your Monique attack. You're stepping up, man. Strategy and timing and guile, with th—"

I got up. "Thanks for the knob job, homie. Let's hop to."

Nigel got up too and started for the door. "Don't mention it and I won't. Gotta work on those teeth, boss. I think you swallowed some of my skin."

I raised my fist and he ducked. When Nigel opened back up and got to work on his first job of the night, I watched the street patterns, looking for ripples. It looked like it was going to be reasonably quiet, which for once was good news. I told him I'd check in later and he gave me the double wink on Lenny, so I went back to my office, put the box of Bling's pill cash in a paper bag, and headed out to my car. Two of Lenny's boys were on the corner a block down pointed our way, so I went home to lie low.

It was dark by the time I pulled up in front of my place. I sat in the car for a while, listening to the soft patter of rain on the roof, thinking. I went in and greeted the cats, flipping lights as I passed through. There was a stack of mail on the floor in front of the drafty mail slot. I tossed it on the dining room table and put the bag with the cash box on the floor next to the curio cabinet.

I turned on the AM jazz station on my big antique radio and got out the Roland Norton flash again, surveying it one last time. I didn't even know why. The old Navy and Merchant Marine garbage made a little more sense, but the flat, dimensionless flowers of unknown genus, the kid drawings of skulls, all the rest . . . in the end I had to grudgingly admit that it was what so many newbies and hacks in the field call "solid and well designed" as part of their phony stone-age worship mantra because they couldn't draw and needed the line. I was being critical because I didn't like the style, in the same way that I'm instantly critical of modern country music. Norton could have been their one-eyed god if he had made another hundred sheets. I shook my head. It was still amazing what Nicky Dong-ju wanted to pay for it. I didn't know what to make of it all, but if the city came down on me hard in the near future, I would have to sell it back to him if he was still in the market. I might not have any choice.

A few years ago an old customer of mine had moved back east and left me his gun safe as a parting half-gift, as in he couldn't afford to move it even ten feet. It was a six-foot, half-ton monster the size of an industrial refrigerator. Moving it myself was out of the question, so for reasons of my own I'd obligingly taken over his storage space. After Bling's theft, I'd copied most of the valuable pieces of flash and stored the originals in it. When I'd put all the good originals in the half-ton metal closet for safekeeping, I'd put my other two Norton pieces in with them, mostly because the way the cats sniffed at them whenever they got into the closet I'd tossed them into made me suspect they had them pegged as a pee target. Many customers had a habit of leaving me other things when they moved, often trading for a final tattoo session or two. I had two broken motorcycles I still didn't know how to fix stored with the safe, a driving lawn mower with a busted rototiller attachment, a crate of single-cask bourbon I didn't want to keep at home because I'd get drunk every night, a huge Styrofoam monkey head from a parade float, and various other oddities.

I didn't have any plans for the evening, so I decided to put the Roland Norton flash into the gun safe, as well as all of Bling's cash. It didn't seem like a good idea to leave either lying around the house with pissed-off feds and eccentric gangsters sniffing around. It was a perfectly shitty night for it, though.

I carefully wrapped the Norton flash in plastic wrap and then put it in a trash bag and taped it shut. Then I put the entire thing back in Dong-ju's fancy portfolio and zipped it. The gun safe was airtight, but you could never be too careful. If it hadn't been for Bling's pill money, I might have put the trip off for another day.

I opened the money box and took out a small stack of bills and put them in the antique meat grinder in the back of one of the kitchen cabinets, then taped the box closed. I considered it very possible that Dong-ju and Bling had had a chat after my last visit and that one way or another Bling had disappeared again, in which case I was a little richer. If I told Delia that I'd entertained the notion of returning any of the money, she'd probably slap me half to death. Nigel and Big Mike would both probably quit, reasoning that I had finally lost the rest of my mind.

The drive to the storage space was a somber one. I went down Burnside and took a right on MLK, headed north. I followed it to Broadway and took a left down toward the river. When I hit the interstate, I went north again, into the heart of the riverside industrial zone.

It was a bleak place with rambling, Stalinesque buildings of indeterminate function ringing the railroad switchyards. The Seed Factory was there, a blazing art co-op built in the shell of a desperately shabby brick building of esoteric historical rumor. The slow, wide Willamette reflected the lights of the downtown skyscrapers west across the water. Bright halogen lamps illuminated a muddy, rain-swept landscape dotted with clumps of rusting machinery and abandoned construction material. Nigel and I had spent a fine drunken evening wandering around the entire place, working our way through the undersides of the bridges and through the muddy lots. It had been a semi-traumatic evening in that we'd both been wearing suits. I'd been out on a date that had gone disastrously wrong when the woman in question had revealed herself to be a born-again Christian, and that the nature of our evening together had been a ploy to bring about my salvation. Nigel had been on a simultaneous date of similar quality, cut short for completely different reasons. The stripper for whom he'd bought two expensive bottles of wine, high-end caviar, and truffle pate to woo over a romantic twilight picnic, a true rarity for him in the romance department, had shown up for their rendezvous coked out of her mind with her super-pissed-off boyfriend/pimp. When my phone rang that night, I was dialing his number to see if he'd wanted to get loaded and help me find my way back to Satan. He'd been calling me because he was been afraid he'd broken his arm. We'd met at a bar minutes later and gotten half drunk, and then gone down to my storage unit to look at my motorcycles and drink Nigel's wine. We ate the caviar and pate with our fingers because he'd lost the crackers. Nigel had declared the motorcycles to be crap and after the second bottle and some of the single cask we'd gone exploring, too drunk to drive, and Delia couldn't be reached for extraction. The midnight exploration had ruined both of our suits and I'd wound up at one point washing my hands in a puddle he later informed me that he'd peed in moments before. A bonding experience between men. But I knew my way around what was over the fences and around the corners down there. It wasn't pretty.

The U-Store-It was a giant yellow one-story concrete building abutting the underside of the Steel Bridge. It had probably been a storage facility for boat parts in the Second World War and converted for civilian use sometime afterward. My unit had outside access, so I parked directly in front of its roll-up metal door. It was raining a little harder. I cut the engine and got the flashlight out of the glove box. The wiring inside the place had burned out years ago or been shut off at the breakers, so there was no juice inside.

I gathered up my packages and sprinted the ten feet to the door. I was soaked by the time I got the two massive, crusty padlocks open and rolled the rusted door up high enough to duck under.

I thumbed the flashlight on and walked over the cracked concrete floor to the gun safe. The small space was cold and smelled like engines and rat poison. I'd completely forgotten about the bundle of deep sea fishing poles, the banjo, the old carousel horse with two broken legs, and the beanbag. All four tires on my riding mower were flat. I wished I'd brought gloves as I spun the heavy dial on the steel door of the gun safe with my frozen fingers. When I finished the combination, I pulled the hinge bar down and the heavy metal door swung open silently. I played the flashlight over the contents.

The stack of lumpy, bumpy Arnie Kirby flash was on the left. Next to it were my four Owen Jensen pieces, which I liked. One bitchin' Cliff Raven. There were twenty or so others, mostly from Rex Nightly's stylish LA hotrod set. I thought about opening the packaging on the Owen Jensen pieces to look at them again, but it was too cold and my wet hands were streaked with rust.

I put Bling's box of cash on the empty ammo shelf at the top of the safe, wiped my hands on my pants for the tenth time, and then took the Roland Norton flash out of the rain-speckled portfolio. The plastic-wrapped parcel was dry, so I placed it inside next to the one of the two pieces of Roland Norton flash Bling hadn't stolen. On impulse I took one of them out and looked at it in the dim light.

It was the sheet of flash that had been at the very bottom of the box I'd found the collection in, stuffed away in Wally's comically sloppy style in the back of the Lucky Supreme's lounge, which at the time was just an extremely filthy storage room. It was so warped and water damaged, so mildew streaked and bent that I'd almost thrown it away along with the other one, which was almost as bad. It was also the crudest piece of them all, with a chubby, moth-like butterfly and the bust of a cross-eyed, big-chested woman with an empty banner underneath it. Most of the remaining surface was empty, like he'd run out of ideas after those two masterpieces.

The thick flashboard itself was peeling apart. I looked at the fraying edges and thought about the facing Dong-ju had done on the other pieces. It could be worth it to try and restore the last two and toss them into the collection for a few extra bucks. I turned it around and examined the upper right hand corner, the worst part, and frowned. The paper was delaminating into multiple layers. I struck my thumbnail into the center and gently pried it open to test the glue.

The thin sheets on the inside were . . . greenish. I angled the flashlight into the crack I'd opened and the light revealed a short sequence of faded black numbers. My heart thumped and I licked my lips. The wheels in my head were finally getting traction.

I peeled the front of the flash off in one smooth stroke. Behind it were layers and layers of treasury bills and bearer bonds, all of them circa 1955. Most of them had been destroyed by time and the water damage, but some of them were still intact. I looked at the amounts. Two thousand. Ten thousand. Twenty-one thousand. Five hundred. I had no idea what they were worth today, but I'd bet it all that Dong-ju did. Every piece had been stacked like this, I was sure. The new facing, the new edges . . . They had all been mined except for these two, the very last pieces in a million-dollar-plus collection. It was the best smuggling operation I'd ever heard of, but at some point everything had evidently gone horribly wrong, and Roland Norton's operation had somehow been lost in time, shuffled away into boxes that wound up in the back of the Lucky Supreme and a few other places around the world. There was no telling how many pieces other than mine and Wes Ron's Dong-ju had acquired, and who else knew about them. The people who had been looking for them for over fifty years would never have found mine if I hadn't hung it up, if Bling had never crossed one of them. I looked up into the darkness and the memory of the blind fish in the slimy water swam up again.

Panama, 1955. President killed at a racetrack. The canal changes hands. Panic in the underworld and the overworld both. Dmitri and his theory of economics as the only true sociology. Movement in money, and when money moves fast and quiet it always moves through the underworld, especially if it came fresh from a crime.

Bling said he'd been set up. Then the feds had told me that Dong-ju played people like bongos. Milo the driver said Dong-ju owned people and that he played eight games of chess at a time in his head. And that I was too stupid to understand what he was trying to say. The hair on the back of my neck stood up. The rotting piece of loaded press-board in my hand suddenly felt very, very cold.

At some point shortly after I'd hung the Norton flash, Dong-ju had found out about it, probably because he had feelers periodically cruising through any tattoo shop with history. And that's when Bling's troubles had started. Dong-ju had been playing us like puppets, and Bling had been center stage until it was my turn. And my turn was almost over.

Obi was in danger. Bling had been dangled out in front of him. Dong-ju had put Bling right in one of Obi's favorite surf spots. He evidently knew all about me, right down to my standard chatter with Flaco. We'd been playing some kind of game for two years, and it had taken me that long to realize it. Two years, and most of it with me hunting Roland Norton flash through all of my connections, tattoo world connections he would never have access to, doing his work for him and sending out a Roland Norton beacon signal for anything he might have missed. That was the worst, most galling, damning part of it all. And now there I was, alone at night, looking right at what he wanted, the final move to Dong-ju's checkmate. The feds were distracted, looking for whoever had been watching Dong-ju. Delia was right. Dong-ju was always been one step ahead of everyone.

A car pulled up behind my BMW, and I heard the engine cut off and then a door slam. I stuffed the Norton piece back in the safe, closed the door, and spun the dial. On my hands and knees, I crawled between the motorcycles and peered out under the door.

There, standing in the rain in a black tracksuit, his dripping face fixed in an unblinking expression of monk-like tranquility, was Nicky Dong-ju.

20

"Darby Holland," Dong-ju called over the static of the rain. "Hello again. I know you're in there, so what say we have a little chat?" I peeked out around the flat wheel of the motorcycle I was hiding behind. It was hard to tell, but it looked like Dong-ju was holding a gun down along his leg on his right.

"You're surrounded, you dumbass sister-whoring pervert," I yelled back. "Only a suckdog fake-ass fuckin' monkey would fall for something this stupid! Drop the gun and bend over the hood of your car before you die from four directions and we take turns raping your corpse! Now!"

The first bullet skipped off the pavement and slammed into the front of the riding lawn mower. The second one tore past my right ear like a hornet and ripped through the tank of the motorcycle beside me. I smelled gasoline and felt something dripping onto the back of my jacket.

"Enough!" Dong-ju screamed in a high voice. "Get the fuck out here!"

"Okay," I yelled back. "Okay! I'm coming out! Just don't fucking shoot me!"

I took a ball bearing out of my pocket and then held my hands over my head. I ducked slowly under the rolling door and rose to face him. His calm had vanished, and now the rain ran down the hellish mask of a psychotic coke-demon.

"Idiot," he snarled, pointing the barrel of the gun at my face.

"It's in a safe," I said quickly. He paused, his expression of hatred mingling with a sudden, predatory curiosity. The rain didn't make him blink.

"I know why you want the Roland Norton flash," I continued. "I have two originals left and I just peeled one open."

"It took you this long?" Dong-ju laughed harshly, his perfect white teeth glinting in the low light. His curly hair was plastered to his scalp from the cold rain, but he showed no sign of discomfort. "More than a few people have known what you do now for decades, you miserable fucking moron. In all this time, how many more sheets have you gathered for me? Bling described you as a cunning man, Mr. Holland. Resourceful. Connected. Half right, minus everything. I knew you would come to a place like this when Bling told me you'd taken his money. A man like you, a simple man, can only keep track of one hiding place."

"You won't be able to figure out how to open that safe if you shoot me."

Dong-ju lowered the gun a little. "Open it or I shoot you in the kneecap."

"All right." I began to turn, very slowly, my hands still held above my head. I had one shot. As Dong-ju lowered the gun, I flicked the ball bearing out of my hand with a vicious snap.

Dong-ju's nose exploded in a red cloud and he toppled backward, howling with surprise and rage, like a strong animal touched on the nipple with a cattle prod. I dove past the front of my car and ran flat out for the bridge. I'd gone about thirty feet when the gun erupted behind me in a rapid succession of shots.

Maybe it was the rain, and maybe it was the fact that I'd just shattered Dong-ju's nose in a terrible way, but I made it to the fence without feeling anything punch through me. He trumpeted something incomprehensible as I sprinted up to an old forklift and climbed it at a run, then catapulted over the fence all in one continuous terror-fueled scramble.

The dripping belly of the Steel Bridge was stretched out above me. I knew the territory and Dong-ju didn't. I slogged through the mud, falling heavily once, and then got to the first of the ladders leading up to the train trestle that ran along the underside of the structure. I started to climb.

Through the slimy rungs, I watched Dong-ju neatly hop the fence. He ran in my general direction, a martial figure that made much better time through the mud than I had. As I scrabbled up, I noticed my huge shadow, cast from a halogen floodlight under the base of the trestle. Dong-ju had evidently noticed it too. So much for the home field advantage.

"I see you!" he sang in a wrecked nasal, helium falsetto. I froze, unable to help myself, anticipating the bullet that would blow me back down into the mud and rusted machinery below. When it didn't come I started climbing again, taking the rungs two at a time.

"I see you!" Dong-ju sang again. He reached the bottom of the ladder just as I reached the underside of the trestle.

I flopped out of his view, gasping for air and reeling with vertigo.

I was lying on a one-and-a-half-foot mossy ribbon of old wood that was part of a long-neglected maintenance and inspection walkway under the rails. I rose unsteadily and grabbed the bent handrails that were more than fifty years old and pitted with exposure. It was at least a forty-foot drop to either side. Ahead of me was the cold, sluggish river. The walkway led almost a third of a mile to the other side before the next ladder. I started moving.

Dong-ju scaled up behind me with cocaine-fueled athleticism and a total disregard for his mortality. I'd gone twenty paces when he reached the top.

He screamed, an incoherent blast of pure rage and violence, and then he sprinted along the slick walkway, his arms pumping at his sides, handrails untouched. He'd lost the gun or tossed it away when it ran out of bullets. I could never outrun him, so I stopped and turned rather than get tackled ten seconds later.

"It's over," I yelled, facing him. "I'll give you the combination!"

A horrible smile spread over Dong-ju's ruined face and he stopped ten feet away from me. A flap of tissue was blowing back and forth around his shredded nose in time with his breath, and there was more blood on him than I'd thought could fit in a face. He was covered, and I could see all the way into the black, weeping cavity of his sinuses. His brain must have been bleeding. Dong-ju turned sideways and flexed his callused hands.

"Too late." His low growl had a hollow quality.

He came at me with the mincing steps of a trained killing machine, balanced at every instant.

"Don't," I cautioned.

He sneered with bloody teeth and kept coming.

I threw my second and last ball bearing at almost point blank range. It smacked into his sternum with a dull crunch and Dong-ju stopped and clutched his chest with both hands, eyes wide. I crouched and raised my fists. Dong-ju coughed raggedly and came on.

His opening blow, a straight fist, hit me square in the base of the neck. I pivoted backward and barely avoided a crushed throat. My hands snapped up and I grabbed his wrist and his elbow, clamping down on nerve clusters with the bruising strength developed from years of tattooing. It was like trying to crush a steel cable.

Dong-ju's knee slammed into my right hip, and we attempted a head butt in unison. Because I was shorter, my forehead rammed into his shattered face and he let out a strangled gasp. I dropped to one knee and delivered a hard, straight right to his crotch.

Dong-ju staggered back and fell, sucking air. The blow to his sternum had done something after all. He rose slowly to his feet and grasped the handrail. We studied each other in the bad light, my breath coming in panting plumes of white, his in something more like tiny hiccoughs.

"Fuck," he wheezed. He drew himself together and came at me again, telegraphing a kick of some kind by leaning back on his right leg.

I snapped out with an engineer boot and caught him square in his right knee. He folded and dropped again, losing his grip on the handrail. As he collapsed, I punched him hard across the cheekbone, driving down into it. His fingernails made long gray tracks through the soggy wood as I savagely kicked him over the side.

Dong-ju hung for an instant from one clawed hand. In that tiny fraction of time, I almost grabbed his wrist, but a final look into his mad, ruined face made me consider. I drew my hand back and Dong-ju dropped, his black eyes trained on my face as he fell. He hit the ground forty feet below with a muddy splash. One of his legs spasmed, bent at an unnatural angle, and then he was still. His eyes were open and unblinking, staring up at me.

I don't know how long I remained frozen, staring down, the drips long and slow and gold as they fell through the halogen, the curtain of rain and black night beyond, there in that suddenly churchlike space. My legs were shaking so badly that I could barely stand when I finally rose. I grabbed the handrail and lurched a few feet, then looked back down again. I couldn't stop myself. Dong-ju remained motionless.

I walked unsteadily back to the ladder and slowly climbed down. My hands and face were cold and almost immobile, so I had to hug many of the slimy rungs for seconds at a time. When I finally got to the bottom, I staggered through the mud to where he lay. I was out of ball bearings, so I picked up a rusted segment of old rebar to fight with. It turned out I didn't need it.

Nicky Dong-ju was cold and broken and dead.

I sank down in the mud next to him and stared at his body. He was clearly broken inside from the fall. One of his ribs was poking up through his track jacket, a surprisingly slender finger of splintered white with a pink core. His leg was twisted so that the foot was upside down. His eyes were wide open, staring up at where I had been moments before. I almost wanted to close them like they always did in the movies, but when I reached out I couldn't touch his face. The gaping cavity of his nose was hard to look at. A foam of fine pink and red bubbles had welled up in it.

The wind had been pouring around me as I knelt there and I started to shiver. Eventually I rose to my feet and spent a long minute lighting a bent cigarette with my muddy hands, then I looked around, dazed.

The underside of the bridge was a mess. I splashed around in the mud until I found a rusted roll of chain link fence. My breath was a torrent of white as I dragged the heavy roll over to Dong-ju's body. It wouldn't flatten out properly, so I weighed the corners down with random chunks of rotten concrete. When I was finished, I pulled Dong-ju's twisted body into the center, took his wallet and keys out of the pockets of his bloody track pants, and rolled him up, concrete and all. Then I braided the ragged edges with my nearly numb fingers, securing his body in a metal and concrete burrito. With the last of my strength, I rolled the entire thing over thirty feet of mud and then finally into the cold, sluggish river, wading in after it until the bottom dropped off and the grisly parcel tumbled down into a deeper place.

I don't remember wading out of the water or climbing the fence again and walking back to my car. Maybe I was too cold. Some part of my memory goes black around then. The next thing I knew I was standing by my car. Dong-ju's rental was parked behind it, a black Ford Taurus. I closed the rolling door on my storage space and locked it, then climbed into my car, revved the engine, and cranked the heater to the max. Sometime later, I took out my cell phone and called Delia.

"About fucking time," she answered. I could hear loud music in the background.

"Where are you?" I rasped.

"I'm out! Drinking!"

"Go to the Lucky and get some latex gloves, then go to my house and get me some clothes, shoes too. You still have my key?"

"Yeah," she replied. The music quieted as she exited wherever she was.

"I'm at the U-Store-It." I gave her the address. "Hurry, and don't bring anyone with you." I hung up.

Delia arrived twenty minutes later with everything I'd asked for in a trash bag. Wordlessly, I changed in the rain, standing on the wet pavement and shivering again, and then put my old clothes in the trash bag. I'd burn them later. I put the gloves on and took out Dong-ju's key and unlocked his car. The rental invoice was in the glove box. A Hertz from the airport, rented to William Liu. I walked back to Delia's little Falcon and she rolled the window down.

"Follow me," I said. "I need a ride back here."

She nodded.

We drove out to the airport and I parked Dong-ju's car in the darkness at the edge of the Hertz lot. It was closed for the night, so I locked it and threw the keys at the kiosk. I didn't care where they landed. For a moment I was almost too tired to move, but I turned and walked back to Delia's car and got in.

It smelled like bubble gum and weed inside and it was warm, almost hot. I peeled my gloves off and leaned back in the seat as she drove us back to the freeway. After a few minutes, she lit up two smokes and handed me one.

"Long night?" she asked softly.

"I killed Dong-ju. Then I rolled his body up in some fence and dragged him into the river."

She didn't have anything to say.

We drove in silence back to my car. When we pulled up behind it, Delia cut the lights, but left the engine running for the heater. She turned in her seat and faced me. I looked back at her, exhausted.

"Pinky bit me on the nose while you were gone. It really fuckin' hurt, too. You owe me a drink."

I smiled for the first time in a few days. Her eyes were warm and soft and wet and large. I reached out and ran my index finger down the bridge of her nose. Something caught my eye and I cupped my hand under her jaw and gently turned her head to the side.

"Delia, you sweet little monkey, that is the ugliest earring I've ever seen."

She smiled hugely.

"I was gonna make one for you too, but the other one got chipped." She gave my hand a soft brush with her cheek and snuggled around in her seat. "Where you takin' me to get loaded?"

21

A week later the feds came by the Lucky Supreme. They weren't too pleased.

Agent Dessel was as haggard as ever, a teenage momma's boy at the end of a multidimensional bender. Pressman's scowl could have turned wine into vinegar into sticky red sand.

The gang was all there. Delia was wrenching on one of her tattoo machines, cursing hex magic. Big Mike was on the phone, Nigel dicking around with a design he had to do later that night. Alex was just finishing some work on a pinup on some skater kid's forearm, and Dwight was breaking his station down. The feds had caught us right in the middle of the Friday shift change.

"Mr. Holland," Dessel said. He gestured at the door. "A word."

I'd been sitting at the front desk going over bills. My foot was still sore from a cut I'd received the night I'd killed Dong-ju. Big Mike had come over that night and stitched it up, and Delia had come up with some leftover antibiotics for her friend Biji's dog, plus I had penicillin left over from a scab gone wrong on Chops. I didn't want to limp in front of them, so I wheeled around in my chair and hit them with a smile.

"Dudes," I said, shaking my head. "Where the fuck are your umbrellas? You're dripping on my floor." It was raining outside. Clean, silvery rain, a thing to dance in, mouth open to the sky.

"We need to talk," Dessel said. Pressman just watched. I guess that was most of his job, punctuated by little spurts of being a dick.

"Go ahead," I said. Nigel and Big Mike walked into the back. Alex followed them, head down. Dwight gave me a nod and went out into the first part of the evening, headed home. Delia hopped up on the desk at my side and crossed her legs. She was wearing lime plastic pants, a Butthole Surfers T-shirt and giant imitation snakeskin cowgirl boots with spurs. One big heel clunked rhythmically into the old desk. I didn't need to look up to know the expression she was dealing out to Dessel and Pressman.

"Dong-ju's gone," Dessel said shortly. "Vanished."

I shrugged. "Fuckin' who cares."

"Any idea where he went?" Agent Pressman asked, giving me his x-ray. Delia stiffened beside me. I patted her skinny plastic leg.

"Mexico," I replied easily, "or maybe southeast Asia. Florida. Isn't that where people go when the feds are after them?"

"Maybe so," Dessel said. He cocked his head a little, trying to avoid Delia's glare, focusing on me alone. Pressman had clearly met his match. He was looking away. "The question is, how did he know? Why did he go from lawyered up but cooperative to gone?"

"You think maybe I ratted you out?" I asked. I leaned back in my chair and crossed my hands behind my head.

"No. That's not what I think." Agent Dessel looked at me like Pressman had for the first time, really watching.

I realized then what Delia had evidently picked up on already. I'd been wrong about those two. Pressman might have been good, but he was the old man with the bad numbers on the team. It was Dessel who had been running the brain department from the start. He was brilliant at what he did, on a level that had cleanly slipped past my face-reading skills. I'd been outmatched in a game I played well. He'd been all over me, using Pressman's surly demeanor as a distraction while he mopped up my reactions. He was doing it right then. Only the orientation of Delia's body had tipped me off. She was pointed at Dessel like a cobra the snake charmer had failed to hypnotize. I was lucky he hadn't busted me on something with that huge brain, but it was that kind of month.

"I need to get back to work," I said, showing the sheaf of bills. "Gimme a little heads up when you need to use me as human bait again, Dougie. In fact, you still owe me a favor, as I recall. So I guess no in advance."

"We're even," Dessel said. "For today." They walked out without looking back.

"I'd watch out for that kid," Delia said, hopping off the desk. "He's a smartypants."

"Thanks for the tip."

The truth was that if a scumbag like Dong-ju disappeared, his empire would be gobbled up by his lackeys and butlers and stagehands. The feds would have plenty to do just keeping track of which new kings came from where. These would be the new suspects, who would figure large in the eyes of all the feds I hadn't smarted off to, including Pressman and Dessel's superiors. Nicky Dong-ju had been slated for a mysterious burial and they all knew it. The how and why might have mattered to someone at some point, but in the end, when everyone went home with their list of new names, after one short week, the truth of it would only matter to me.

Gomez and I had a contractor customer of mine go through the Lucky Supreme, the Rooster Rocket, and the Korean mini-mart next door. He gave us a laundry list of violations, from glaring electrical hazards to makeshift plumbing repairs, all of it in the Lucky and Gomez's place. The old Korean lady had done much better over the years. We had to call in a translator to deal with her and her family. It turned out that they thought the Lucky was a hair salon. They'd never peeked in. They thought Gomez and Flaco ran the new incarnation of the porno theater that had been there before them. They had taken the news that the Rooster Rocket was a bar and that the Lucky was a tattoo parlor with an indifferent shrug, and as an afterthought one of them had asked that Flaco discontinue selling tacos. No one ever knew why. The grand total bill to fix it all was a little over fourteen thousand dollars. Gomez and I reluctantly split it, as Dmitri flatly refused to even listen to me when I approached him. Roland Norton and Jason Bling paid my half and the repairs were done in five days on the down-low, mostly at night. There was coke involved, and everything else was paid in cash. No inspectors hit up the Lucky during construction, and when they finally did, they grudgingly gave us permission to carry on for the time being.

When I called Obi to check in with him, he had interesting news.

"It's gone, boss," he said. "The Teething Hot Dog Tattoo Stand was gutted in the night about a week ago." A week to the day after I'd rolled Dong-ju's body into the river. "Even the sign is gone. I talked to one of the women at the hair salon next door. She came in last week and it was like a midnight fire sale had happened. I guess the building might be getting sold, too, though she didn't really know."

I told him where Bling lived and he went over to the apartment and found it empty, too. The neighbor, a very pregnant woman with bad acne, told Obi that she was on the lookout for Bling as well. He owed her fifteen bucks and change. I hadn't seriously considered returning the money I'd taken from Bling, but I had considered it. He was probably gone for good this time, so I sent Obi five hundred bucks of it to give to Bling's pregnant former neighbor.

On Halloween, which fell on a Monday night, I had an old tattoo artist friend of mine from Salem watch the shop, and I took the entire crew on a trip up the river on the *Portland Spirit*, a cruise boat that plied the Columbia with a fancy restaurant, a decent bar, and a shitty cover band. It was weird to see my people dressed up. Nigel wore a perfectly tailored vintage Italian suit, Big Mike some kind of upscale mall deal, Alex and Dwight off-the-rack Men's Wearhouse. Both Alex and Dwight were still going to quit after everything that had happened, but not tonight. I wore my favorite black Armani, stolen from Sachs by a treasured old client. Everyone's wives or girlfriends looked like models with real asses.

Delia wore a skimpy black dress, shiny six-inch pumps, and an imitation mink coat. Her date was a dirty punk kid in a rumpled tuxedo, none other than the lead singer from Empire of Shit. She introduced him as her dildo, but his name turned out to be Hank. We all called him Hank Dildo from then on, and the name stuck.

When we passed under the Steel Bridge, I looked across the river at the east side, at the distant pools of yellow light and vast rectangles of midnight, the black water that flowed through those shadows and the untold ruins of decades and secrets beneath it. Delia plopped down in my lap and stuck her boozy tongue in my ear, so we got into a tickling fight and knocked over the table and some chairs. When we passed under the bridge a second time, I didn't even notice which bridge it was.

We all got roaring drunk. Alex threw up. Dwight's wife did too, and almost fell over the side. My date was a gorgeous redhead who waited tables at a bistro around the corner from my apartment. We'd been flirting forever, but when she got that first real look into my personal life, she decided to latch on to the bass player from the band.

Delia was in rare form even for her, and got so loaded that she fell off the causeway and broke her ankle after we'd finally been kicked off the boat. Hank Dildo took her to OHSU in her car, and I planned on heading up there later after the worst part of the screaming and biting was over. It was the perfect time to present her with the Shuckins Taxidermy T-shirt I'd been holding in reserve.

That night I got back to the Lucky just after closing. My night shift stand-in David Knoll had finished up and gone out into the world to party before the holiday finally went to sleep. There was always a stand-in, a replacement, a sacrificial lamb. The Lucky didn't take nights off, and it never would. I sat down in the dark lobby and lit a smoke, then leaned way back and stared out the window, upside down. Late at night, you could see all the wires in the sign out front, and the old girl seemed a little like a cadaver with her tendons showing. When I slowly sat back upright, I let my eyes play along the walls, the bright images muted and glossy in the faint rays of the permanent neon. High above me were the framed copies of the Roland Norton flash. I wondered about the mind of the man behind them again. I'd gone back to my storage space a few days before and peeled out all the treasury bills and bearer bonds in the final two pieces. A banker customer of mine had looked them over and told me that I had a little over a hundred thousand in redeemable paper. The rest, worth a fortune had they been salvageable, were too badly damaged. The seventeen that Dong-ju had stripped, mine and Wes Ron's and the other one from San Diego, if that really was all he had found, had netted untold millions.

I was going to take the copies down in the morning. The final sum total of Norton's life and work would reside forever in a gun safe in a storage unit. I couldn't have it on the walls. Roland Norton was long dead, but even the things he had made with his own hands, his art, however bad, would then vanish forever. The only person who would ever see it again was me, and I didn't even like it. I couldn't risk the interest of another Dong-ju, another monster on a treasure hunt. Norton would die the true, most final death of any artist, and become something forever forgotten in the long, blurry history of the Lucky Supreme.

I took a drag. Norton and Bling. Two generations of dirtbags who never even knew each other, Roland Norton moving panic money out of Panama and Jason Bling slinging pills and chlamydia. Time had not been a barrier for them, and the two turn-and-burn stencil jockeys had managed to stretch their hands out across countless miles and six long decades to steal each other's watches and drop flies in each other's drinks. I wound up killing someone. The murderer in such a long, long story was me, and I'd used my symbol, my ball bearings, objects that had meant something to me, to do it. I never found them that night. I never looked.

Accidents of that magnitude always made me feel like an accident myself, a shade in the shade of an anonymous Old Town. In that quiet period between closing time and the turning of the sign again, sitting alone in the dark and breathing in the perfumes that trailed from the ghosts of the long and dreaming day, I never thought anyone looking through the window would see anything but an empty chair. But on that rainy night, the ghosts were so real, and the red neon had changed for me in some way. I couldn't help it in the end. It had finally become the color of my memory.